## Don't miss the other books of The Bridesmaid Chronicles

### Praise for the novels of Karen Kendall

"Sassy and sexy . . . a writer to watch."
—Susan Andersen

"Effervescent . . . witty . . . fresh . . . fun."
—Christina Skye

"If you find a Karen Kendall book up on the shelves, don't hesitate to grab it. You'll enjoy it, guaranteed."
—A Romance Review

"The incomparable Karen Kendall is back with yet another rollicking comical romance, which will have the readers laughing their hearts out. . . . [She] is indeed a masterly writer."      —Road to Romance

"Will leave you howling with laughter."
—*Affaire de Coeur*

"A terrific love story . . . filled with laugh-out-loud humor."      —Reader to Reader Reviews

"Smart, sassy, and sensational, this is the contemporary romantic comedy of the year."
—Romance Reviews Today

"A fast-paced, amusing and heart-warming romp."
—The Romance Reader's Connection

"Fans of amusing yet serious relationship dramas will delight in Karen Kendall's *I've Got You, Babe*."
—The Best Reviews

**Visit her Web site at www.karenkendall.com**

# First Dance

## The Bridesmaid Chronicles

## KAREN KENDALL

A SIGNET BOOK

SIGNET
Published by New American Library, a division of
Penguin Group (USA) Inc., 375 Hudson Street,
New York, New York 10014, USA
Penguin Group (Canada), 90 Eglinton Avenue East, Suite 700, Toronto,
Ontario M4P 2Y3, Canada (a division of Pearson Penguin Canada Inc.)
Penguin Books Ltd., 80 Strand, London WC2R 0RL, England
Penguin Ireland, 25 St. Stephen's Green,
Dublin 2, Ireland (a division of Penguin Books Ltd.)
Penguin Group (Australia), 250 Camberwell Road, Camberwell, Victoria 3124,
Australia (a division of Pearson Australia Group Pty. Ltd.)
Penguin Books India Pvt. Ltd., 11 Community Centre, Panchsheel Park,
New Delhi - 110 017, India
Penguin Group (NZ), cnr Airborne and Rosedale Roads, Albany,
Auckland 1310, New Zealand (a division of Pearson New Zealand Ltd.)
Penguin Books (South Africa) (Pty.) Ltd., 24 Sturdee Avenue,
Rosebank, Johannesburg 2196, South Africa

Penguin Books Ltd., Registered Offices:
80 Strand, London WC2R 0RL, England

First published by Signet, an imprint of New American Library,
a division of Penguin Group (USA) Inc.

First Printing, August 2005
10  9  8  7  6  5  4  3  2  1

Copyright © Karen Moser, 2005
Excerpt from *First Love* © Julie Kenner, 2005
All rights reserved

 REGISTERED TRADEMARK—MARCA REGISTRADA

Printed in the United States of America

PUBLISHER'S NOTE
This is a work of fiction. Names, characters, places, and incidents either are
the product of the author's imagination or are used fictitiously, and any resemblance to actual persons, living or dead, business establishments, events, or
locales is entirely coincidental.

The publisher does not have any control over and does not assume any
responsibility for author or third-party Web sites or their content.

This book is dedicated to
Displaced Homemakers' Associations and
Greyhound Rescues everywhere.

## ACKNOWLEDGMENTS

I could not have written this book without the systematic torture of numerous attorneys who probably still duck and run when my e-mail address or phone number appear! So a huge thank-you to Julie Kenner, Terri Bakowitz, Kim Peterson, Amy Kaye, Kathryn Bell-Moss Campbell, Jason Wakefield and "Mad Max" Hagan. Thanks especially to Lisa Canterberry who read the whole manuscript to identify and weed out bloopers. You guys are the best!

I also want to thank my editor, Kara Cesare, Rose Hilliard, and everyone at Signet who works behind the scenes to produce and market wonderful books. Last but not least, thanks to Sally Franklin, production editor extraordinaire.

# Chapter One

Vivien Shelton kissed the five doggie noses arrayed at varying heights in front of her and backed out of her Manhattan apartment. She clutched a tape roller and her computer bag in one hand, and a tall espresso-strength coffee in the other. Ellis whined mournfully, and Brooklyn gave a sharp, disapproving bark.

She looked regretfully at her gaggle of greyhounds. "I know, guys. But I can't stay and play. Klein, Schmidt and Belker pays me for my legal expertise, not my Frisbee skills. Tabitha will keep you company, okay?" She glanced at the tiny blond walker, still incredulous that the dogs didn't pull her right off her feet.

"Queenie has a two p.m. vet appointment, remember. Just have them send me the bill—forty-three greyhounds later, they know I'm good for it."

"Will do." Tabitha crunched down on a Granny Smith apple and waved goodbye. "What about the couple who's interested in Brooklyn? What should I tell them?"

"I'm not comfortable with him going to them. There's something 'off' about those people. Tell them he's already been placed."

"Okay. Have a good one, Viv."

"You too!" She dropped another quick kiss on little Mannie's speckled pink nose—he was practically an albino—and he licked her cheek, probably taking off half of her makeup. Mannie was the latest in her long line of rescued greyhounds, and he hadn't left her side all day on Sunday. She felt guilty leaving him, but he was in good hands. Cranky old Schmidt would have a stroke if she brought Mannie anywhere near the office.

Viv glanced at her watch and galloped toward the elevator, madly tape-rolling the little white hairs off her left trouser-clad thigh. She did her lower left leg while waiting for the car to arrive, and her right leg on the way down from the seventeenth floor to the first. A slurp of coffee, then the right front of her jacket. Another slurp, and the left front.

Mr. Duarte from the eleventh floor watched eagerly as the roller skimmed over her breasts, and she sent him a quelling look. This only made him look hopeful that she might punish him. Duarte gave her the creeps.

Once they got to the ground floor, Viv waited for him to scram. Then she sidled over to Timmy, the doorman, raised a come-hither brow, and dove down the service hallway. Timmy appeared within seconds, she presented her backside, and he tape-rollered her from nape to ankles.

"Oooooh, Timmy. Was that good for you, darling?" She winked at him once he was done. "Because, as always, it was *sensational* for me."

"You're lucky I'm here to service you, Miss Viv." Timmy winked back.

"That I am," Viv agreed. "That I am. Thank you!" She popped the tape roller into her bulging computer bag and rushed out the door just as the firm's car and driver appeared.

Viv had once thought that the chauffeured car was a nice perk of working at Klein, Schmidt and Belker: a luxury. She now considered Maurice and the Lincoln Continental to be her jailer and paddy wagon, respectively. Maurice made sure she was working hard to generate the big bucks for Schmidt and Belker by seven forty-five a.m. each weekday morning, and by nine forty-five a.m. on too-regular Saturdays. (Klein was technically out of the picture, after he'd dropped dead at a urinal in the men's room three years ago. He'd left behind a spectacular courtroom win ratio and an exposed trouser snake that bent even farther right than his politics.)

"Good morning, Maurice," Viv said crisply as she stepped into the Lincoln. "And how are you today?" The usual nauseating smell of wintergreen gum and tropical fruit carpet freshener assailed her nostrils.

The wizened little man looked at his watch and frowned. "Better, now that you're in. Four times around the block today, Miss Shelton!"

"Four, really? How frustrating. Were you early?" Viv was never late. Not by as much as thirty seconds. And tardiness in others was one of her biggest pet peeves.

"Early, schmurly," grumbled Maurice, lurching forward and left in the heavy traffic and cutting off an irate and vocal Middle Eastern cabdriver. Then he floored it for all of eight feet before dodging right again, barely missing a bike messenger, and slamming on the brakes.

Viv took it all in stride. She had a strong suspicion that Schmidt and Belker awarded Maurice an annual bonus for delivering her hundred-and-thirty pounds of flesh before eight o'clock each day. She and the other five attorneys on his run were his responsibility.

She had at least fifteen minutes to kill before the car got from her Upper East Side building to the law offices in midtown, so she checked e-mail on her Palm Pilot.

Please, she prayed, let there not be any more wedding horrors awaiting her. Since the troubling news that her best friend Julia Spinelli was getting married to some redneck she'd only known a month, Viv had tried to digest the fact that she'd have to be a . . . She shuddered, unable to wrap her mind around the concept.

A *bridesmaid*. Vivien didn't want to be anybody's maid, not even for a day. The whole concept was foreign; it implied servitude and worse; it spanned all the possibilities of polyester.

She'd already had to leave a deposition one day to find a full-length, strapless foundation garment in her bra size. Julia had then commanded that she purchase a pair of satin Manolo evening mules and a flaring *petticoat*. Viv had never in her life worn something as fussy as a petticoat, and she dreaded seeing the hideous taffeta creation that went over it. Oh, God! Please let her not have to wear anything with a bow on the butt . . .

Under any other circumstances, she'd laugh her ass off at the idea of one of Manhattan's top divorce attorneys moonlighting as a bridesmaid in a wedding. But all the humor went out of it immediately when *she* was the top divorce attorney in question. Viv had represented some high-profile clients, and she only hoped the papers didn't get hold of this. She could see the headlines now: RAPTOR IN ROSE-BUDS! WILL SHELTON SERVE GROOM PAPERS AT RECEPTION?

Viv shook off what she knew were selfish thoughts under the circumstances. She should be a lot more concerned about Julia than she was about herself. She'd already questioned her delicately on the phone about this guy Roman. She'd also told Julia that coincidentally she knew his sister, Kiki Douglas. Unfortunately Viv had represented her ex-husband in their Manhattan divorce three years ago.

"Listen, hon," she'd said to Julia. "If Roman is anything like Kiki, you want to be careful."

"Roman is nothing like Kiki!" Julia had exclaimed, even though to Viv's knowledge she'd never met her.

Viv had closed her eyes to ward off a migraine—impossible—and sent an urgent e-mail to Sydney Spinelli, Julia's older sister.

Today there was a reply, and Vivien scanned it quickly.

Subject:   Re: Your little sister has gone crazy!

From:     numbersgeek

To:       vshelton@kleinschmidtbelker

Tell me about it! Yes, I've met him, and there's something fishy with the guy. What kind of Texan speaks Italian, wears designer clothes, and has a vineyard??? And Viv, here's the really awful part: the ring he gave her is FAKE!!!!!!!!!!!!!! I think he's marrying her for the $$$. But I can't talk sense into her.

Syd

*"Fake?!"* Viv said it aloud, with enough force that Maurice squinted at her in the rearview mirror. *"What?* She has *got* to be kidding!"

Viv typed a quick reply. She'd call Sydney as soon as she got to the office.

Subject:   FAKE ring???

From:     vshelton@kleinschmidtbelker

To:       numbersgeek

What do you mean, the ring he gave her is fake?! HOW COULD HE??? I'm speechless. xoxoxo, Viv

*party is not authorized. If you are not the intended
recipient, be aware that any copying, disclosure, distri-
bution or use of the contents of this transmission is
prohibited. If you have received this electronic transmission in error, please notify us immediately. Thank you.*

Sydney was obviously online at the same time, because before Viv had finished reading one of the
work e-mails her reply popped into the mailbox.

Subject:   Re: FAKE ring???

From:      numbersgeek

To:        vshelton@kleinschmidtbelker

Viv, supposedly it's not his fault. The grandmother
sold it way back when and he didn't know. (Do
you believe this? Not sure, myself.) But it doesn't
matter! Our Julia has got it bad: she's STILL
WEARING the ring, and says she doesn't care that
it's fake. Why? Because HE gave it to her. I give
up . . . I'm going home. Can you at least get her
to sign a prenup? I'm serious!!!!!!!

Syd

Viv stared in disbelief at the text. Julia was still
wearing a fake ring! She logged off and shut her
laptop with a snap. This was insane. This Roman guy
must be damn good in bed to have her so deluded.
He sounded like one hundred percent bad news, and
if he was related to Kiki Douglas, whose face had

been *all* over the tabloids lately, then he was a prize schmuck.

Julia needed a prenup, all right. The question was how to convince her of that. People in love and planning a wedding did not want to think about the ugly death of that love and the dissolution of the wedding. You couldn't really blame them.

Viv shuddered at the idea of grabbing Julia and telling her that the fabric, cut and design of her gown didn't matter, because she'd be burning it in a backyard bonfire in less than a year.

"Julia, honey," she saw herself saying, "don't worry that the doves they delivered for the event are both male. You'll be roasting them on the barbecue with veggie kabobs by Christmas." Or . . .

"Sweetie, don't bother freezing the top of that cake—unless you want something heavy and icicle-encrusted with which to brain your husband after he absconds with your trust fund." Or . . .

"Lacy white bridal lingerie imported from France? Don't spend the money—unless you've got some red or purple dye on hand. You can transform them for your divorce trousseau."

Viv winced. Julia, the poor thing, wouldn't want to listen to any of this. But Vivien had seen the rough side of marriage. She dealt with it every day: the ugly accusations, the dirty little secrets, the infidelity, the asset hiding, the custody squabbles—even the occasional kidnapping of the miserable couple's children by one spouse.

Viv had seen some strange things. She'd attended a Divorce Dirge for a client of hers and downed a dirty martini as a doll of the ex-husband was burned in effigy.

A caterer client had baked a large, penis-shaped chocolate cake for a luncheon, serving a stunned Viv a good chunk of the balls on a china plate. The client had then thanked her in front of everyone for her great work.

And during one case the cheating SOB of a husband had propositioned Viv right in front of her client, his wife!

But Viv's mistrust of marriage went far deeper than her job. Not only were her own parents divorced, but their parents before them. She simply did not believe in marital bliss.

As the Lincoln pulled up in front of Klein, Schmidt and Belker's building, Viv pulled her things together. She got out with an unenthusiastic thanks to Maurice, who gunned the engine and pulled away before she even had the door closed. Then she schlepped inside.

The first face she saw that morning belonged to grumpy old Schmidt, whose yarmulke hung precariously from a bobby pin attached to one of three final strands of combed-over hair. Now, in Schmidt's favor, he'd been married to the same woman for forty-eight years.

But Viv had a suspicion that Mrs. Schmidt hung around more out of inertia and fear of the man's divorce-law expertise than out of any burning passion for him. And she'd long ago decided that Schmidt stayed with *her* due to a fondness for her chocolate babka cake and light touch with potato latkes. He was also far too fond of his money to part with any of it in a divorce.

Schmidt grunted at her and she nodded back as she passed him on her way to her office, navigating the sea of dark mahogany tables, tasteful green plants and leather seating.

Belker, the younger partner, had covered the walls of the firm with his dour, very minor, old-master Flemish paintings, which Viv referred to collectively as the sourpusses. Belky, unlike Schmidt, had been divorced twice and had given each wife a considerable amount of money for his freedom. But since the firm dumped more on him by the truckload, he didn't seem to mind overly much.

Unfortunately Belky had a thing for Viv's assistant Andie, a former client whom she'd hired in an unwise moment of sympathy. She'd negotiated a fabulous settlement for Andie, the bulk of which was her husband's 2.3-million-dollar house. Unfortunately he'd stopped making the insurance payments on it and burned it down with himself inside it.

Andie was terribly sweet and had a way with Viv's usually upset female clients, whom she plied with tea and sympathy and great gossip.

Belker was sitting on the corner of her desk with his scrawny knees apart when Viv appeared, his chest puffed out like a rooster's. "I had the judge in the palm of my hand," he said, eyeing Andie's plump assets in their tight black sweater. "Had her *purring*."

"Good morning," Viv interrupted him, hardly able to refrain from rolling her eyes.

" 'Morning!" Andie sang.

Belker nodded coolly and removed his vile, skinny buns from their perch. "Ah, Vivien," he said. "I have something to discuss with you."

*Ugh.* She didn't want to discuss anything with Belky other than a promotion and a raise—or taking some of the six weeks of vacation owed to her by the firm.

"Certainly, Howard," Viv told him, accepting the stack of phone messages Andie handed her.

Belky followed her into her office, picking at the dead skin on his left hand—caused by his psoriasis.

She averted her gaze and crossed her arms in front of her, waiting for him to begin, as tiny little flakes of his flesh spiraled toward her carpet. The same carpet she walked on in stocking feet when she worked late.

"You may not be aware, Vivien, that I've just taken on the divorce case of one Samuel Buckheimer."

"Congratulations," she said, infusing her voice with just the right amount of cordiality.

"Yes, well. Sam owns a couple of large operations both here in New York and in Florida. Greyhound tracks. And he happened to come across your name as a large donor to—"

Viv felt her face freezing. "Oh, he did, did he?"

"Yes. He was very pointed in his questioning. Frankly, it was embarrassing."

"Howard. While I feel for you being put in such a position, I must respectfully say that my personal donations or activities outside the firm are a private matter."

"I'd just like you to think about it, Vivien. Okay?"

"He's also being represented by *you*, not me."

"He's concerned about any of his money adding to . . . er, your bottom line. Since you two are philosophically opposed," said Belky smoothly.

Viv gritted her teeth. "Yes, that we certainly are. I don't think that the torture, starvation and neglect of animals for profit is acceptable. Do you?"

Her boss ignored the question. "Great work on the Alderson case, by the way," he said to soften her up.

"Thank you."

"See you at the meeting later."

"Yes."

Viv glared at his hunched little back as he left her office, trailing more tiny bits of his decayed flesh. This wasn't the first run-in they'd had over work she did outside of Klein, Schmidt and Belker. As far as he was concerned, pro bono activities were a waste of time, unless they were accompanied by the firm's name in huge letters and reported in the media.

She'd learned that it was useless to lobby Klein, Schmidt for charitable contributions, unless they involved a fat tax write-off and good spin.

Vivien sighed and began to return phone calls, eyeing the towering stack of briefs and files on her credenza. Just a little light reading to pass the time . . . She glanced at her watch. She had less than twenty minutes before her first appointment.

She'd resolved a couple of issues with one client and left a message returning another one's call when Andie buzzed through. "Miss Sydney Spinelli is on line four."

"Okay, thanks." Viv punched the button. "Syd? I was just going to call you."

"Vivien! How are you? How's your mother?"

"I'm fine. She's fine. You?"

"I'm . . . great, actually." And Syd—*Syd!*—actually giggled. "I'm still here in Fredericksburg. I've, uh, met someone."

"Well, I hope you're not going to marry the guy after a week," Viv said dryly.

"Not yet," Syd chirped.

Syd never chirped. She, like Viv, had studied the entire time that Viv, Julia and Sydney had spent at boarding school in Massachusetts. Well, she'd played field hockey, too. She'd never gotten into trouble, that was for sure. And she'd never been upbeat and bubbly, like her sister. But today, Sydney's voice could almost be mistaken for Julia's.

"Syd, what is going on down there in Texas? Julia's wearing this fake rock, and she believes this BS story about the grandmother hocking it without anyone's knowledge?"

"Yup. And I can't talk any sense into her. I've been accused of jealousy and meddling. And now that I've met Alex, I especially can't say anything to her, because she throws my own romance into my face. Viv, you're Julia's best friend. You're the Ball-Busting Bitch of Manhattan. The *New York Post* said so."

Viv glanced at the framed copy of the article that she'd proudly hung on her wall. Her lips twitched at the unflattering photo, which made her look like Dracula's trailer-trash mistress on a bender.

"You have to come down here and reason with

her," said Sydney. "At least get her to sign one of those ironclad prenups of yours. This Roman guy says he's head over heels for Julia, but he's expanding the family vineyard and looking for cash to do it—I heard him say it myself. He thinks we're like a blue-collar version of the Hilton sisters: the Marv's Motor Inn heiresses."

"Syd, if she didn't respond well to *you* talking with her, she won't listen to me, either. I'm not even family."

"She'll listen to you because there's no sibling rivalry involved. And you're so frighteningly business-like. You just tell her you want to protect her legally. You say, 'Here, Julesy, sign on this dotted line and I'll take care of the rest.'"

Andie buzzed through. "Mrs. Bonana is here for your eight thirty."

"Okay, thanks," Viv told her. "Can you put her in one of the small conference rooms?"

"They're all full."

"Oh. All right. Send her in." Viv went back to Sydney. "Look, hon, I'm glad you think I'm frightening, but I doubt that even I can scare Julia into doing something she doesn't want to do. That dent in her chin means, as you very well know, that she's stubborn. And she's also a bona fide romantic. Plus, as usual, I'm up to the eyeballs in work right now, and I'll be lucky if I can get away to be there for the wedding."

Andie brought a dubiously sun-streaked brunette to her office door. Viv nodded and held up a finger.

"Please, Viv. You've got to do something."

"Syd, it sounds as if you might need a prenup soon yourself, doll."

"Oh, no. Alex is completely trustworthy."

Viv groaned. "See what I mean? And you don't think your sister will have the same reaction?"

"No, really, this is different."

How many times had Viv heard that before? "I've got to go—I have an appointment."

"Please say you'll think about coming down and talking to her. I can't do anything else. It's all up to you."

"I'll think about it," Viv promised, more to get off the phone than anything else.

"Okay. Thanks."

She hung up the phone and smiled reassuringly at Mrs. Bonana, who looked a little manic and frayed around the edges. "Hi. I'm Vivien Shelton. What can I do for you?"

# Chapter Two

Twenty minutes later, Viv had a full-fledged migraine from hell, and Mrs. Bonana was half hysterical and sipping a fourth cup of coffee, which wasn't helping her nerves.

"Let me get this straight," Viv said, removing her black, rectangular glasses and rubbing at the bridge of her nose. "You legally *married* a chimpanzee. With a judge present, and signatures on an actual, binding document."

"Yes. I married Seltzer to protect him, and so I could have him in my house in spite of the zoning laws, and now—"

"What was the judge smoking at the time of the wedding?"

"Pardon?"

"Never mind."

"Now Seltzer has bitten my neighbor, who was only trying to put back some of my mail that went to her house by mistake. And she's always been so sweet. She used to make him banana cream pies! But now she wants to sue me, and so I've got to get a divorce. *Instantly.*"

"Mrs. Bonana—is that your name or, uh, Seltzer's?"

"Well. I gave it to him so he had a legal surname. But then I changed mine through the courts to match his."

"I see." Viv massaged her temples. "Well, the thing is, that married or not—and I'll need to check for sure, but I strongly doubt this marriage is valid—Seltzer is an animal. A pet. Which technically makes him your property under New York law. And even if you divorce him now, he was still your property at the time of the biting incident. Which makes you responsible for his behavior, and therefore vulnerable to your neighbor's suit."

"But what if Seltzer and I were legally separated at the time?"

"You were still technically married. And even if that marriage is invalid, he's still your pet, which makes you liable for his actions." Vivien's head was starting to spin. "Wait. I have to ask. How did you get a judge to legally marry you, and what was his name?"

"Oh, he was the sweetest thing, and he thought it was a great joke."

Viv's heart sank. She had a feeling she knew who it was.

"His name is Barclay Phelps."

"Disbarred in 1998 for being drunk off his a—uh, bench during court for months at a time. I know Barclay." *He's even asked me out.*

"Isn't he a doll?"

"A doll. Yes. Oh, absolutely." There was no reasoning with this crazed woman. And she definitely didn't want to know anything further about this happy couple's personal life together . . .

"So what am I going to *dooooooo*?" wailed Mrs. Bonana, gazing piteously at Viv. "My neighbor wants my husband *executed!*"

That did tug at Viv's heartstrings. She didn't want to see the animal put down for defending his territory. "Does Seltzer have rabies?"

"Absolutely not."

"And the neighbor came into your yard."

"Yes."

"Was she threatening Seltzer in any way?"

"Just waving my mail."

"Could he have taken that as a threat, perhaps?"

"I suppose so."

"Good. Is the yard fenced, with a gate she had to open?"

"Yes."

"Excellent. I don't think that she can legally force you to put Seltzer down. Only the state can decide that, and we'd have a pretty good case under the circumstances."

"Oh, thank God!" Mrs. Bonana dabbed at her eyes with a monogrammed hankie.

"Now, about this bite. Is it infected? Has it caused any type of blood disease or the amputation of the arm?"

"I don't think so. But she's claiming trauma and mental anguish or something. She has a weak heart. It may have worsened her angina, she says."

"Mmmmm. Mrs. Bonana, I'm a divorce attorney, and quite frankly I'm expensive. You don't need a divorce for an invalid marriage, and this is not my area of expertise. Though Klein, Schmidt and Belker can certainly handle the case for you, you may wish to look elsewhere for representation." Viv prayed silently. *Please scram, you wacko.*

Mrs. Bonana sniffed and stuck out her lower lip. "But . . . I *like* you, Ms. Shelton. You're nice and frightening—in a good way, you understand—and you have quite the reputation." She gazed pointedly at the *New York Post* clipping. "Andie says you're the best."

*Thanks, Andie.* Vivien sighed inwardly. *I am so screwed.* The woman wasn't going to go away. "I, ah, like you, too, Mrs. Bonana."

After another appointment, Viv was able to snarf a protein bar at her desk and down half a bottle of lukewarm water before heading to one of the now-free small conference rooms to take a deposition from client Siegfried Klempt. She hoped that dear Sieggie wasn't going to get *ver*klempt during the process. His wife had left him for another woman.

Sieggie, as it turned out, was far, far from ver-klempt. He was dancing a green-faced Andie around the polished maple conference table, much to her dismay.

"What is going on here?" Viv demanded.

Sieggie released Andie, who coughed, gagged and fled. "Ms. Shelton! How sharming to zee you again." Klempt staggered toward her, wearing a suit that looked as if he'd slept in it for the last three days. His eyes were bloodshot, his face covered with graying bristle, and she had a feeling she *really* didn't want to touch the hand he extended.

But Klempt's breath was the crowning horror: It positively blew the hair off her head. No wonder poor Andie had turned green and gagged. She deserved combat pay.

"Mr. Klempt, you are in no condition to render a deposition this morning."

"Ssshharp as a talc," he said solemnly.

"Yes, I can see that." Viv went to the phone. "Andie? An entire pot of black coffee, please. You can send it with one of the male runners, doll. Thanks."

"Care to danssh?"

"*No*, Mr. Klempt. Have a seat." Viv eyed him sternly and wondered just how bad this day was going to get. Her frightening-in-a-good-way image served her well in this instance, since he pulled out a chair with an unsteady hand and collapsed into it.

"She's gone," he announced to nobody in particular. "Doggone."

She assumed he was speaking of his wife. "Yes, I'm sorry. She is. But there are other barracuda in the sea, Siegfried. She wasn't very nice to you."

"Neither was my first wife. I liked—*hic*—the familiarity of that."

Viv patted him on the shoulder, standing upwind of his breath. Her next call was to the receptionist, Cleo. "Cleo, it's Viv. Could you please call Maurice and get him to swing by here for a, um, incapacitated client? He'll need to take him home and probably put him into his bed. I know that's not in his job description, but he'll have to get over it. Yes. Thanks."

Viv didn't bother trying to reschedule Siegfried's appointment just yet. He wouldn't remember it. The runner arrived with the coffee, and she left him to babysit until Maurice's arrival. Perks of the job . . .

Back in her office, there was a note from Belky: *Buckheimer walked. Thanks for your team efforts.* Viv balled up the piece of paper in her hand and threw it angrily into the trash. Jerk. Belky was one of the reasons she disliked her job. He was always trying to throw her a curveball—and it was thanks to him that she'd ended up having to defend Kiki Sonntag Douglas's ex-husband in court. She had no fond memories of the man she'd dubbed Walter the Wanker, but he was a golfing buddy of Belky's.

The image of Kiki's Texas attorney (who'd worked with her New York attorneys) appeared far too often in her mind's eye—even after three years, J.B. Anglin had the power to haunt her. She hadn't been so nice to him the last time they'd seen each other, which was another reason she didn't want to go anywhere near Fredericksburg, Texas. As the Sonntag family attorney, the man would no doubt be at Julia's wedding!

Viv didn't blush—it was physically impossible for her to do so, since nothing shocked her—but her heart beat faster at the thought of encountering J.B. again. God had been unjust to women when he'd fused the looks of Matthew McConaughey with those of Jude Law, put the result in cowboy boots and turned him loose. Yes, God had played a cruel joke, but it got even worse: Viv had seen J.B. Anglin naked.

*Do. Not. Think. About. That. Man.*

To distract herself, Viv glared again at the wadded piece of paper in her trash can. She was not going to be intimidated or coerced out of her charitable donations to causes she believed in. Speaking of which—she looked at her watch—she'd better get the rest of those phone calls returned, since she had a luncheon to attend for the Displaced Homemakers' Association of New York.

She worked mostly for women, deliberately so. And she found it very disturbing that many of them, in the event of divorce, were so ill prepared to return to the workforce after years of being wives and mothers. Viv did everything she could for her local chapter, from making financial contributions to leading training seminars and doing pro bono legal work.

Viv returned all her calls, adding to the latest game of phone tag with one opposing counselor who refused to speak with her in person and whose legal secretary left obtuse messages with Andie.

She was pushing back from her desk and grabbing her purse when Andie buzzed through again with Syd Spinelli on the line.

"Have you thought about it?" asked Sydney.

"Syd—"

"She's been there for *you* when you needed her."

"Yes, she has, but I can't just leave work in the

middle of the week." Viv's gaze fell on the balled-up note from Belky again. Or could she?

"Why not? You hate your job anyway."

"Pretty much everybody hates their jobs sometimes. That's no excuse to—"

She saw little scraps of skin falling on her carpet first. And then Belky's custom-made wing tips. Oh, not again! What did he want now? Why couldn't he get some kind of intestinal disorder and be trapped on the throne, away from her?

"Viv, I made you a flight reservation for this afternoon. You fly out of JFK at four twenty-two p.m. on American. At this point we only have two weeks to either stop this wedding or at least get Jules's signature on a prenup. I hate to be pushy but she needs you."

It was true. She owed it to Julia to at least *try* to protect her.

"Vivien," Belky began pompously, without waiting for her to get off the phone. "I need you to appear in court for me tomorrow on the Bleckner case."

Her ire rose. "One moment, Ms. Spinelli," she said crisply to Sydney. "Howard, I can't do that. I have a conflict."

A tic began in his left eye. "Please reschedule so that you don't."

His arrogance and calm certainty that she'd leap to accommodate him were the final straw. Honestly, her decision had nothing to do with her subconscious remembering what J.B. looked like—and felt like—naked.

Viv's chin went up. "I'm afraid that's not possible, Howard. I'll be out of the state, on an urgent personal matter. A relative of mine isn't well."

They locked gazes. Vivien knew it was just a matter of time before they'd lock horns for good, and as senior partner with his name on the shingle, Belky wasn't the one going anywhere.

"Very well, Ms. Shelton." His fingers twitched and a few more flakes of the little lizard's skin fell on her carpet. He was very displeased.

She couldn't care less. She wasn't his lackey. Viv raised a brow, looked pointedly from him to the phone, and resumed her conversation with Sydney. "Fourish, did you say?"

Belky and his peeling skin retreated under her glare, and Viv's lip curled. "So, Syd, you just upped and got me a ticket. You're not shy, are you, hon?"

"Nope."

Viv chuckled. It was classic stubborn Syd. "You're leaving me with an hour to get home and pack a bag, and I'm going to have to skip a luncheon. Not to mention the fact that I just dissed my boss."

"You enjoyed it, though. I could tell by the tone of your voice. See, I gifted you with the opportunity."

"Nice, Sydney. Very nice. You owe me a drink when I get there."

"I don't owe you a thing." Sydney laughed. "You're traveling on *my* frequent-flier miles."

"First class?" asked Viv hopefully.

"Sorry, darling. You're in steerage with the common folk. Suck it up."

24

\*    \*    \*

J.B. Anglin placed his booted feet on the corner of his desk, leaned back in his worn, comfy leather chair, and folded his hands behind his neck.

"So do you think I have a case?" asked the very pretty blonde in his visitor's chair.

J.B. smiled at her, and she smiled back—but she wore a disturbingly covetous expression. And what she coveted had nothing to do with his legal expertise.

"No, darlin', I don't. Yes, Ted Kimball's emu flock should be penned. And it is—most of the time. He can't help it that somebody's cutting his fence just to watch the featherworks."

"He's still liable for those stupid giant chickens."

"Well, yes. But, bottom line, that curve you skidded around is marked by a big yellow sign: SLIPPERY WHEN WET."

Her eyes widened and she licked her small, pink lips.

J.B. groaned inwardly. Mindy Baker *would* take a road sign as a sexual come-on. "And so, whether or not there was an emu pile on the tarmac, you should not have been traveling at the rate of sixty miles an hour on that portion of road. Know what I mean? In fact, the speed limit there is thirty-five."

"I wasn't going sixty!" she exclaimed indignantly.

"Wes said you had to have been, judging by the state of the Blazer."

"Wes can't judge anything but a pie."

In spite of his friendship for their local law enforcement, J.B.'s lips twitched. "How fast do you estimate you were goin'?"

"No more than fifty miles an hour."

J.B. rubbed a hand over his jaw. "Sweetheart, that's still a good fifteen miles per hour over the speed limit. You don't have a case, emu poop or not."

"Jeffrey is *sooooooo* mad at me for totaling the Blazer. I just wanted to see—"

*. . . if you could pawn off your mess on somebody else. Someone like my friend Alex's uncle.* J.B. refrained from saying that Jeffrey would be a whole lot madder at her if he found out how she was spending her time. She seemed unable to choose a stained glass pattern for her front door, and had been "consulting" with Denny Stoltz for hours and hours when her husband was away.

Now it looked like she was bored with Denny and exploring her options with J.B.

She didn't have any.

Since his divorce, J.B. hadn't been a big fan of women in general, but he thought cheating women were lower than, well, emu poop. As for women who made serial cheating a hobby, he didn't even have a word bad enough to describe them. He wanted Mindy Baker out of his office.

Instead of obliging him, she crossed one long, tan leg over the other, managing to hike her short skirt up even more. She dabbed at an eye with a tissue, careful not to smudge her turquoise eyeliner. "My insurance company is going to non-renew me," she whined. "Isn't there anything we can do?"

*Yeah. Stop driving double the speed limit.* But J.B. didn't say it aloud. "I can look into a defensive driving class for you."

"I've already taken two."

J.B. sighed inwardly. "I didn't realize that, Mindy."

"I'm *soooooo* stressed out right now."

*Maintaining a brand-new house with a three-car garage and a pool will do that to you. Especially when you have no kids and no job. Must be exhausting.* "I'm sorry to hear that."

"I need to relax." She leaned forward and placed a hand on the tip of his boot.

J.B. wanted to kick it off. "You should talk to your doctor, Mindy. Maybe get a prescription for Xanax or something." He glanced at his watch. "Would you look at the time. I've got just enough of a window to grab something for lunch and then get back here for a twelve-thirty appointment." He swung his feet off the desk, and she had to let go of him. He stood up and moved to his office door.

"Oh. Well. I'll come with you!" she said brightly. "I'm starved."

*Great.* It'd be all over town that he was nailing Jeffrey's wife. He really could do without that. J.B. opened the door for her without enthusiasm, and whistled for Harley, his black Lab.

Harley bounded to his feet, leading as usual with his tongue. He gave a great big canine yawn and shook himself awake.

*Lick her, boy. Lick her. She'll hate it.* "Harley, meet Mindy. Mindy, Harley."

"Nice doggie. Eeeeeuuuuwwwww!" Mindy squealed, as Harley slurped her. She stepped away from the dog. Harley just extended his tongue and followed. "Nice—nice doggie. Stop that!"

Mindy's golden drumsticks were now spackled with dog drool, and J.B. couldn't have been more pleased. "Come 'ere, boy. Stop that." But he scratched Harley's head and ears with approval.

J.B. aimed a subtle eye-roll at his receptionist, who also happened to be his widowed mama. Still handsome and trim in her late fifties, she had ash-blond hair the same color as his own and wore it clasped at her nape in a large barrette. Though she owed a little bit to L'Oréal these days, they were unmistakably mother and son.

She raised her brows, asking telepathically if he needed help extricating himself. He shook his head with an evil grin, and she narrowed her eyes as if to say *What are you up to?*

"Bye-bye, Mrs. Anglin. *Soooo* nice to see you!" gushed Mindy. "You take care, now."

"You, too." His mama was a plainspoken Texas woman, and though she was unfailingly polite, she didn't believe in false enthusiasm.

J.B. led the way out to his pickup truck, went around to the passenger seat, and opened the door. He whistled. Harley bounded up, almost knocking Mindy over, and sprang into the vehicle, where he turned around three times before sprawling all over the passenger seat.

Mindy blinked. She looked from his black, shedding body to her white silk skirt and knit top.

Harley gazed right back at her, letting a big dollop of drool plunk between his paws.

Keeping an utterly straight face, J.B. said, "I need you in the seat belt, but Harley needs to hang his head out the window, otherwise he gets carsick. So unfortunately you may end up somewhat trampled."

Mindy ran her fingers through her heat-set curls. "I, uh, just remembered that I have a manicure appointment. And I'm already five minutes late! I guess I'll have to take a rain check. But thanks for inviting me."

*I didn't.*

She flashed him a toothy white smile and an eyeful of cleavage. Waggling her fingers at him, she made full use of her hips as she walked toward her own car. "Bye-bye!"

*You got that right, lady.* J.B. shut the door on Harley and turned on the ignition and air for him. Then he walked back into his office. "Ham and cheese on rye with a pickle?" he said to his mother.

"Perfect. That girl is bad news. How did you get rid of her?"

"Harley was happy to do his part. She's not a dog person."

"Phew. For a minute there I thought you'd lost your judgment to her legs."

"You know me better than that."

"Speaking of legs, Corinne called. Wanted to know if you'd swing by after work and hang a replacement door for her. She says the back one's rotted." Mama kept her face completely devoid of expression.

Corinne was his ex-wife, now divorced a second time. "I'm not her handyman."

His mother just looked at him.

"I'll think about it. I don't know if I have time— I'm meeting Alex and Roman at Cuvée after work."

"Okay. I'll pass that on when she calls back."

"Thanks."

As J.B. drove to get their sandwiches, his jaw tightened and his stomach clenched. Corinne had a nerve. She also had half of his earnings from his short-lived pro ball career, thanks to a shark of a divorce attorney and J.B.'s inability to care about the money at the time.

He'd been too shell-shocked at her departure. J.B. was the only person in his entire family, past and present, to have gotten divorced. When Anglins married, they did it for keeps.

They didn't just walk away when things got tough and the magical fairy dust of romance got vacuumed into some void. Every Anglin he knew prided him- or herself on keeping the family together. They believed in unity, problem-solving and respect.

Not that they were squabble-free, or that there hadn't been two or three Anglin couples who'd had separate bedrooms and even, in one case, a separate house. And J.B. had heard about a great-aunt who really did bash her husband's skull with an iron skillet. He went deaf on the side she hit, and she had to nurse him out of a bad concussion, but they stayed married.

Even J.B.'s second cousin, whose wife bore him two sons by another man, had stayed married to her. While he'd gone and beat the tar out of the other guy once he found out, the cousin had raised the children as his own. After all, it wasn't their fault.

J.B. didn't want to think about Corinne. He didn't even know what he felt for her anymore. He'd been almost celibate since the divorce four years ago. Almost. Only one woman had tempted him, gotten under his skin—or at least on top of it. And he was damned if he knew why.

Vivien Shelton. Long, lean, graceful and fierce. She'd reminded him of a Doberman in court, as opposing counsel during Kiki Douglas's divorce. Out of court, and out of her clothes, she was . . . something else.

He'd never see her again. But in the unlikely event that he did, he had a score to settle with that woman.

# Chapter Three

Vivien made her flight with only minutes to spare and reluctantly slid into a middle seat about halfway back in the plane. She was squashed between an enormous man with a bag of unshelled peanuts and a ten-year-old boy with more gadgets and beeping gizmos than she could count.

When Viv traveled for business, she normally went first class, since the firm had a seemingly limitless supply of frequent-flier miles on the corporate AmEx card. She told herself that she was not a snob, but she looked longingly toward the curtained-off area at the front of the plane, thinking of the wide, plush leather seats and the solicitous service.

Her traveling companion cracked another shell, and particles scattered again over the brief she was trying to read. Again, she brushed them off while he crunched and munched.

*Bleep! Blip, blip, blip. Bleeeeep!* On the other side of her, the little boy was killing something violently on a minivideo screen.

Behind her, a baby awoke and began to cry, probably feeling pressure in her ears.

Viv ordered a glass of Chardonnay and slipped off her pumps. Maybe it wasn't first class, but it was still better than dodging Belky and insane clients in the office. And though this was to be somewhat a working vacation, at least it was a vacation.

She wondered just what Fredericksburg, Texas, was like. She wondered what Roman Sonntag was like. She wondered how she was going to bring up the subject of a prenuptial agreement with Julia. And she couldn't help but consider the possibility of seeing J.B. Anglin.

If she did, what the hell would she say to him?

*Hi, remember me? The woman who . . .* Viv closed her eyes and swallowed half the glass of Chardonnay in her hand. *The woman you unnerved so much that . . .*

*The woman who, to all appearances, used you for sex and immediately kicked you out when she was done?*

How could he *not* remember her? She still recalled the shock and disgust on his face as she shut the door, leaving him standing shirtless in the hotel hall.

It had not been her proudest moment. Even though, in theory, it should have been. All she'd done, really, was even out the score between the sexes. How many men kicked women out of their beds, once they were done?

Viv told herself she should be proud. Stand tall. Shake her fist for womankind. Instead she had a horrible feeling that J.B. hadn't deserved that kind of treatment.

Oh, BS! Pretty much all men deserved it. Even her maternal grandfather and her own father had been pigs, cheating on their wives and then disappearing. In her father's case, he'd returned to town long enough to take her mother, a certified Park Avenue Princess, for half what she was worth. Half had been a very sizable sum, since Mummy was a toothpaste heiress.

Viv's mother had brought her up to be defensive and wary of men. Anna Shelton spent a third of her life desperately in love with one unsuitable man or other, and two-thirds of it crying, cursing the latest man, or constructing voodoo dolls of him.

The voodoo, in particular, gave Vivien the creeps. Mummy was a matched-pearls-and-gray-cashmere-twinset person, not really the voodoo type, but she'd had a Haitian housekeeper as a girl and had observed her more intriguing habits.

Viv drank the rest of the icky Chardonnay from the plastic airline cup, and managed to drift off to sleep. When she awoke, her papers were covered with peanut shell particles, and the plane was landing at the Dallas airport. From there she had only a short hop to Austin, where Sydney would pick her up and take her to Fredericksburg. Being a born-and-bred city girl, Viv had never learned to drive. Having your own car in Manhattan was just an expensive headache. Garaging it alone cost almost as much as rent.

The lack of a driver's license never bothered her until she left the Big Apple for somewhere like Los Angeles, where there was no public transportation to speak of. At those times, she had to hire a car and driver, but since the firm picked up the tab it didn't concern her much.

When she got off the second flight in Austin, Syd rushed her in baggage claim. "Vivver! I wasn't sure you'd actually get on the plane. How are you!"

They hugged and stepped away from each other for a brief inventory—neither had seen the other in over three years. Syd looked radiant. Her hair was loose and flowing over her shoulders, her eyes sparkled and she carried herself in a more open, confident stance. "You look beautiful," Viv told her. "And I like the Western wear." Sydney had become a new woman—a new woman sporting some very mod, hand-tooled cowboy boots.

"So do you! Check out the designer suit and the three-inch heels on you. If I hadn't seen your Snoopy nightshirt and bedhead at school, I'd be petrified of you!"

"Why does everyone say that? I'm frightening. I'm intimidating. I'm scary-in-a-good-way. I dress professionally, that's all. I am a professional."

Sydney laughed. "Viv, it's the way you walk. And talk. You just reek of Park Avenue and private schools and the best of the best. There's nothing wrong with it—you're no poseur. It's just you. But some people don't know how to take it."

Viv shrugged. "Whatever. To me, I'm just me. Non-scary, very human, have-to-pee-like-everyone-else. Now my mother—she's a scary woman. But me?"

"Come on, let's grab your bag and hit the road."

As the two waited for the luggage to tumble off the carousel, Viv had to ask. "So . . . what do these bridesmaids' dresses look like? How ugly are we going to be? Will we look like little floral upholstered sofas? Or are we doomed to be torrid in taffeta? If she's got us in peach tulle, I'll be sick."

Sydney threw up her hands. "Beats me. All I know is that I'm sick to death of tasting white cake. Julia's veered from floor-length black satin to white tailored tuxedo tops with bell skirts and cummerbunds. From floral cotton to peacock blue silk minis. From tea-length, buttercream yellow linen to Pepto-Bismol pink shantung sheaths."

Viv shuddered at the idea of a pink sheath. They'd all look like oversized tulip buds. Her bag appeared before the nightmare could grow to horrific proportions in her mind: little green pillbox hats with stems on top, and matching green kid gloves and shoes.

The airport, well-air-conditioned, did not prepare Vivien for the heat, which slapped her face and knocked the breath out of her. She stood in shock for a moment, trying to suck some oxygen from the sticky air.

Sydney cast her a look of sympathy while she set down her things and stripped off her summer-weight Escada jacket. Any weight at all was too much for August in Texas. It was brutal.

New York in the summer, with its acres of black macadam and walls of concrete, was no picnic. But Texas made the City seem cool by comparison.

Syd was driving a car about the size of a soda can,

but Vivien managed to cram her small suitcase into the trunk and wedged herself and her computer bag into the passenger seat, fumbling for a way to move it back so that her forehead didn't press against the windshield. She was afraid that, like a leaf under a magnifying glass, she'd spontaneously combust.

Besides the heat, though, nothing in particular had announced her arrival to the Wild West. Viv didn't know what she'd expected. Not a gigantic yellow wall of roses, or a public building shaped like a Stetson. But something. Oversized Remington bronzes?

She decided to ask Sydney.

"Oh, you missed the gift shops in the Bergstrom airport. You can get a chili-pepper necktie, a Texas Chardonnay, or a Tex-Mex cookbook with a big-haired lady on the cover. You can also buy a plastic model of the Alamo, or a coffee cup in the shape of a boot. Should we go back and get you one of those, or would you like to pick it up on your way out of town?"

Viv raised a brow. "I don't think I can live without a coffee cup in the shape of a boot."

"We'll find you a matched set," Syd promised. "And a chip 'n' dip tray where the salsa sits in a Mexican sombrero and the handles are made of little ceramic 'ropes.' "

Viv nodded. "Mummy would adore one of those," she said in tones drier than dust. "I'll have it gift-wrapped and sent to her. I'm sure she'll place it right next to her Limoges and Sevres porcelain on the mantel of the formal living room."

"Texas," Syd said, "is actually a very cool place. I've never had so much fun! And you're going to love Fredericksburg."

"I am?"

"Guaranteed. It's pretty much impossible not to like it. The place is so cute. And so clean. No enormous black Dumpsters everywhere. No stink of rotting garbage. No scaffolding or detours. And everyone is nice! Even construction crews are polite."

"Impossible."

They'd gotten onto the highway now after weaving through the airport maze, and Syd had the little soda can car speeding like a bullet toward Julia and her crazy, impromptu wedding plans. The double yellow lines pointed their trajectory. As they raced into town, Vivien worried about the looming, difficult conversation she needed to have with her best friend and the unnerving possibility of seeing J.B. Anglin again.

Should she look him up? No, not a brilliant idea. He'd probably spit on her if she did.

They passed working ranches, peach orchards and wineries—though Viv didn't have much faith in Texas wine. But when she said as much to Syd, Syd told her to withhold judgment until she'd tried several varieties. "Texas wines are being served in the White House these days, Vivver."

Viv restrained a snort.

They passed barbecue places and odd little holes in the wall and taxidermists by the dozen. Finally they turned down Main Street and into a town that could have been a Hollywood set. Fredericksburg was one hundred percent picturesque Texas village, lined with shops and restaurants and tourists. To Vivien, it could have been Mars.

The streets were wide and the buildings low—most of them one or two story. Flowering trees framed the broad avenue, and what looked like wisteria climbed posts here and there. An old bathtub served as an unusual planter outside one shop, and wooden benches dotted the sidewalks for tourists who needed a rest. Many of the buildings that housed storefronts were historical and wore preservation plaques. Wooden plank porches and railings added to the general movie-set feeling.

Viv almost felt she needed a bonnet, a blue gingham skirt and a pair of granny boots. She exchanged a glance with Sydney, who punched her lightly in the arm.

"You're not in Manhattan anymore, Dorothy."

A woman walking across the street rapped on Viv's window, and she lowered it suspiciously. "Do y'all know whayere Cranky Frank's Barbecue eeyis?" She could barely understand the woman.

"Cranky Frank?" She looked at Sydney, who shrugged. "We're a couple of escaped Yankees. Sorry."

"Well, thank you, ma'am." The woman turned away.

"Wait!" Syd said, frowning. "I think it's on South 87. Go down Washington, headed south, and it'll become 87."

"Oh, okay." She waved as the light turned green and they accelerated.

"So just how cranky is Frank?" Viv asked.

"I don't have a clue. You'll have to ask Julia. By the way, I've booked you a room at our very own Marv's Motor Inn on Orange Street. Luxury accommodations for the discriminating traveler."

Viv swallowed. She'd heard Julia's opinion of the Inn when she'd first arrived. "Uh, that's okay—I wouldn't want to put you guys to any trouble—"

Syd aimed a mocking grin at her. "No trouble at all, doll. I'm staying in room 239, and Julia herself is in number 116. With you there, too, it'll be just like old times at school. Except with more brown and orange. You'll love it, I promise."

*Great.* "Syd? Didn't Julia actually find a family of rats in one of those mattresses?"

"Yup. And fleas in the carpet. Some old guy had leased the room long term, and he had a couple of incredibly lazy cats. I guess they used to watch the rats run around at night just like guys watch televised sports."

Sydney laughed at Viv's expression. "Don't worry. Julia tore out most of the carpet and replaced the funky old mattresses. I think she even used her own money to upgrade them, because Marv would only order the cheapest of the cheap, if he were footing the bill. He'd purchase the kind of bedding where the coils spring through in the middle of the night and impale unsuspecting guests."

She steered the little soda can around the corner onto Orange Street, and there it was in all its bad seventies' glory, Marv's Motor Inn with its flashing neon sign: the arrow that pointed toward the familiar slogan, COUNT SHEEP FOR CHEAP.

Viv blinked. Not once in her lifetime had she

stayed at a hotel of this caliber. Mummy would have run screaming from the place: hitchhiked back to the Hamptons with her monogrammed Ferragamo luggage.

"Viv, unbuckle your seat belt and step out of the car. It's not the Ritz, but you'll survive. What's a little asbestos poisoning to you, huh? And the lead paint problems will bolster your immune system."

*What doesn't kill me will make me stronger.* Viv disentangled herself from the safety harness, opened the passenger side door, and stepped out into the blaze of heat again. The air petrified in her nostrils before she could suck any oxygen out of it, and her skin immediately blossomed with sweat.

"The AC works in there, right?" She didn't want to think about how many toxins and molds and germs were recycled through the ductwork. She just wanted it to be cold. She turned to grab her computer bag—Syd had her suitcase—when she heard an excited shriek.

"*Vivver!*" Julia erupted from behind the brown smoked-glass door of the Inn, and shot toward her like a pretty little blond cannonball. "Vivver, Vivver, Vivver! I can't believe you're *here*! In the middle of a workweek! Did Sydney bribe you to come initiate my divorce even before the ceremony?"

*She's not stupid, is she?*

While Syd laughed a little too loudly, Julia grabbed Vivien in a surprisingly strong bear hug and twirled before letting go. "You look wonderful! Like Courteney Cox-Arquette . . . dressed as Dietrich. My God, you look—"

"Intimidating? In a good sort of way?"

"How did you know I was going to say that?"

"Just a sixth sense. You look gorgeous yourself, as always." Viv eyed Julia's crisp, cool little sundress. *Perfect on her. Me, I'd look like a florally impaired moron. Not to mention the fact that I'm so sun-starved that I glow in the dark.*

"You're just completely uptown New York," Julia told her. "Escada. Kate Spade. Sleek hair. Platinum Tiffany earrings. Minimal makeup. A don't-get-in-my-way expression. Competence radiating from every pore. Scares the stuffing out of lesser mortals."

"You've never been a lesser mortal. You're one of those annoyingly sunny little goddesses."

Julia laughed.

"And now you're going to be a married one. Let me guess: You're going to throw the biggest, most elegant wedding this town has ever seen."

"Oh, you can count on it. Roman's family has been here for generations, so I want to do it up right."

Viv touched her shoulder. "You're sure about this, Jules?"

"I'm sure about it." She stuck her tongue out at Sydney. "Don't listen to the Evil Redheaded Sister. I'm betting she's told you all about the ring. Don't bother denying it. You're good at keeping a deadpan face, but she's not. Syd, you blabbed!"

Sydney blushed and couldn't deny it.

Julia put her hands on her hips. "Go play with your new boy toy, Alex. Get yourself pregnant, why don't you? Just for the look on Marv's face. Just kidding! I *am kidding*. Well, sort of."

"As a matter of fact," Syd said, "I do have a date

with Alex later. And before you get too cute, why don't you thank me for getting Viv at the airport?"

"Thank you, Syd. Except that I know you well enough to sense you're up to no good. This involves a plot of some kind." She looked suspiciously from Viv to Sydney and back again. "Let me guess. Viv is the Voice of Reason, brought down to talk me out of getting married since you failed so miserably."

"No such thing!" Sydney exclaimed.

"I'm here purely out of friendship, Jules." Viv said it in calm, diplomatic tones. "And yes, I wanted to see for myself that you're of sound mind and body. This has all happened so fast. Come on. Let's go somewhere for a drink and a catch-up chat."

"I secretly booked her a room," Syd called to Julia as she got back into the mobile soda can. "The presidential suite with the panoramic view."

"Very funny," said Julia, taking Viv's suitcase. "Give me that—it's twice your size."

They argued over it companionably until they got to Vivien's deluxe accommodations, which featured an appalling polyester quilted bedspread, festooned with dying flowers in shades of brown and mustard yellow. The room also sported a pitted mirror, bad particleboard furniture and a serigraph of a constipated duck in a poisoned lake.

However, it was scrupulously clean and the toilet paper was folded into a little "V." She was sure this was due to Julia's influence. Viv opened her mouth to say something along the lines of *Very nice*, but she just couldn't. She put her computer bag on the bed and nodded. "Looks . . . comfortable."

"Viv, honey, free beats ambience any day, don't you think? And don't worry, all the rats and fleas are gone. I *promise*. Now, let's go get you a decent glass of wine."

Julia looked so happy, so irresistible, so adorably Reese-Witherspoon-with-messier-hair. Did she not realize that she was entering into a contract to pick up this Roman person's dirty socks, run his errands and never see her toilet seat in the "down" position again?

But Viv kept quiet until they were settled into a nook of Cuvée, a combination bistro, market and wine bar. She slowly sipped a fantastic Australian Chardonnay that made her cringe at the memory of the airline wine.

"So," she said to Julia, who cocked her head and smiled more mysteriously than the Mona Lisa.

"So?"

"What makes this guy Roman different? What makes him your One and Only? The one man for whom you'll forsake all others?"

"Viv, it's not something I can really explain. You know I tried when we talked on the phone. It's just a feeling of coming home. An understanding on a very basic, almost primal level. As if I know what he's thinking and feeling just when he's discovering it himself."

Well, that sounded genuine. "Do you think that he knows what *you're* thinking and feeling just as *you're* discovering it?"

Julia nodded.

"So he shares your excitement over the new fall collection by Prada or Herrera?" Vivien asked.

"I said this is on a *primal* level. He's a man, so there are obvious differences. But yes, he does appreciate good design. And good wine—just like you. He's a great businessman and incredibly romantic—"

"What about this whole ring business? Yes, Syd told me. Because she's worried. So don't be mad at her."

Julia's small hand curved into a surprisingly fierce little fist. "I explained this to her. And I'll explain it to you. This ring"—she flashed it at Viv—"belonged to Roman's great-grandmother, and then his grandmother. Social life and keeping up appearances were very important to Olga Sonntag, but not to her husband, who complained that she spent too much money. Apparently they fought over money a lot. So at some point Olga got desperate to have some funds of her own, and she had the original stone removed from the ring. She sold it, and had the diamond replaced with a crystal copy. But nobody else in the family had any idea. So poor Roman goes and gets the ring from the bank vault and proposes to me with it, having no clue that the stone isn't genuine! Of course Sydney the bloodhound had it tested, and has now decided that he's a first-class creep.

"Roman wants to get me another ring—but I'm fine with this one. He proposed to me with this ring! And it's like a fun secret . . . I'm wearing the family skeleton on my fourth finger."

*That's one way to look at it,* Viv thought and just

shook her head. "But a diamond is the symbol of eternity. What does a crystal signify?"

"Anything we want it to. Look, if I'm fine with my big fake ring, why should anyone else worry about it? Whose business is it, really? Poor Roman is mortified, but I *don't care*."

Viv took another sip of her Chardonnay and gazed at Julia's mulish expression. "Okay, then. I won't bother you about it anymore."

"I don't want you to think Roman is some kind of con artist, or cheapskate. He's a wonderful man. I want you to love him, just like I do."

"Well, maybe not *just* like you do," Viv teased. "That would be a little odd, don't you think?"

"You know what I mean."

Viv nodded.

"So have you done any more designer divorces?" Julia asked. "It was great when you got the free clothes from that one woman. What was her name? It was exotic . . ."

"Something extremely common, spelled backwards. Like Scaasi and Isaacs. And no, it's a shame, but I haven't had any clients recently from the garment sector."

"What you need," said Julia, holding up her index finger, "is to handle the case of a truly fabulous shoe artiste. Is Louboutin married? What about Manolo?"

"I don't know."

"Maybe Joan and David are on the rocks. Send Joan a business card, why don't you?"

"Julia, honey. Underneath all that innocent blond hair is the mind of a serial shoe whore."

"People who live in glass houses, Imelda, should not throw stilettos!"

Viv just flashed her best Cheshire cat grin and switched the subject. "So have you heard from anybody lately?" *Anybody*, they both understood, meant classmates from school.

"Yup—Claudia and Daisy both expressed shock at my whirlwind wedding plans, no surprise. Frances e-mailed me from the Australian outback—God knows how—and tells me she's tracking the behavior of some sort of critter with a hot man Down Under. Tally and Hunter are still running that catering business in Westchester. They'll all be at the wedding except for Frances. She's short of funds, gets sick on long flights and would have nothing to wear except for cargo shorts and a fishing vest."

"Too bad. She'd have been the life of the party."

"No, honey. *I'll* be the life of the party. The walking, spotlighted star. But she probably would have cast a line at the bouquet and reeled it in before I could throw it for anyone else."

Viv laughed. "Somehow I don't picture Frances married, even to a Jeff Corwin type."

"You never know. She'd solve the baby problem by just having a big pouch sewn on her, like a kangaroo."

Midsip, Viv snorted bubbles into her wineglass.

"Has Mummy seen that table trick?" Julia teased.

"No, and she never will."

"How *is* Mummy these days? You should get her to the wedding and we'll hook her up with Marv and Myrna just for sport."

47

Viv's eyes widened in horror. Mummy had once expressed her concern that Julia and Sydney, while "well-behaved girls," were not "top drawer." Viv had told Mummy what a horrendous snob she was, and that she might wish to join the real world, whereupon Mummy didn't speak to Viv for a month.

She knew without a doubt that her mother would go into strong hysterics if forced to mingle with Marv and Myrna Spinelli, who probably wouldn't even *have* a drawer in her social highboy.

"Mumsy is just peachy. I think she's coming out of her latest melodramatic breakup with Mr. Unsuitable Number 97. Clara told me she found his dummy in the bathroom wastebasket last Friday, which is always a good sign. When she throws away the little voodoo replica, she's on the mend."

Clara was Mummy's longtime Irish housekeeper.

"Should I even ask what horrible malady Number 97 succumbed to?"

"You should not. It involved elephantiasis of his—"

"Oh. My. God!"

"Yes."

"You know it's just creepy that she does that. And even creepier that it seems to work."

"Ask me why I never want to make Mummy too angry. She'd probably give me elephantiasis of my left breast, right in the middle of a high-profile case."

Julia shuddered. "Well, at least Number 97 is due for some relief now. The poor man."

"Yes. Of course, Clara also mentioned that Mummy bought new lipstick, which could be a bad sign that Mr. Unsuitable Number 98 is blowing her way."

"Didn't you once tell me that the gardener was in love with her?" Julia asked.

"Paolo. The Brazilian who comes once a week to tend her exotic jungle in the solarium. Yes. He's adored her for years, and he just shakes his head over the voodoo thing. But, desperate ex-housewife that she is, she's never given him the time of day. Too bad. He's hot for a sixty-five-year-old man."

"All that repotting and pruning, I guess."

"Yes. I *have* seen her check out his rear view before, not that she'd ever admit it."

Viv didn't really want to talk about her mother. She was undoubtedly the motivation behind all her work with the Displaced Homemakers' Association. She just wished Anna Shelton would do something more productive with her time and money. She'd let her bitterness corrode her.

Julia leaned forward conspiratorially. "Gossip time. So tell me about Kiki's divorce."

"What do you want to know?"

"Everything."

"You know I can't tell you everything because of attorney-client privilege and all that. But what I can tell you is that I called her ex, my client, Walter the Wanker. He was a primo schmuck. I don't know what she ever saw in him—besides money and contacts in Hollyweird. But there's no accounting for taste—and maybe he had more hair when she married him."

"Roman said he wore a rug."

"Well, that explains everything. A little superglue held the toupee in place when she stayed overnight. She didn't find out the bald truth until she woke up *Mrs. Walter the Wanker*."

"Now, you two aren't going to get into a tiff at my wedding, are you?"

"A *tiff*? You're joking, right? Manhattan attorneys don't get into tiffs, sweetie. We rush for the jugular, crush the windpipe and hack off the legs at the knee."

"I mean, there won't be any unpleasantness, right?"

"Well. She may be tempted to assassinate me." Viv smiled. Then she had to ask. "Her attorney won't be at the reception, will he?"

Julia looked blank for a moment.

"J.B. Anglin?"

She brightened. "Oh, J.B. That darling man. Yes, of course he'll be there. He's one of Roman's dearest friends."

*Uh-oh.* She should have known. "So, Julia. You don't mind if I attend your wedding by videoconference, do you?"

"Very funny." Her friend eyed her curiously. "Why? What happened between you and J.B.?"

"Nothing, nothing," Viv assured her hastily. "It was just a rough case, that's all. Feathers got ruffled all around."

Julia folded her arms and sat back from the table. "Viv, let's order dinner. And then, while we're eating, you can tell me the truth. You're a *very* convincing liar, but I've known you too long to ignore the signs. You get extra impassive and your eyes go carefully blank, when you're telling half-truths.

"It's an expression I remember from school—like the time you covered for me with the headmistress when I'd snuck out to meet Richard Carlisle. And the time you swore up and down that you had no knowledge of how the grain alcohol got into the punch—some boys from St. John's must have done it."

Viv remembered. She'd had the Everclear bottle duct-taped to her thigh during the whole conversation with Mrs. Burlock. The tape had ripped tiny hairs out of her leg later, when she disposed of the evidence in the Dumpster, and she'd been unable to get the sticky residue off her skin in the shower.

But all she said was, "Julia, you're imagining things."

"I'm not. What happened between you and J.B. in New York?"

# Chapter Four

Vivien ordered a carb-laden pasta dish swimming in a full-fat cream sauce—and another glass of the Australian Chardonnay. *What happened between J.B. and me in New York is going to stay safely tucked away there, three years and two thousand miles away.*

Julia, being disciplined about her figure before her big day, ordered a salad. That done, she repeated her question.

"Nothing happened between us," Viv lied.

Julia's lovely blue eyes narrowed. "I'm going to order the biggest, fattest, rhinestone-covered bow and Velcro it to your butt—yours alone!—on my wedding day if you don't tell me everything."

"I'm calling your bluff. You want an elegant, tasteful ceremony."

"Then . . . I'll put Little Bo Peep bonnets on every single one of you bridesmaids, and make you carry a stinky live lamb."

Viv shook her head. "There's nothing to tell!"

Julia played her trump card. "Pink," she hissed.

"Rayon. With mammoth cabbage roses and a matching *wreath* on your head."

"*Noooooooo,*" Vivien moaned.

"And I'll send a close-up of you to the *New York Post!*"

"Okay, okay. You could say Anglin and I had a mutual attraction thing going."

"You saw him across a crowded courtroom," Julia said, her eyes shining.

"Yes. Wearing a giant condom hat, because he's a—"

"No, he's not. He's a really nice guy. Did you know that he used to play pro football? And that his wife left him when that didn't work out? That was about three and a half years ago, I think. Roman said he hasn't even dated anyone since then."

*Great. Oh, perfect. That would be around the time I was so nice to him.*

"So you exchanged sizzling glances in court, while you both attempted to destroy the characters of each other's clients."

"Something like that."

"And then you dated clandestinely outside of the case."

*Dated? Nooooo. Not exactly. One steamy, acrobatic encounter does not a date make.* "Well, no," she said aloud. "He was invited up to some black-tie thing that Kiki's New York firm was sponsoring, after the case was settled. He needed a date; a 'worthy conversational adversary,' is how he put it. He called me and we made a brief appearance at the party."

"And?" Julia prompted.

*And then I had the best sex of my entire life, but he scared the hell out of me because he was too intense.* "And then . . . we had a drink."

"Viv! You're worse than a clam. Spill!"

"Okay, fine. One thing, as they say, led to another and we ended up at the Plaza."

"I'm shocked at you, young lady." Julia grinned and shook her head. "You of all people, getting it on with a cowboy like J.B."

"He's got a good seat." Viv's lips twitched.

"I'll just bet he does. So what happened then? Did you see each other again?"

"No. Come on, Julia. I live in New York. He lives in Texas. Get real."

Their entrées arrived, thank God, so Viv didn't have to go into detail about their parting. She didn't want Julia to know how she'd come close to losing her heart to a man she'd known intimately for only an hour. She couldn't reveal to her friend how she'd panicked and, true to form, overcompensated for her insecurity with an Ice Queen act.

These just weren't the kinds of confidences Vivien shared. She kept personal humiliations private. She was happy to share triumphs, but preferred that debacles stayed under wraps. Why advertise your shortcomings and failures? There were plenty of people out there who were more than happy to throw them in your face, or even make some up if they couldn't discern any.

Once the waiter was gone, Julia pounced again.

"So you had a one-night stand with J.B. Anglin but never spoke to him again."

*More like* he *never spoke to* me *again. For good reason.* Viv shrugged. No way in hell was she going to admit that she knew the man's office mailing address by heart.

Then Julia said something horrifying. "Well, since J.B.'s a groomsman and you're a bridesmaid, I'll have you walk down the aisle on his arm to make amends."

Viv's mouth went drier than her skin in a New York January. "He's a groomsman?"

"Of course. I told you that he's a good friend of Rome's. Since you've already taken more than his arm, you won't mind, right?" She smiled sweetly.

Viv swallowed a couple of strands of linguine whole and glared at Jules, who looked far, far too innocent. Like butter wouldn't melt in her mouth.

"And after all, he'll be clothed."

"Julia! Brides are not supposed to indulge in fiendish laughter. You people focus on sugar and spice and everything nice."

"Listen to that! *You people.* You people? Like brides are Martians or something. Beings from another planet, in a galaxy far, far away." Julia waved a slice of cucumber at her.

"Where no sane person has gone before," Viv said solemnly. "And you guys *are* Martians."

"Venusians. We like lace and veils and sequins and roses . . ."

"Stop! You're giving me hives." Viven swatted at Julia.

". . . champagne and moonlight and heart-shaped doilies with little chocolate kisses on them . . ."

"Julia, you're getting feverish and delusional and I'm worried about you."

"Sydney says it's due to a steady diet of white cake sampling."

"Sydney is right!"

"She says my brain is becoming a giant Swedish meatball."

"You should listen to her."

"Cynicism will get you nowhere."

"Optimism is foolish."

"Trade you some salad for some pasta?"

"No way. But I'll give you some. Even though this is as good as anything I've had in New York. This place is amazing. What are they doing in Podunksville, Texas? They could be anywhere in the world with this food and wine."

"Maybe you're discovering that this particular Podunksville is a hidden treasure." Julia smiled. "And wait until you have dessert—you will die, but happily."

"Dessert? Are you trying to give me a heart attack?"

"One dessert won't hurt anything. Besides, your work habits will affect your heart before your diet will. Vivver," she blurted, "don't you ever want to get married and have kids?"

Viv put down her fork. "No, I do not want to get married. I do think about kids, but there are perfectly good test tubes out there for making those."

"You can't have a test-tube baby!"

"Why not? I'll just have them stir one up and pop it in an incubator when I'm ready."

"Viv! You act like you can just buy it off a grocery shelf, like a Duncan Hines cake mix. It's not that easy, and this is a little *person* you're talking about."

"Yes?"

"A little person who needs a mother—"

"I'm right here."

"—and a father—"

"I'll rent one occasionally. I don't want one underfoot."

"You're impossible."

"Not at all. I've thought this through, really."

Julia covered her face with her hands. "You've thought this through? What kind of example will you be setting for this child?!"

"A great one," said Viv. "I'm teaching him or her that women can be independent and self-sufficient. They don't need to rely on men for their happiness, their financial security or their life directions."

"Fabulous theory. But a little flawed and sterile, hon. What about teaching that little person how to love and share and compromise?"

"I will love her to distraction, and she'll be sharing a life with *me*. As for compromise—why? Women compromise far too much, in my opinion. *Men* need to start doing that."

Julia looked at her for a long time in silence, then reached out and touched Viv's shoulder. "Do you think maybe your job is getting to you? Making you a touch nihilistic?"

Viv thought about it. Had seeing women dumped

because they hit age forty or gained twenty pounds made her bitter? Had objecting to wives being used as punching bags changed her views? *You bet.*

Had she wanted to scream when a client told her about being on an "allowance" from her husband, or having to ask his "permission" to go to lunch with a friend? *Of course!*

And what about the men who bought expensive jewelry for their girlfriends on the side, while claiming that they couldn't afford a cleaning service for their wives who worked seventy-hour weeks *and* took care of the children? Did that make her bitter? *Unavoidably so.* However, it did not make her nihilistic.

Viv said to her friend, "To be nihilistic I'd have to believe in nothing at all. I believe in lots of ideas and principles. But not always traditional ones, Jules."

"You're just arguing with me. You know what I mean."

"Look. Has marriage made your parents happy? Because it didn't bring a lot of joy to mine. Or their parents, either. And I handle divorces every day."

"Viv, you're supposed to be the smart one here. Miss Harvard Law. And I'm just the little blond fashion merchandising major. But happiness should *not* be a noun! It should be a verb. You have to work constantly at it. Maybe it's not that our parents weren't happy—they just got *lazy*." And Julia tossed her napkin on the table, disappearing to the ladies' room.

Viv just stared after her, while the waiter appeared with dessert menus. She noticed that a woman in the corner, with bright orange hair, was staring at her. Viv stared right back until the woman finally looked away.

She decided to take refuge in a mocha-hazelnut cheesecake. How could she refuse such a dessert?

When Julia returned, Viv hissed, "Who is the scary woman with carrot hair?"

Jules didn't even need to look up. "That's Thelma Lynn Grafton, town gossip. We haven't been officially introduced yet—and I'm glad—but Syd's met her."

They ordered dessert and cappuccinos in pensive silence.

At last Julia asked, "You're not serious about this test-tube baby thing, are you?"

"Yes, I am, actually. I have yet to meet the man I could tolerate living in my space on a long-term basis. A man I would share a bathroom with, or whose laundry I would do." *And you don't even want to know about the ugly things I've seen men do in and out of court.*

For example, she didn't tell Julia about the custody case in which a husband paid several women to falsely testify that they'd had relations with his wife.

She didn't tell her about the guy who'd murdered his estranged wife midtrial, and left her to be discovered, half clothed, in the most horrifically undignified position possible.

And Viv didn't mention the disgusting, brutal details of incest and child abuse that she sometimes encountered—because she had to block them out of her own mind, and work at not killing the male perpetrators with any means available, "fair trial" be damned.

No, none of that belonged in this conversation. She'd stay on the somewhat light side.

Viv took a large, inelegant bite of her cheesecake and waved her fork at Julia.

"Do you realize that when you marry Romulus—"

"*Roman.*"

"Right. When you marry Roman, *you will never have your own space again.* He will always be breathing your air, eating your food, using your toilet, shaving in your sink. He will always have control of the television. He will never admit that you are right. He will throw his underwear on the floor and wait for you to pick it up and wash it. He will snore in your ear. He will fill up your refrigerator with beer—"

"Wine," corrected Julia. "And that's fine by me."

"Wine, then. But let me finish."

"I doubt you ever will." Julia smirked.

"He'll bring fattening man-food into the house and you'll gain thirty pounds just by looking at it—"

"Vivver, you're *such* an only child. I get the idea. Eat your dessert."

Viv realized her tirade was hopeless and stuck another unwieldy bite of cheesecake into her mouth. Behind her, Cuvée's front door opened and she noticed a smile spreading over Julia's face. She heard footsteps approach.

Sheltons didn't corkscrew their necks. Like members of the royal family, Sheltons waited until a subject approached before deigning to extend a hand. She figured this was Redneck Roman, and he'd show himself soon enough. She savored the cheesecake in her mouth before having to formally greet him.

"Vivien," Julia said, "I know you've been dying to meet Roman. Roman, meet my dear friend Vivien Shelton."

Viv looked up at a handsome, refined-looking guy as he kissed Julia's cheek and then nodded. Cordially, she held out her hand.

Then another, very broad-shouldered man came into view. All bronze skin, dirty-blond wavy hair and loads of attitude, this man stared her down.

J.B. Anglin asked her softly, "What's a bad girl like you doing in a nice place like this?"

He could have knocked her down with the contempt written across his face. His intense green eyes pinned her into place. The color of Savannah moss, they were shot through with little golden flecks—and hostility.

Viv froze for a split second. Then she tried to gasp for air, finish swallowing and make a sarcastic retort all at once.

Central Command couldn't process all those messages simultaneously; she sucked cheesecake crumbs into her lungs, swallowed air and coughed the sarcastic retort.

When her body tried to recover, it malfunctioned yet again. The cheesecake went down, but it stuck, and she began to cough and choke in earnest.

"Viv, are you okay?" asked Julia urgently.

She nodded but then shook her head and put a hand to her throat.

J.B.'s eyes narrowed on her, while her own began to water and bulge as she fought for air.

"Christ, she's choking!" yelled Roman, stepping toward her. But J.B. beat him to her.

He grabbed Viv unceremoniously by the waist— Escada suit and all—and hauled her out of her chair, against his body. He clasped his hands together in front of her, and jerked her back hard, hitting her square in the diaphragm with his fists. When that didn't work, he did it again.

The piece of cheesecake lodged in her throat flew up, and unfortunately out, landing in Julia's coffee.

Viv gasped air into her lungs and hung weakly over J.B.'s right arm, slowly registering the breezy scent of his laundry detergent, the clean fragrance of Ivory soap, and the earthy man-smell that was peculiarly his own. He rubbed her back with his free hand, sending comfort and pleasure eddying through her body in spite of the circumstances. A deep shiver spiraled through her.

"You okay?" he asked gruffly, just as Roman voiced the same question and Julia thanked God aloud.

"Fabulous," she managed. Coffee dripped into her open-toed sling-back, and J.B.'s warmth and toughness seeped through her clothes. Viv made sure she wasn't going to lose her balance in the puddle of coffee and then stood up and pulled away from him.

Immediately he took a couple of steps back, then shoved his hands into his pockets. The contempt slowly crept back into his expression. It settled along his high cheekbones, dripped along the grooves etched from nose to mouth and pooled in his dimples.

J.B. was all straight shoulders and long, lean legs. He had a physique honed by years of long, sweaty hours on the practice field and a quiet, innate confidence that owed nothing to others. His nose had definitely been broken near the bridge, which gave him a faintly pugilistic look.

His remarkable green eyes had held a lot of humor and self-awareness three years ago. She remembered running her hands through his hair and recalled the only soft part of him: his earlobes. She'd held them between her forefingers and thumbs, stroking the velvety texture—until he'd playfully bitten the tip of her nose.

Sexual awareness flashed through her, bizarre at this moment since she was still recovering from almost choking to death. Utterly inappropriate timing. Worrisome.

She took a deep breath. "Thank you," she said, her hand reflexively reaching for her throat. "You're a good man to know in an emergency."

His gaze moved over her body openly and she felt her blood heat. He'd seen every part of her, and licked it, too.

He lifted a brow. "Emergency? And here I thought it was just a little ballroom dancing. The old Heimlich Tango, sweetheart."

She paused. Nobody, but *nobody*, called her sweetheart. Under normal circumstances she'd be tempted to deck him. However, these were far from normal circumstances. He had just saved her life. She supposed she should demonstrate a little grace and allow him his patronizing term of endearment.

His sardonic gaze deepened into an open smirk as he clearly read her mind. "So how are ya, Vivvie? It's been a while since we've seen each other." He scratched his head like a yokel and fell into a slouch. "And I seem to remember," he drawled, "that you were wearing a lot less."

# Chapter Five

All of the gratitude and goodwill Vivien had felt for J.B. drained from her once his words, said tauntingly, were delivered like a slap in public. As if he needed to take back his human, sympathetic response to her choking and throttle *it*.

She fixed him with her coldest courtroom stare, while behind her Julia said, "Yikes." Roman looked as if he'd rather be anywhere else. J.B. just smiled blandly.

"At least I wasn't dangling my meat in a hotel hallway, Sweet Pea," she volleyed back. At the next table, a heavyset man with a handlebar mustache spit water all over his salad, while his wife looked as if she might faint.

In fact, the entire restaurant looked on with great interest, but Vivien refused to blush, or bat an eyelash. She remained as white and shameless as Sargent's famous painting of Madame X.

"Nice return," J.B. said, nodding.

How dare he be magnanimous? "Dirty serve."

"Well, what would you expect from those of us

who didn't grow up on Park Avenue? You know, the Great Unwashed."

"A little Southern courtesy."

"I'm polite as can be to a *lady*, darlin'. You don't qualify."

Viv noticed that even the chef's mouth was agape, and the flambéed whatever-it-was he held had become a raging culinary fire. What the hell. She'd play his game. This was nothing compared to some of the divorces she'd handled.

"Actually, I do qualify," she shot back, needing to win, as usual.

"Pardon me?"

*Oh, don't say it, Viv. You're just giving him free ammo.* "Since my father is an earl, I inherited an English title." She didn't mention the part about how he'd been a broke earl, who badly needed an influx of American cash to ward off selling his ancestral pile in the English countryside. It was a story straight out of a Regency novel.

J.B. actually laughed. "I should have guessed. The Divorce Diva has an effin' *title*." He made a show of bowing to her. "Charmed, milady."

"I don't use it." *I don't even like the concept of a title. It's embarrassing. . . . Why am I explaining this?*

He rocked back on his heels and looked down his nose at her. "But you sure did use *me*, didn't you, darlin'? I guess you got me confused with one of the servants."

A long pause ensued, and Viv looked away, trying to calm her blood down from boiling to a mild simmer. *I am not going to explain my actions in front of a crowd.*

Then Roman said quietly, "Maybe you two should take this outside, J.B."

Anglin rounded on him, his expression mock genial. "Aw, c'mon. Let's play court. We've got two lawyers: Vivvie and me. We've got a built-in jury—" He gestured to Cuvée's patrons. "And we can introduce all the evidence. Julia, here, can act as judge."

"That's enough, Anglin." Viv's voice, to her own ears, could have frozen vodka. "Roman's right. We need to take this outside."

"Suddenly shy, Counselor? You're used to center stage. Hitch up your skirt and let's dance." His eyes blazed a challenge at her.

Sheltons didn't back down from challenges. They normally issued them. However, this was neither the time nor the place to verbally dance with the man.

She raised her chin. "Bring it outside or I'm leaving."

"So leave."

She tossed some bills onto the table. "Roman, it was a pleasure to meet you. Julia, I'll see you later." She moved to the door.

Anglin opened fire again. "I'm surprised to see you run away, Your Majesty."

"Don't try to manipulate me. I'm not running. I just don't see the point of discussing this in public. And why did you just save my life, only to assassinate my character?"

"For fun," he drawled. "Pissed because you feel

like a *puppet*? That's a shame. It's not a pleasant feeling, is it, Vivvie?"

She opened the door.

"What comes around goes around, Counselor. You just remember that."

Viv walked calmly out of Cuvée and headed for Orange Street and Marv's Motor Inn. Julia ran after her.

"Would you care to explain to me what that was all about?"

"No." Viv lengthened her stride.

"I've never seen J.B. obnoxious like that! What did you do?"

Viv stopped and turned. "Never? And you've known him for what, three weeks? Yet you assume that I did something to deserve that."

"Vivver, it's not his style. And what did you mean, he dangled his meat in the hotel hallway? Come on. I'm your friend. Just tell me."

"Isn't it obvious? I'm a cold, evil, ball-busting bitch. I used him for sex and then threw him out naked into the hallway. Just for fun. Just because I could." She clenched her jaw.

"No. I don't believe that."

"He does."

"So why don't you set him straight?"

Viv sighed. "What's the point?"

Julia actually stamped her tiny foot. "You are the strangest person. Obviously it hurts you that J.B. thinks that. But you won't do anything about it? You're a lawyer, for God's sake. You talk for a living.

So go and talk to him and tell him why you did whatever you did. And if you don't tell me what it was and why, then I will dye your *hair* pink for my wedding. I'll sneak in while you sleep!"

Viv had to grin at Julia's latest threat.

"You're like a guy when it comes to your emotions. Did you know that? You just clam up and won't talk. It's *maddening*."

"Like a guy?" Viv thought about it. "I suppose, given my mother's histrionics, I chose the polar opposite tack."

"Well," said Julia, "it's not healthy."

Viv threw up her hands. "I'll start shrieking and practicing voodoo on men right away. Just for my health, you understand."

Julia folded her arms and waited.

Viv sighed. "We went back to the hotel after dancing a little at the black-tie event. We . . . you know. And he . . ." Viv paused, trying to block out the memories. "He made me cry. I kicked him out."

"What do you mean, he made you cry? Did he *hurt* you, Viv? Oh, sweet Jesus—"

"No! No, not at all. *Hell.* I'm not sure I can explain this." She closed her eyes and rubbed at her lids, trying to massage the tension out of her head.

"Try," ordered Julia.

"He was incredible. So tender and giving and . . . and not a wimp about it, if you know what I mean. He—Julia, I'm not going into it, I'm not the kiss-and-tell type, but I'll just say that he made me, um, very happy. But before I knew it, I was in tears. I was about to lose it—I don't know why. And all of these images flashed into my mind: me, addicted to this guy like crack; him disgusted by it, and turning mean and leaving. I could see the end of our relationship, the very messy end, before it even began. I felt hysterical, nutso.

"He asked me what was wrong, and I told him I suffered from allergies. I got up and went into the bathroom, closed the door, and turned on the water faucets full blast. I shoved every one of those crazy feelings right back down my throat to internalize them and got hold of myself." Julia put her hand over Viv's.

"Except I still felt as if I were going to explode. If he said one more sweet word, if he touched my hair, if he kissed my shoulder—all hell was going to break loose with me and I wouldn't be able to control it. *I* had to get him out of there. I didn't want him to think I was some kind of psychotic!

"He came to the bathroom door and said if I'd fallen in, he wanted to come swimming with me . . . 'swimmin',' " he said. You've got to love that accent, don't you?" Viv smiled sadly. "I. Had. To. Get. Him. *Out*."

She took a deep breath. "So I let the ax fall. In the coldest tone of voice I could dredge up, I complimented his performance and said I was done with him now."

"No-you-did-not." Julia's hand fidgeted over her mouth, her eyes wide with shock. "What did he *do*?"

"Oh, God, Jules. There was the longest, most pregnant pause, and then he said, '*Excuuuuuse* me?' " Viv sank down on one of the wooden benches that lined Main Street, and Julia joined her.

"I know it sounds awful, and it was—*I* was. But I can't begin to explain the urgency in me to get rid of him before it was too late and I was hooked. So I opened the bathroom door, no sign of emotion on my face, and said that he'd been magnificent but he had to go now.

"His jaw dropped so low that I thought he might trip on it. He looked at me with total disbelief. And then hatred. And then . . . contempt.

"He said, 'Well, don't I even get a tip?' And he grabbed his clothes and yanked open the door. He gave me one last incredulous look. Then he said, 'It was nice *fucking* you, darlin'.' And he walked out."

To her surprise, she was shaking. She didn't even realize it until she saw Julia's hand vibrating on her shoulder.

"So." Julia took a deep breath. "So you didn't want to act like a psychotic, huh? Instead you . . . acted like a psychotic. That was a good swap, there, Vivver."

"Yes, wasn't it?" She laughed weakly. "So now you understand that ugly little scene back there. I pretty much deserved it, even though I'm not the type to take an attack lying down. You know me. I'll fight, even when flight is the smartest thing to do."

"Viv, honey." Julia's brow furrowed, her perfectly groomed eyebrows drawing together. "I'm worried about you."

"Well, I'm worried about *you*. I don't think you know what you're signing up for."

"And I don't think you know what kind of void your life is becoming. You cannot just exist in a vacuum without other people!"

Viv got up. "I have plenty of other people in my life." *There's Andie, and Mummy and Timmy and, ugh, Belker. There's old Schmidt. There are my pups: five distinct doggie personalities. There's Tabitha and crabby old Maurice.*

She kept naming names to herself, to prove her point.

Julia nodded. "And do any of them make your life worth living? Would you feel desolate without one of those other people?"

"Feeling desolate is a waste of time," Viv said.

"You're right. Efficiency is everything," Julia told her. "We can't waste precious minutes being human. Being unproductive. I mean, gosh, those aren't billable hours."

"Hey, hey, hey. Easy, now. Let's move back to you, for a moment. You're making a major life change in less than two weeks. You're getting married. And regardless of any concerns I may have about that, it's your decision to make," Vivien reminded her.

"Why, thank you," Julia said with a grin.

"But. You are what Mummy would call 'a woman of means.' A chick with bucks. And speaking as not only your friend but your attorney, I recommend that you protect yourself."

Julia opened her mouth but Viv held up a finger.

"I'm talking about a very simple document called a prenuptial agreement—"

"No!" Julia said furiously. "Damn it, *that's* what

Syd's been cooking up. What both of you are plotting. No, no, and if I didn't make myself clear, *no*."

"Jules, it's for your protection and nothing else. It's not a curse, not an insult, and of course it doesn't mean that it will ever be necessary—"

Eyes flashing, Julia snapped, "What it *means* is that I'd be entering into a marriage without a key ingredient, and that is *trust*. If you don't have trust, then you don't have love. You have *nothing*. I am not going to ruin my marriage before it starts, Vivien."

"I think you're overreacting. A prenup is not necessarily about mistrust; it's about planning for the future, okay? Just like when people buy burial plots. It doesn't mean they're going to keel over and croak the next day. They're just planning."

"*No.*"

"You're planning a wedding, correct?"

"Yes."

"Because you have a vision. You want the event to unfold a certain way."

"Yeah . . ."

"Doesn't that mean you don't trust someone else to do it for you, the way you'd want it?"

"Viv, you're twisting this. I am not a witness in a courtroom, okay? I'm not under cross-examination here. I am telling you point-blank that I refuse to sign a prenup. Don't push this any further. And let me warn you that it's not okay with me for you to go and talk to Roman about this. In fact, if you do, I won't be speaking to you any longer. I'm serious. Don't push this, Vivien. I understand that you have my best interests at heart, but it is *my* heart. I'm not going to wave some horrid piece of paper in Roman's face and demand that he sign on the bottom line. Do you understand?"

Viv looked at the stubborn dimple in Julia's chin and knew it was hopeless. She might be cute, she might be blond, but she knew her own mind. They walked in silence back to Orange Street.

# Chapter Six

J.B. wished the waitress, cute as she was, would get the hell away from him and Roman. But she hovered and giggled and, very unsubtly, jiggled. He was an easy target. Fredericksburg was a small town, he was unmarried and he still had hair.

Finally in desperation he hunched a shoulder at her and said loudly to Roman, "I know you need to get back soon, so let's talk business."

She took the hint and their order to the kitchen while Rome stared at him like he had three heads. "Would you like to tell me what just happened in here and why you've transformed into a complete dickhead? And was it really necessary to do that to Vivien in public?"

"No, and yes." J.B. tipped a healthy amount of red wine down his throat and wished it were beer. The food at Cuvée was incredible, but he didn't share his friend's passion for the grape.

"What bit you in the ass?"

"She did. Three years ago. Right after we settled

Kiki's divorce. C'mon, Rome, you had to have caught that much."

"And?"

"I watched her in depositions and at court. She's amazing. I was fascinated. I made the mistake of thinking she might just carry that passion and wit and beauty into her personal life. That she might be warm and human—not just fake it. I wanted to get to know her, date her. Don't ask me why her, or bring up the distance thing. It wasn't a choice. It had nothing to do with practicality. I was just drawn to her for some reason."

Rome nodded his understanding.

"So I asked her to this black-tie thing I had to attend while I was in New York, working with Kiki's Manhattan attorneys. And before I know it, I'm getting lucky with her. Little did I realize that I was just a goddamn mechanical bull and she was a woman with a quarter."

His friend looked like he wanted to laugh, and J.B. didn't appreciate it. "What are you smirking at, you son of a bitch?"

Roman hid his mouth with his hand. "It's just that in high school, that would have been our ultimate fantasy. Life is cruel, isn't it?"

"I'm glad you think this is funny, Rome. But she was unbelievable. I was just a piece of meat to her. Get this: She told me my *performance* was *impressive*! Can you beat that for sheer gall?"

"Hey, at least she didn't tell you that you sucked."

"No woman has ever said that. No woman ever will." J.B. cracked his knuckles.

"Well, damn, J.B. I'm flattered to be sitting with a

gen-u-wine, certified Sex God." Roman laughed at his friend's extended middle finger. "So I take it she didn't send you flowers next day?"

His answer was a baleful stare.

"And your ego's a bit burned."

"This has nothing to do with my ego. I'm pissed about my lack of judgment. I swear I saw something in her, something rare. But obviously I was wrong." He fell silent, grateful that Rome didn't point out that he'd been wrong in his choice of wife, too.

"You wore a raincoat, right?"

"Of course—I'm not nuts."

"Then why are you still worried about it?"

J.B. clenched his jaw. "I'm not *worried*, Rome. I'm just starting to question my ability to gauge women—my capacity as a judge of character. And seeing her again just brought back the anger."

Roman casually swirled the wine in his glass. "You wanted her, too, buddy."

J.B. shot him a glare. "Just because I performed the Heimlich on her doesn't mean I wanted her."

"Sign of true love." Rome grinned. "Mouth-to-mouth is next, mark my words."

"I wouldn't touch that woman again if you paid me."

The answer he got was a raised brow.

"Or if I did," J.B. amended, "you can bet it would only be to teach her a lesson."

Vivien awoke that morning at 2:58 A.M., homesick for her dogs and thinking about a woman named Susan at the Displaced Homemakers' Association.

Susan had come in for a job training program after her husband left her with their three children to run off with another man. A wealthy stockbroker, he'd bypassed the typical midlife crisis for an entire midlife meltdown.

Doug had, without Susan's knowledge, drained their life savings on a Miami-docked yacht, plastic surgery for his lover, and designer wardrobes and a trainer for them both.

He'd left Susan with a monster mortgage that she couldn't pay, three young girls, and a Mercedes that promptly got repossessed.

Viv was working her case pro bono, and had even, in a moment of madness, suggested to her mother that she might enjoy taking care of the girls a couple of days per week as a "fun little charity project." If Susan was going to get job training, she needed time away from her little ones, and her own parents couldn't do it every day.

Viv was disappointed, but not surprised, that so far Mummy's answer had been a resounding silence. Perhaps, however, she could use that to guilt her into funding a day-care center for the Displaced Homemakers' Association.

With this thought, Viv flipped on the bedside light, and wished immediately that she hadn't. The mustard and brown flowers converged on her, spinning her into a 1970s nightmare.

If Julia had succeeded in replacing all the Inn's mattresses, why hadn't she done something about the décor?

Oh, yes—she had Marv to reckon with, the man

whose checkbook creaked when he opened it, at least when it came to business decisions. She'd never noticed either Sydney or Julia lacking for anything at school.

Viv kicked off the dead polyester garden and reached a toe out cautiously for the burnt orange carpet. She hadn't thought to pack slippers, and there was no avoiding the contact unless she pulled the pillowcases over her feet. She thought about it, but dismissed the idea when it occurred to her that she didn't want her face to touch the naked pillow, either.

She pressed down into the spongy, musty petroleum product with her foot, revolted to discover that it was faintly damp. She was not at the Stanhope, that was for sure.

Viv put her other foot down into the sea of orange and scuttled for the bathroom before anything could jump up out of the rug and attack.

She missed her happy hounds and their bulk around her at night. She missed the city noises; it was unholy quiet here. You could actually hear insects chirruping outside, and a breeze blowing through the trees, even coyotes baying in the far distance.

Where the hell was a nice, noisy bus when you wanted one? Some honking to relax to? Car alarms and rude comments yelled across the street?

Once in the bathroom, she took a swipe at her tangled mop of dark hair and checked out the deep circles under her eyes. Very attractive. J.B. must have been salivating. Viv peed and then, for lack of anything better to do, rebrushed her teeth. She ran her tongue over the smooth enamel surfaces, feeling vaguely like a night creature, polishing her fangs for nefarious purposes—maybe to take a bite out of J.B. for being so rude.

She sighed and tiptoed over the carpet again to the bed, stopping first for her laptop. She might as well check e-mail.

A pending client had made a decision to retain her services and was notifying her that she'd mail a check.

Another client wanted to go ahead with the restraining order they'd prepared against her estranged husband.

Mrs. Bonana wanted some reassurance.

And speak of the devil! Or think of her, anyway. Mummy had finally responded.


Subject:   Your Odd Request

From:     AShelton

To:        vshelton@kleinschmidtbelker

Vivien Anthea,

I must say that I find myself quite taken aback at your suggestion that I frolic with unknown children twice a week! Does this woman not employ a housekeeper? Does she possess no relatives? Don't scandalize me by telling me she has no nanny!

As you know, my health is delicate, and children positively swarm with germs. It's not that I don't adore them, love—they are delightful, particularly little girls. But perhaps I can take them to tea one day instead, along with their nanny?

A few butter cookies, some chocolate-dipped strawberries, perhaps a raspberry tart or a fresh scone! Delicacies such as these go a long way toward making a child feel special, abominable father or not. And they could wear lovely little pastel dresses!

I think this is a much better solution, don't you? Provide me with this Susan's telephone number, and I'll give her a ring. Oh, must fly! I have an appointment at the hairdresser's.

xoxoxox. Toodles, Mummy

"Oh, perfect," Viv said wrathfully. "Sure, Mum. Taking them to high tea will solve all of their problems!"

Fingers flying over the keyboard, she wrote,

Subject:   Re: Your Odd Request

From:      vshelton@kleinschmidtbelker

To:        AShelton

Mummy, it's very kind of you to offer to take the girls to high tea, and I do hope it's not too great an inconvenience for you. I'm sure they have some pretty dresses to wear for the occasion.

However, Susan's greatly reduced circumstances do not allow for a nanny or a housekeeper, and her parents are elderly. She is currently trying to

scrimp and save enough money to be able to purchase a car, since hers was repossessed.

My suggestion that you spend a couple of days
a week with the girls was only made because I
thought you could all help each other out. I worry
that you may get lonely sometimes, Mum. And
Susan and so many women like her are in desperate circumstances.

Which leads me to bring up a fabulous idea!
What if you were to found the Anna Shelton Day-
Care Facility at my chapter of Displaced Homemakers? I could match you, 33% to your 66%, of
the cost. And Gerald would be thrilled at another
tax write-off, the old skinflint.

So think about making both your CPA and your
daughter happy at the same time! Think about the
relief you could provide to hundreds of women
while they receive job training. Let me know.

In the meantime, I've taken a brief trip to Texas:
Julia's gotten it into her head to marry a man from
Fredericksburg. Why, I don't know.

xoxoxo, Viv

Shaking her head at her mother, Viv snapped out
the light again and fell upon the bed face-first. What
was she doing here? Anglin would cheerfully run her
over, and Julia refused to sign a prenup. She should
have just stayed in Manhattan.

*So why don't you set him straight?* Julia's voice
echoed in her head.

*I think it's a little late for that.* She turned her

thoughts back to Julia and her impulsive decision to get married. Even if Roman wasn't the creep Syd suspected him of being, things could go wrong. People fell out of love every day. They hurt each other. And in revenge they went after the other party's money.

Julia had forbidden her to talk to Roman about a prenup, and Viv would honor her wishes. But still she searched for a way to protect her friend. Under Texas law, the property that a spouse came into the marriage with stayed his or hers, unless there was extensive commingling of funds. That was all well and good, but with Roman expanding a business and Marv getting on in years, and the possibility of children—things got complicated.

What if Marv the Motor Inn Mogul passed on and Julia inherited a huge chunk of change after the marriage? Forty hotels or so? Roman would be entitled to half the revenues from the chain, plus half of any increased value of the real estate, from the day Julia inherited. And things got more complicated if the properties were mortgaged, which they almost certainly were for tax purposes.

Roman having a claim on this wasn't acceptable. She had to do something.

Viv lifted her head and stared at the impossibly ugly headboard of her borrowed bed. Some factory run amok had drilled "designs" in the quality particleboard and then wrapped it in vinyl faux woodgrain.

Disgusted, Viv punched the fiberfill pillow against the headboard and came to an unpleasant conclusion.

She couldn't talk to Roman, but she could talk to Roman's *attorney*.

Well, as long as he didn't forcibly evict her from his office she could talk to him. But surely he'd be willing to discuss something of an important business nature, pertaining to his client. The man was a professional.

And perhaps . . . maybe . . . she'd get the chance to tell him what had really happened in New York.

Viv rolled over and stared at the lumpy, textured popcorn ceiling. Out of the corner of her eye she saw that it was now 3:37 A.M. and her body showed no signs of wanting to fall back asleep. She might as well work on the problem of world peace, because counting sheep—even for cheap—wasn't going to do her any good.

J.B.'s mocking face swam into focus. Did she really *want* to explain her behavior to him? As she'd told Julia earlier, what was the point? Rolling over and exposing your soft, white underbelly was a stupid move—especially stupid to show it to a man who wore steel-toed boots and showed every sign of wanting to kick her.

*Let him think I'm a ball-busting bitch. I don't give a damn.*

She was awakened by some cheerful asshole whistling "The Yellow Rose of Texas"—all the way down the brown hallway. Viv had slept a total of about an hour, and resentment propelled her out of bed and to the door. She opened it, stuck her bedhead out and sent the old gentleman a Death Stare.

He blinked. "Mornin', ma'am."

Beyond speaking, she pulled her head in again and shut the door. She squinted past the menacing polyester garden on the bed to the mocking red numbers on the digital clock radio and moaned. "Six seventeen a.m.!"

Outside, an evil early bird cheeped in excitement as he went for his worm. And sunshine winked through the heavy mustard curtains.

Carpe frickin' diem. Would that it were possible to seize the day and shove it under the bed until she was ready to face it.

Viv staggered to the shower and tried to soap herself into something recognizable as human. She slipped on the slick bottom of the tub and made a mental note to tell Julia this was a lawsuit waiting to happen. They needed to put in rubber grips.

Feeling marginally better, she climbed out, dried off and tried to mentally prepare for facing J.B. this morning.

*I'm here in the interests of your client*, she'd say—as long as she got past reception.

She chose her clothes carefully: black trousers, crisp white blouse, strappy sandals, power-red lipstick. The crisscross Tiffany earrings said *Keep out*, and her posture would do the rest. She looked like a New Yorker in a position of authority: no bullshit or fools tolerated. She *felt* like microwaved death.

Viv grabbed her computer bag, unloaded the heavy laptop from it and slid it under the chair cushion for safekeeping. Then she tottered for the door in search of real coffee, because that weak crap in the packet in the bathroom wasn't going to do the trick of waking her up.

She walked to the stairs and clutched the banister for balance on the way down. On the first-floor landing, a woman with almost clownish makeup and monstrous silver-and-turquoise earrings smiled at her. "Good mornin'!"

Viv blinked at her and managed to nod. Everyone was so cheerful in Texas. Really, it was disgusting.

Well, everyone but J.B.—and she supposed he was motivated. But hell, he should get over it. Wasn't no-strings sex every red-blooded man's fantasy? What was wrong with him?

Part of her wanted to avoid him. She didn't normally go into business meetings knowing what her adversary looked like naked, down to the tiny constellation of freckles right on his—

"Good morning!" sang another Marv's guest, and Viv winced. What kind of gauntlet did you have to run here to get a freakin' cup of coffee?

This woman wore orange lipstick and brutally frosted hair, and she was so friendly as to be scary.

"Aah like yore earrings, hon," she said, taking a step closer to peer at them.

"Thank you," Viv said, taking a step back.

"Tiffany?"

Viv hesitated, then nodded.

"You know, you coulda got knockoffs just over the border in Nuevo Laredo. Good silver, too. A fraction of the price."

She blinked. It seemed a little snotty to point out that the earrings were platinum and had been a graduation gift from her mother. "Oh. Well, I wish I'd known that. Thank you."

"I bought three necklaces, a bracelet and a couple pairs of earrings the last time I was down there. This set I'm wearing is from that trip." The woman dug inside her pocketbook and came up with a dog-eared card for a store. "Here you go."

"Um. Thank you." It was nice of her, yet Viv didn't wear earrings the size of satellite dishes or necklaces with links big enough to tow a boat. She accepted the card with a smile, though, and headed for the little alcove where she'd seen a coffee urn the day before.

She stood by the machine and downed two cups, black, in quick succession. Then she took another for the road. She slipped out a rear door so she wouldn't run into Julia yet. She hoped she'd assume Viv was still sleeping.

Yet another cheerful Texas lady greeted her, and Viv asked her where she could get a cab. Her answer was a blank stare. "We don't . . . really have many of those around here, hon. You're not from here, are you. Where do you need to go?"

Before she knew it, she was being herded toward the woman's minivan, over her protests that she couldn't impose.

"J.B.'s office is just a few blocks over, but you don't want to walk there in those shoes."

Being a New Yorker, Viv had gym shoes shoved into a side pocket of her bag. She pulled them out. "I'll just put these on."

"Good gravy, hon, no! Forgive me, but they don't go with your outfit *at all*. Put those away. I'll just drop you off, and he can have someone run you back.''

*He's more likely to run me out of town.* But Viv got into the passenger seat of the lady's minivan, trying to avoid the raisins, oyster crackers and plastic toys scattered on the floor. Grandchildren, she presumed. She did her best to imagine herself hitching a ride with a total stranger in the City, and failed utterly.

The lady introduced herself as Glenna Sue and had Viv on J.B. Anglin's doorstep within three minutes. After thanking Glenna Sue and having her heart blessed, she steeled herself to go inside and face Bluebeard.

# Chapter Seven —

Before she could touch the handle of the door, it opened and a stunning blonde about Viv's age strolled out, a frown of annoyance marring her golden-peach brow. She had wide hazel eyes that narrowed on Viv briefly, gave her face and body a professional scan and immediately priced her jewelry. A slight lift of the blonde's left brow indicated that her inventory was complete. She nodded in a not-unfriendly way, said "Hi" and brushed past.

Viv, still getting used to this Texan business of greeting complete strangers, just blinked.

J.B.'s office was very pleasant inside, without being oppressive and stuffy like so many law firms. The walls were lined with wall-to-wall bookcases, blond instead of the usual dark cherry or mahogany. Furniture was also blond and Scandinavian in design, upholstered in tasteful fabrics of mostly blues and greens. Legal reference books took up most of the shelf space, but along the very top level a collection of beautiful modern glass paperweights caught the Texas sun.

A handsome older woman sat at the reception desk, a pair of reading glasses perched on the bridge of her nose. "Corinne," she murmured, "I'm sorry but he really can't be disturbed right now."

She had ash-blond hair that came close to matching the furniture, and she reminded Vivien strongly of someone. When she looked up, Viv faltered; the woman had the same wide green eyes as J.B. He just didn't have the habit of wearing mascara or grooming his eyebrows.

"Oh, I'm sorry. I thought you were—may I help you?" the receptionist asked, with a welcoming smile.

"Yes." Viv walked forward, channeling Marlene Dietrich, and extended her hand. "I'm Vivien Shelton, of Klein, Schmidt and Belker. I'm here from Manhattan for a brief time."

The woman took off her reading glasses and her smile widened a bit. "Ah. The cheesecake girl, I presume?"

Viv opened her mouth and then closed it again. Finally she said with a tight smile of her own, "That's me."

"This is a small town. Word gets around, hon."

"Right. Well." Viv really didn't want to think about the implications of this. How much detail was she acquainted with? "I credit J.B. with saving my life. It's a good thing he was there."

"Yes, I'm very proud of him. I'm his mom." The wattage of her smile got just a little too bright.

Viv paused. "A pleasure to meet you, Mrs. Anglin," she said, without a blush—even though she was now sure Mom knew last night's conversation word for word, and was highly intrigued. *Great.* She took a deep breath.

"Well. Though I don't have an appointment, I wondered if Mr. Anglin—J.B.—was available to discuss some business pertaining to one of his clients."

Mom's smile brightened another twenty watts, and Viv could practically see her ears prick under the ash-blond helmet.

"If you'll have a seat, Ms. Shelton, I'll be happy to check."

Viv wondered what had happened to *He can't be disturbed,* but shrugged.

Mrs. Anglin pressed a button on the intercom system. "John Bryan? Are you free to see Ms. Shelton for a few minutes?"

No response. The door to his office opened after what seemed an interminable pause, and J.B. stood there, leaning his rangy body against the jamb. He appraised Vivien coolly while she stared right back.

"Miz Shelton. To what do I owe *this* honor?"

"You owe the honor to Roman Sonntag. May I come in?"

"Well, sure, honey—as long as you're already slummin' it."

His mother looked from one of them to the other. "I'll hold your calls," she said.

He nodded. "Thank you."

Viv smiled tightly and walked into his office with her head held high.

He nudged the door shut with his boot. The man dressed for the office as if it were a country and western bar: snug denim, the same boots of the day before, and his white, buttoned-down shirt open at the neck, the sleeves rolled up to just below the elbows.

Inside the room, a scent of lemon oil mingled with the essence of new wood. The bookcases extended around the entire well-lit room, supporting hundreds of leather-bound volumes. A modern oil painting stood on a blond wood easel near the window. His desk, a work of art in itself, was in the center of the floor. It looked like a piece by Henry Moore, if the English sculptor had designed furniture. Smooth, abstract, rounded pieces of polished wood supported a massive slab of thick, beveled glass. Anglin's tan leather office chair rolled up to it on one side, and two visitor's chairs sat on the other side.

He did not invite her to sit down, but she did anyway.

"Well, make yourself comfortable, Vivvie."

"Please don't call me that. Viv is fine. Vivvie is not." To soften that a little, she said, "I like your office."

"I'm so glad you approve. I renovated it myself."

"You did?" She gestured to the shelves, the beautiful six-inch moldings. "All of this?"

He nodded. "Yep. Sad to say, some of us do have to learn manual labor."

"Look, J.B., I don't appreciate the whole rich-bitch angle."

"I didn't appreciate it, either."

"You think my background had anything to do with what happened between us in New York?"

"Yeah. I think you went slummin' with a cowboy and then, once your itch got scratched, you sent me on my way."

"You're wrong."

"You know what? It's water under the bridge." He strode toward her and leaned on the desk, looking down so that she felt dwarfed. "Why are you here in my office? What's this about Roman?"

"I want to talk with you about something related to the wedding," she said, getting up so that he didn't have such a height advantage. In spite of her heels, she still had to tilt her chin up to look at him.

"Julia and her sister will be very wealthy women one day, as the daughters of Marv Spinelli and inheritors of his motel empire. As Julia's legal adviser, I have urged her to protect herself with a prenuptial agreement."

"Oh you have, have you?" There was a definite edge to his voice, motivated by an ugly little scuffle they'd had during Kiki and Walter's proceedings—a scuffle that she'd won. J.B. didn't care for prenups.

"Yes. And as Roman's attorney, I'd think you'd advise him to do the same, considering the fact that he's got a family business that's still very much on the ground floor. One that he's in the process of expanding. In the event that Julia and Roman part ways, he will not want Sonntag Vineyards impacted. Especially since his parents' money is involved in the venture as well."

"How do you know that?"

"I do my homework, Anglin."

He nodded, and then his mouth twisted. "How

can you have the nerve to even mention the word 'prenup' in my presence?"

"I guess I just have a lot of nerve," she said calmly.

"You know damned well that Walter tricked Kiki into signing that piece of crap. And yet because you went to law school with the judge's niece—"

"The burden of proof was on you, Anglin. Don't blame me for doing my job."

"I don't blame you for doing it, Sweetness. I blame you for *how* you do it. And snuggling with the judge isn't in my rule book."

"Snuggling? Excuse me? That's uncalled for."

"He stared at your—"

"Drop it, J.B. Think about your client, here. It's in Roman's best interests to sign a prenuptial agreement. Plain and simple."

"No, darlin', it's not. I don't know how much 'homework' you think you did, but Marv Spinelli is easily worth about thirty times what Sonntag Vineyards is. Which would make his daughter worth fifteen times what Roman is, in the event of Spinelli's death—and that's a conservative estimate. So you do the math.

"If old Marv kicks the bucket after the wedding, then it's most certainly *not* in my client's best interests to kiss millions of revenue dollars goodbye. So you can take your Park Avenue ass right out of here, because I may be country, but I'm not stupid."

"Doesn't Roman have any pride? Would he really screw her out of money that was her father's? What would people say? He needs the peace of mind that a prenup can offer him: proof that he didn't marry Julia for her money."

J.B. threw back his head and laughed. "No, the peace of mind argument is not going to fly."

"Really? Are you aware that he gave Julia a fake diamond, and that her sister is enraged and convinced that he's after her inheritance?"

"He did no such thing."

"Ask him." She folded her arms and glared at him. "This prenup might just save his reputation, because when that story gets out—if it's not all over town already—his name will be mud."

He narrowed his eyes at her. "Vivvie, darlin'. Why aren't you in *Julia's* face, pushing this prenup? Or for that matter, why not go straight to Roman? Why come to me?"

She shrugged and tried to finesse it. "I felt it was more aboveboard to iron it out with you first."

"I'm betting that's a bald-faced lie."

"*Bold*-faced."

"Don't change the subject. Here's what I think, Vivvie. You've already brought up this subject with Julia, and she was outraged. I don't know her well, but I do know she's a romantic. I'm betting she got into a real tweak about this prenup idea, and she said no. And furthermore, I'm betting she told you to drop it and that she'd kill you if you talked to Roman. So here you are, in my office."

She kept her expression utterly deadpan.

"It's not going to work. And you know what? Your gall knows no bounds, babe."

"I'll take that as a compliment." Viv knew when the gig was up. She hitched her computer bag onto her shoulder and headed for the door. She'd reached it and opened it two inches when his boot kicked it shut again. He grabbed her shoulder and spun her around to face him. He leaned one hand against the closed door, his arm still nudging her shoulder, and shoved the other one into his pocket.

J.B. stared down at her with an inscrutable expression, the corners of his mouth inverted.

She could feel his breath on her face, smell the clean starch in his shirt. He wore the lightest touch of outdoorsy cologne that conjured images of pine trees and crisp autumn evenings. The laugh lines around his eyes had gone serious, punctuating the mossy green with faint diagonal shadows. But it was his mouth that hypnotized her.

She remembered that mouth on her body in New York—still could feel the roughness of his jaw as he slid down her rib cage, trailing from her breasts to her belly and hips. She remembered the magic of his lips.

She also recalled the urge to leave before she was left—the sheer discomfort of knowing she was investing too much in pleasure, letting it rise up like a warm bath until, too unwary and relaxed, she feared she'd drown in it.

"Why did you do me that way, Vivien? Hmmmm?"

She fought the urge to rub her face against his chest, feel his arms go around her, have his fingers weave through her hair. "You wanted me to do you."

"I mean, why did you kick me out."

*Do you want the truth or a nice lie? If I tell you the truth, won't you think I'm deranged?* If there was one thing she knew from living with her mother, it was that men despised weak women.

How in the hell could she tell this guy that she'd been afraid she'd need him after an *hour*? That in itself seemed insane.

Viv said, "I try not to be sentimental about these things, J.B. We wanted each other. We had great sex. You were magnificent, so don't get your shorts in a wad—"

"I don't need you to tell me that. Your body told me what you wanted and how much you loved what I did. I don't need your patronizing reassurance. What I need is to know how and why you turned into a robot."

"Robot?"

"Devoid of expression. Devoid of emotion. Devoid of anything human or sensual. You turned off a spigot and your soul was gone."

"We'd had sex. We were finished! You got what you wanted: into my pants. I didn't need you to stick around and pretend to hold me afterwards, okay?"

"Jesus, that's cold."

"I'm not one of those women who needs cuddling and sweet nothings whispered to me. That's all they are: *nothing*s. Don't tell me I'm cold just because I see through this stuff! You're pissed off because I wouldn't play the game—pretend to be snowed by your charm and wait by the phone while you decided whether or not to call."

He opened his mouth, but she overrode him. "You're nursing your ego, Anglin, because I treated you like men treat women! And I'm supposed to know my place and not do that, because I don't have a dick and you do. Well, get over it. I used you for sex. So what? It happens in reverse every day. You've done it hundreds of times, I'm sure."

J.B. looked at her in disgust, but this time it was tinged with something sad. "I have never treated a woman like that in my life," he said quietly. "And I never will."

Viv didn't have a rebuttal for that.

"You've obviously been hanging out with some really nice guys."

Mortification climbed inside her, dug its claws into the lining of her stomach.

"So do you do that often?" he asked. "Use men for sex and kick them out when you're done?"

"No!" She was starting to feel trapped. She wanted to push him aside, open the door and run outside to breathe.

"Good. Because it's a little dangerous these days." J.B. took his left hand out of his pocket and leaned it against the door, too, so that she was effectively caught between his arms. Her pulse kicked up and her skin heated. She fell into his eyes, drowning in the green of them, unable to catch her breath.

Then J.B.'s mouth took hers, swallowing her very unlawyerlike squeak, which developed into a full-fledged moan and then a sigh. The second his lips touched hers, he awakened a hunger in her. She opened to him, melted into him, felt him mate with her tongue and drink in her warmth. She couldn't control her instinctive response to him.

J.B. cupped her chin as he pulled away, looking surprised at himself. "Tell you what, Vivvie," he said. "You just come use me for sex again while you're in town. You know, for old times' sake."

# Chapter Eight

Viv didn't dignify his suggestion with a reply. She put one hand on his chest and shoved, while she groped behind her for the doorknob with the other.

While she didn't succeed in moving the large J.B. an inch, he did get the message and backed away from her, shoving his hands in his pockets again. New Yorker though she was, she noticed that he didn't open the door for her, and his previous comment about her not being a lady rankled. It was this that motivated her next comment.

"Thanks for the offer, J.B., but I travel with my vibrator and plenty of spare batteries." She opened the .door as he responded with typical cowboy arrogance.

"I don't think your little toy makes your toes curl the way I did, honey. I had you beggin'."

She winced as she saw his mother's face in the reception area, and cast a look behind her at J.B., who turned brick red.

Mrs. Anglin did her best to pretend she hadn't heard, but her glazed expression gave her away.

Mortified but highly entertained, Viv made her exit. J.B. had a long day ahead of him, working with Mom.

Outside the office, she found a bench and sank down on it, her hand to her bruised lips. How they'd gone from sparring to devouring each other, she didn't quite know. But one thing was for sure: The attraction between them still blazed. Not that she planned to take J.B. up on his generous offer. She wished she did travel with a personal pleasure device. She wished she even owned one. It would be most welcome right now.

Viv slipped off her high-heeled sandals. She put on her running shoes instead, laced them up and popped the sandals into her bag. Then she headed back in the direction of the Motor Inn by way of Main Street. She needed to distract herself from thoughts of Anglin and her reactions to him.

She poked her head into a couple of shops, discovering the Tea Rose's quilts and buying a small one for Tabitha, her dog walker, as a thank-you gift. She fell in love with Dogologie, a wonderful emporium of canine accessories. Five doggie toys and five doggie fleeces got shipped to New York.

She ignored the odd looks her footwear received. It soon became apparent to her that she was in the South, where no woman would be caught dead wearing running shoes with business clothes. They'd just suck it up and acquire ten blood blisters—a senseless exercise to Viv.

Comfy in her high-tech rubber soles, she wandered on and fell in love with Homestead, Room No. 5, and Idle Hours, shops full of whimsy and beautiful items for house and garden. She had to laugh at herself: She lived in the shopping capital of the world, and yet here she was, making her purchases in rural Texas. A box of lemon-scented candles joined the trail of packages headed for New York. Her mother would love them for the summer house in the Hamptons.

As she left Idle Hours, she heard the screech of brakes and the honk of a couple of horns. Looking back toward the intersection of Main with North Llano, she saw a very strange sight: Sydney Spinelli and a tall, thin, older man were in hot pursuit of . . . an ostrich?

Viv squinted in disbelief as two more of the creatures scrambled into the intersection to the tune of more screeching brakes. Heads bobbing and wings flapping, they trotted across Main Street, heading toward Bejas Grill and Cantina.

Sydney, her red hair streaming behind her, chased these two while the older man caught up with the first renegade bird and grabbed it around the chest. He seemed to be talking to it.

"Vivver!" Syd yelled. "Can you help me out here?"

"What the hell do you want me to do?"

"Wave your arms and yell. Stop them."

*Oh, yeah—right!* ATTORNEY TRAMPLED BY GIANT CHICKEN. The *Post* would have a heyday with that one. "You've got to be kidding me! Those things are taller than I am. What *are* they?"

"Emu! Just step in front of them and wave your arms."

"E-who?"

Syd practically leaped on one, wrinkling her nose at the smell. "Snoopy, you're just a born trouble-maker, aren't you?"

*Snoopy? Don't tell me the other one is Woodstock.*

"I got Shaq!" yelled the thin man, from in front of Dogologie.

*As in Shaquille?* Bemused, Viv gulped and stepped in front of the third bird. *Pretend it's a hostile witness.* She formed claws with her fingers and did her best to roar.

The bird stopped in its tracks and cocked its head. It blinked. Then it opened its mouth and stuck out a black tongue at her. *Nice.*

The noise that then came out of its mouth was a weird thrumming sound, and the creature began to bob its head with enthusiasm. Viv started to get nervous.

More honks sounded from the intersection, and then hoots and hollers. The tall man had evidently borrowed a couple of leashes from Dogologie, because he crossed the street with Shaq in tow and tossed one to Sydney.

Woodstock—or whatever his name was—darted his beak forward and grabbed a lock of her hair, still thrumming.

"Ow!"

He kept bobbing his head up and down. She managed to get him to drop her hair but now he started to circle her, and she didn't like the gleam in his eye.

"Uncle Ted!" Sydney yelled. "You need to cut in on Shrub, there, before he tries to mate with my friend."

*Shrub?*

*Mate?!*

Uncle Ted got to her, grabbed Shrub around the neck and fastened a dog collar onto him. Shrub didn't take it very well, making Big Bird noises of protest. Shrub smelled really bad; he was one foul fowl.

Finally Syd caught up and she and Ted stood there with the three steroidal ostriches on leashes while Vivien tried to figure out what planet they were all on. She began to laugh.

"Ted Kimball," the tall thin man said, transferring the leashes into his left hand and extending his right.

"Alex's uncle," Syd added helpfully. "He's an emu rancher. He's having kind of a hard time keeping the birds contained, though."

"Nice to meet you," Viv managed.

"Some jerk keeps lettin' 'em out just for fun. Nothin' wrong with my fences, but I can't help it when they get cut."

"Who could be doing it?"

He shrugged. "Kids."

Sydney asked, "What if it's a cattle rancher who's threatened by the emu industry?"

Uncle Ted scratched his head and thought about it. He fed Shaq and Shrub each a mini–dog biscuit, oblivious to the stares and guffaws of passersby. "I don't rightly know who we'd be threatening. It's not like demand for my birds is high." Snoopy got aggressive about a dog biscuit of his own, and Ted dug into his pocket.

"Alex and I are working to change that, Ted." Sydney said it firmly. "With the Emu Roast and the new Spa Products line, not to mention his barbecue sauce, demand is going to skyrocket!" She turned to Viv. "Hey! Do you think Julia would agree to serve emu at the wedding?"

Viv's brows crawled into her hair as she looked at the homely family of Shaq, Snoopy and Shrub. "No." She started to laugh again. "What are you picturing? Minced emu cakes garnished with tarragon? Roast emu, carved off the bone? Or maybe emu marsala with shiitake mushroom demi-glace?"

Syd glared at her. "It was just an idea. Julia and Roman's wedding will be quite the social event, and if we served emu it could become fashionable."

But Viv was on a roll. "Braised emu shanks, served like turkey legs at Oktoberfest? Cream of emu soup? Or maybe crispy emu à l'orange . . ."

Ted looked thoughtful. "I think you're onto something, girls. I'm going to consult with Susie and then give Breckin, the wedding planner, a call."

Viv stopped laughing. *Julia isn't going to appreciate this . . .*

"But for now," Ted said, "I've got to get these bad boys home."

She couldn't help herself. "Are you going to walk them home or ride one?"

Uncle Ted pinched her cheek, and she felt five years old again. "You're awful cute for a killer attorney."

*How, exactly, do I respond to that?*

"I heard about the pie at Cuvée." He winked.

Syd cracked up.

"Cheesecake," Viv said with as much dignity as she could muster.

"Pie, cheesecake." He shrugged. "It's all the same. So did you really kick J.B. into a hotel hallway in his birthday suit? You feisty little filly, you." Uncle Ted beamed beatifically and slapped his knee. He obviously thought it was a great joke.

*Yes, that's me. One hundred percent feisty filly.* Viv still hadn't formulated a socially correct answer for the man. If one existed.

"Well, there's Susie with the trailer now. Come on, Snoopy. Come on, boys."

And Uncle Ted, the un-pc good shepherd, departed with his flock. Viv watched, amused in spite of herself, as he loaded the birds as if they were cattle or horses.

She and Syd traipsed back to Marv's Motor Inn only to find Julia in the midst of Bridal Indecision. "I don't know," she said into the phone at the front desk. "I just don't know. Ooooh, really? Yes, I do need to take care of that right away. Thanks for reminding me."

She waved at Vivien and Sydney. Syd, wisely, disappeared before she could be sent to taste any more white cake. Viv got collared as Jules hung up.

"Vivver!" Her smile was too white and too bright. It meant she was up to something.

"Yes?" Viv said cautiously.

"Would you, pretty-please-with-sugar-on-top, mind helping me with a teeny, tiny wedding detail?"

*Uh-oh. There are two people in the United States you can't refuse. One is the president. The other is The Bride.* "Sure, Jules. Anything."

Her friend grinned a sharklike grin.

"Anything within reason," Vivien added hastily.

"This is very reasonable."

*Why do I think you're lying through your teeth?* "Shoot."

"All I want you to do is go to this bridal boutique in Austin tomorrow and get fitted for your dress."

"Oh, is that all."

Julia nodded. She looked *waaaay* too innocent. "That's all."

"You remember that I don't drive? Is Syd taking me? She has to get fitted too, right?"

"Syd's busy. But I've taken care of your ride. Can you be ready by nine a.m.? My friend can pick you up then."

"Absolutely." She stared at Julia, who was humming and checking things off a list. "This dress isn't a scary color of pink, is it?"

"All I'm going to tell you is that it's fab. Gorgeous. It will be an amazing contrast with the birds-of-paradise I'm having flown in."

"Do you mean the flower, or are we literally going to be dive-bombed by winged things?"

"The flower."

"That's good. Real birds might fly overhead and add natural ingredients to your cake frosting."

"Viv, that is disgusting. You have to be the single most unromantic person I know! How do you even come up with these warped ideas?"

"They hatch in the Manhattan water."

"Switch to juice, I'm telling you." Julia scanned her from head to toe. "Been sightseeing?"

*Step carefully.* "I went out for a decent cup of coffee and something to eat."

"You're awfully pulled-together for a coffee shop."

Viv shrugged. "Reflex, I guess. I haven't taken a vacation in months. I'm not sure what my casual clothes look like anymore."

"Want to go grab some lunch? We'll get takeout and swing by the winery. You can get to know Roman better."

"Sure."

Viv woke up at three a.m. again. Well, to be precise, 3:07 A.M. Details of various cases had run through her mind until they converged into insomnia and paid her a wake-up call. She also clearly remembered having a dream about J.B. Anglin.

*They were in the Grand Ballroom of the Waldorf-Astoria, doing the rumba, which Viv had never done in her life. Julia was there, too, with Roman. Marv Spinelli danced by with the very proper headmistress of their old school, who was dressed in a toga and downing a pitcher of beer through a crazy straw.*

*Alex and Sydney were doing the limbo, and Walter the Wanker, Kiki's ex-husband, was engaged in the Macarena with First Lady Laura Bush. Just as Viv thought the*

*dream couldn't get any weirder, they all genuflected while
Kiki was crowned Miss America.*

*Then she looked down to discover that she was naked,
except for a glitzy necklace and a pair of Claudia Ciuti
silver sandals. Her scarlet dress had been literally painted
on her bare flesh à la Demi Moore on the cover of* Vanity
Fair. *The only other accessory of interest was Viv's new
Brazilian wax job.*

*She might have a superhuman ability to remain blush-
free, but she sprinted for the ballroom's exit while everyone
pointed. J.B. followed on her heels in hot pursuit—waving
a ·paintbrush.*

When she woke and flipped on the bedside light
to behold the bedspread's Garden of Ugly Delights,
she felt almost relieved. She looked down to find her
"pajamas," a tee and boxers, instead of red flesh.
This, too, was a good thing.

Then she looked around for J.B., but only her laptop stared back at her. That *should* have been a good
thing, but somehow it wasn't.

Viv found herself reliving yesterday's kiss. What
had made him do it? More important, why had she
let him? She could not claim that he'd taken advantage. No, she'd pretty much seized him by the throat
and clamped herself to his face with an airtight seal.
She'd probably made a popping sound when he
pulled her off . . .

She braved the burnt orange carpet again and
prowled the room like a caged animal, fingering the
scary fringe on the lampshades and wondering how
anyone could have come up with a color scheme so

vile. *Earth tones? I don't think so. More like the tones of the fourth circle of hell.*

There wasn't even a minibar to raid for junk food. Work was the only available distraction. Viv sighed and padded over to her laptop. She got a Styrofoam cup of tap water and planted the machine in her lap.

She had an e-mail from Tabitha reporting that the dogs were fine but they missed her. There was another e-mail from Julia reminding all the bridesmaids to be sure they had purchased their foundation garments for the dresses and got their fittings. She assured them she had scheduled manicures and updos for everyone on the morning of the Big Day.

Several work-related e-mails came next, followed by one from her mother.

Subject:   Vivien Anthea! Texas?

From:      AShelton

To:        VShelton

Darling Viv-Ant,

Do explain more about the trip to the Wild West. *MUST* Julia marry this rodeo clown? Seems such a waste. She's very pretty and quite well-behaved, in spite of Those Dreadful Parents. And to be perfectly honest, she could do much better now, while she has no cellulite. I'd be happy to introduce her to some of my B-list friends' boys (sorry, the A-list wouldn't have her with That Background. I'm not being a snob, just realistic, darling. So don't get snippy with me.).

Now, I should tell you that I've met the most wonderful man—even though Dr. Hagan has been utterly useless in regard to my own cellulite. So I'm keeping the lights turned low . . . who knows, you may just have a new stepfather soon! I think he's The One. Picture me blissful.

Phone me when you return! If you drop by, leave the horrible hounds behind. Five of them . . . what are you thinking? Tsk, tsk. Your apartment must smell like a kennel.

All right. Toodles, darling. xoxoxo, Mummy

(PS I have taken your day-care suggestion under advisement. Let's chat.)

" 'Let's *chat*'? And my apartment does *not* smell like a kennel," Viv said aloud, clicking away on a polite, generic reply to her mother.

"Greyhounds are the cleanest dogs ever. As for The Most Wonderful Man, wake up, Mum! He's not The One. He's Number 96. Or Number 97—I can't remember. By next month you'll have a tiny replica of him, prone on the kitchen table, while you paint a mixture of cayenne pepper and mint toothpaste under its arms and in its crotch and probably on the bottom of its feet.

"The Most Wonderful Man will be itching violently and scratching himself in uncouth places— probably in front of important business associates. And you'll be cackling away over your third vodka martini, after which you'll get morose and self-pitying."

Viv sighed and scanned her generic, soothing message about how wonderful it was that Mummy was happy; that's the most important thing; blah blah blah. She urged Mummy again to think about funding the Displaced Homemakers' day care. Viv didn't see any obvious Freudian bloopers that would have revealed her true feelings, so she hit the SEND button and logged off of e-mail.

She opened a research document she needed for a pro bono animal rights suit against a dog-racing track. Though the details of the case (starving, neglected, malnourished greyhounds) made her physically ill, at least it wasn't another divorce.

She settled back into Marv's lumpy pillow, bracing herself psychologically for what she was about to encounter. The words were difficult enough, but the pictures would haunt her: mass graves, dogs who were literally no more than skin and bone, dogs trapped in tiny kennels that they could barely turn around in. How could human beings do this in the name of sport and profit?

As she read, rage and disgust mounted inside her. These greyhounds were defenseless, loving creatures who couldn't hire attorneys to fight on their behalf. They relied on the kindness and civilization of humans, and yet were betrayed by them every day. Viv was going to nail these sons of bitches to the wall if it killed her.

Unable to sleep himself, J.B. entered his workshop at precisely 4:53 A.M., a steaming cup of coffee in his hand and his dog by his side.

"You're gonna get sawdust all over you, Harley."

Harley wagged his tail and didn't seem too worried about it. He made a snuffling lap of the room, enjoying the familiar smells of the shop and fascinated by the unfamiliar ones. He sneezed once, then twice.

J.B. inhaled the scents, too: the earthiness of raw wood, the metallic tang of machine parts, the pungency of wood-stain and mineral spirits.

He yawned and headed for his workbench, where his latest project lay in pieces. A wedding gift for Roman and Julia, it was a bird's-eye maple console table. The two end pieces were subtly shaped like wineglasses, and he'd added a shelf underneath for greater stability. His next step was to sand each piece, wipe it with a tack cloth and carefully stain it in a light cherry, wiping off the excess stain.

J.B. got to work, interrupting the peaceful morning with the buzz of the sander and spraying himself with sawdust. It was messy work, but there was nothing more relaxing or satisfying for him than bringing a piece to life under his hands.

Harley didn't like the noise of the sander or the automatic dust-collecting system, and generally went outside during this stage, but he came over periodically to check on J.B. when he stopped the sander. That's when he liked to roll in the sawdust, paws in the air, a blissful expression on his doggie face.

J.B. cast an indulgent glance his way and used an old T-shirt to wipe off the piece of wood he was working on. Then he switched on the sander again. He'd be at this for a good while, perfectionist that he was.

Predictably, Harley scrambled to his feet and took off, leaving J.B. alone with his thoughts. They turned to Vivien Shelton, her talk of a prenup, and the way her lips had felt under his . . . damn her.

He couldn't get her out of his head, and she was undoubtedly the reason he was awake at this hour of the morning—because he was going to have to spend a great deal of the day in her company. He checked his watch. A couple more hours out here, and then he had to go in and get showered.

Julia was up to something, and J.B. didn't appreciate it. The last damned thing in the world he wanted was to be saddled with Vivien for the next four to five hours. But when your best friend's bride begged you ever so prettily to help her get something done for the wedding, you automatically opened your stupid fat mouth and said, "Sure, honey! Anything! Shoot."

And shoot she had. She'd shot Viv out of a cannon and straight into his pickup for the ride from hell. J.B. didn't want to get fitted for a penguin suit. The last time he'd worn one was three years ago, when he'd squired the lovely but merciless Miz Shelton to that black-tie thing in New York. *Fond memories.*

He refused to *buy* a tuxedo on the grounds that it was a useless rag that would hang in his closet, ignored, for the next ten years. By the time he dusted it off again and tried to wear it, he'd have a paunch, and only three strands of hair left, and the thing wouldn't fit him—nor would it be in style anymore.

J.B. had absorbed with disbelief the news that Vivien couldn't drive. What kind of grown woman had never gotten a driver's license?

At ten minutes after nine, however, he pulled his

cranky ass up to Marv's Motor Inn to behold Miz Shelton glaring at her watch and tapping her foot maniacally on the sidewalk.

He grinned. That's right—she lived by the clock, with every minute accounted for. J.B. lowered his window, and then his shades. " 'Mornin', Honeybun. You ready to go?"

Awareness dawned on her face. "I don't believe this," she said. "I knew Julia was up to no good."

"You ever set your Park Avenue buns inside a pickup truck?"

"No. And I don't intend to do so today, either. I'll call a cab."

"This ain't Manhattan, Sugar Lips. No cabs to call."

"Refer to me as Sugar Lips again and you can yodel for an ambulance. Got that, Anglin?"

He was starting to enjoy himself, he really was. "You are right terrifyin' before coffee, darlin'."

She glared at him. "I've had coffee, thank you."

"Really." He shuddered. "Well, then, my little Morning Glory, hop into the chariot."

Viv muttered something very rude.

"Be nice, now, or I'll make you ride in the bed of the truck, on a hay bale."

"I'll call and hire a car and driver, thanks."

J.B. sighed, put the gears in neutral, and swung out of the driver's side. A few strides and he stood looking down at her. "Get in, Vivvie, or I'll pick you up and toss you in."

She pokered right up. "I dare you to lay one finger on me, Anglin. You so much as breathe on me wrong, and I will slap you with a suit for assault so fast your head will spin."

"Aw, honey. Don't be that way. My head's already spinnin', on account of your radiant beauty and your winsome personality."

"I'm going to puke."

"Such a romantic." J.B. took another step toward her. "Gimme a kiss."

"No!" She took a step backward.

J.B. stepped to the right.

She stepped to the left.

"Just a little kiss?" He backed her another few steps, then blocked her with an arm, resting it on the open passenger door. He almost had her now.

"Get away from me."

"For charity, you know." He stuck his neck out and puckered, only to encounter the palm of her hand. He licked it, and then nipped it.

"Stop slobbering on me, you lunatic—"

He took one more step forward and slapped his other hand on the side of the truck, trapping her. "The way I see it," he said, "you've got two choices. You can kiss me, or you can sit your derriere down on that passenger seat. Which will it be?"

"Aaaarrrrrggghhhh!"

"I'm sorry, honey, but I don't recognize that as a functional word. I think you want a big wet one . . ." And he angled his head.

Viv skittered into the truck like a crab running for the end of a dock.

*Excellent.* J.B. slammed the door on her and

punched the lock button. "Gotcha." He strode around to the other side and climbed in himself.

Her lips fought off a smile. "What are you, part sheep dog?"

"Exactly." He nodded. "And I just had to have ewe."

Viv groaned.

He grinned.

They headed down Main Street, past the light at Goehmann Road, and hit the highway. The windows were partially down, even though the morning was characteristically warm, and he noticed Viv inhaling the fresh air with something that came close to appreciation. A few rays of sunshine bounced across her nose and shone in her hair, revealing unexpected touches of honey in the mahogany color.

*She's one gorgeous woman.*

*Yeah, J.B., and she's packed full of TNT. Do you need to learn this lesson again?*

*Nope. I need to teach the same one to her.*

# Chapter Nine

Viv leaned her head back against the surprisingly comfortable seat. *I am riding in a pickup truck, hurtling down the highway with a bad punster. A bad punster who just herded me into this redneck vehicle as if I were a wayward cow. Worse, I have an appointment with a Bridesmaid's Dress. Will somebody please just shoot me?*

"So," J.B. said conversationally. "What's with a grown woman not having a driver's license?"

"I live in the City. I've never needed one. What's with you Southerners that you don't know how to take public transportation?"

"Honey, in case you haven't figured this out, it doesn't exist here."

"So everyone just drives around wasting tons of gas while we become more and more dependent on foreign oil. That's great."

J.B. ran his tongue over his teeth and cast her a sidelong glance. "Tell you what, Miz Environmentally Conscious. If you'll hand over your trust fund and about a hundred of your closest friends' trust funds, we might be able to get *started* building a transportation system that would be a ludicrous waste for this area. In case you haven't noticed, we don't have quite the same traffic patterns as your Big Apple."

She folded her arms. "People could at least drive hybrids."

He nodded. "Sure. As soon as they come out with hybrids the size of a Suburban, folks around here will jump right on 'em. Until then, good luck."

"Demand creates supply, not vice versa."

"You're just full of wisdom today, Slick. Why don't you stick around and run for mayor? Then you can direct operations for the whole town."

"Very funny."

"See, I think all this finger pointing and soapbox stuff is coming from a personal inferiority complex because you can't drive."

"That's ridiculous," said Viv. "Besides, how hard can it be? Driving is a simple mechanical task that any moron can perform. It's not like you need a university degree to get a driver's license."

"Mmmmmmmm." J.B. said nothing further. He just smirked, which made her a little uneasy.

Viv decided to change the subject. "So have you thought any further about advising Roman to sign a prenup?"

His smirk disappeared. "No. We've had this discussion."

"But—"

"N-O. Word meaning to answer in the negative. No, *nein, nyet, non,* no!"

"Don't you think you should at least consult him? Maybe his opinion will be different from yours."

"I'm not going to bring up the topic with Roman. And let me tell you, Vivvie, that if you go anywhere near my client waving a prenup, I will hog-tie you. I will throw you into the back of this pickup, and I will personally drive your ball-busting butt back to New York. Do you understand?"

"There's no need to be quite so rude about it."

"Yes, there is. I don't want there to be any misunderstanding—anything you can construe as a loophole to wriggle through. You damned divorce attorneys are snakes in the grass."

Her jaw dropped open. "*Excuuuse* me? I don't believe you just said that to me."

"You want me to repeat it?"

"What in the hell did you think you were doing representing Kiki in her divorce, you hypocrite?"

"I represent the entire family, and you know it. You couldn't pay me enough money to do divorces on a regular basis. What a racket—all about ego and paycheck."

"I see. Well, let me tell you something: I'll bet you wished you'd signed a prenup yourself when your ex-wife took you to the cleaners for your pro ball money."

J.B.'s jaw tightened and his mouth went flat. He took a deep breath. "You are *so* over the line with that comment, Shelton."

"And calling me a snake in the grass wasn't?"

"Let me give you a little warning, here. Number one: Mention the word 'prenup' again and I'll put you out on the highway. Number two: The topic of my ex-wife is not up for discussion. Bring her up again and I *throw* you onto the highway going full speed. Understand?"

"Are you threatening me, Counselor?"

"Are you badgering me, Sugar Lips?"

They stared at each other, neither blinking an eye, until Viv noticed that the truck was drifting toward the double yellow line on the highway.

"Why don't you look at the road, and not at the snake in the grass?"

He finally did so, and straightened the wheel.

"Aren't you afraid that I'll slither up your thigh and bite you right in the apples? That's what we snakes specialize in, you know."

"You leave your venom behind, you can slither up my thigh anytime," J.B. said, looking as if he was getting quite a nice visual. "But no biting."

"Aw, you won't let a serpent have any fun, will you?"

"We'd have lots of fun. And you know it."

They were drawing closer to Austin, and Viv gazed out the window at Oak Hill, which looked so new that it gleamed. "Did they order this town from a catalogue?" she asked. "Because there's no dirt anywhere. There's no seediness. Everything shines in this updated, Norman Rockwell way. It's a little creepy."

He glanced over at her. "Missing your Manhattan grime and ubiquitous Dumpsters? The smell of stale urine in doorways? I had no idea you were so sentimental, Sugar Lips."

"Will you stop it already with the icky Southern endearments? Do you not get the concept of 'politically correct' and how it's not okay anymore to call women these patronizing names?''

"But Sweetness, Sugar Lips fits you so well. You're just full of goodness and light, and your mouth melts under mine.''

Viv growled at him.

"I had a dog that used to make that sound,'' J.B. mentioned casually. "Oh, now don't bare your teeth, darlin'—you're starting to look just like him. Not that he wore red lipstick, but there's a definite resemblance . . .''

"Are you calling me a bi—''

J.B. clucked reassuringly. "No, no, no. My dog was male.''

Viv gritted her teeth instead of baring them. *I can't club him over the head, since I have no weapon and we'd end up dead in a ditch.* Really, when she thought about it, the only recourse she had was—

*Oh, no you don't. You are not sleeping with the man again. Not for old times' sake. Not for revenge. Not for any motive at all.*

But it was so tempting to savor the idea of kicking him out into the Marv's Motor Inn hallway naked.

*It will remain a nice vengeance fantasy. That's all.*

Forcing herself to be civil, she asked, "What kind of dog was he?''

"Irish setter. Beautiful. His name was Blarney. Now I have a black Lab, Harley. You like dogs?''

Viv smiled. "Oh, yeah. You could say that.''

"You have one?''

"Five.''

*"Five?"* His voice was incredulous. "And you keep them in an apartment all day? What, are they those little fuzzy toilet-seat-cover dogs?"

"Toilet-seat-cover?"

"You know. Useless. But squish 'em flat and they make a great adornment for your toilet seat."

"That's very warped," Viv said. "And no, I don't have little dogs. I have greyhounds. I work with a rescue."

J.B. raised a brow. "A rescue? Shelton, you do surprise me. That doesn't fit with your heartless image."

"Sorry to disappoint you. And they don't stay in my apartment all day. They get walked for miles."

"But you're at work. Wait, tell me you don't have a dog sitter."

"Well, yes," she said defensively.

He hooted.

"What's wrong with having a dog sitter? They're happier that way."

"It's just very Park Avenue, Sugar Lips."

"Stop it with the snob thing. I'm not a snob. I work very hard. I volunteer. I've personally found homes for almost a hundred dogs, I give a lot of money to my local rescue and its national parent organization, and I take on animal rights cases pro bono. That is"—she cleared her throat—"when I'm not eating babies for breakfast."

He raised a brow. "Jeez, I'm feeling like a slacker here. Only one dog and no rescue work."

"Do you have acreage?" She couldn't help it—her heart started to beat fast.

"Yes."

"So you could take in several greyhounds. Can I have your local greyhound rescue contact you?"

"Whoa, wait a minute—"

She looked at him pleadingly. "These poor dogs, J.B. They're so mistreated. They're starving. They're kenneled over twenty-three-and-a-half hours a day! What kind of life is that? They need you. Your Lab—Harley—he's probably lonely, and Labs get along well with other dogs . . ."

"Harley's pretty happy being an only child."

"He'll be happier with company, trust me. Being an only child is not so fun."

"You speak from experience?"

"Yes." She left it at that. "Now, how many greyhounds do you think you could take? Can you work with them to socialize them? Housetrain them?"

"I—Viv, I don't know."

"You know, you just won't commit."

"Forcefulness is not a problem for you, is it, Viv?"

"Nope. Yes, I am forceful, and I won't apologize for it. By the way, there's so much land around here. Do you have friends who could take dogs, too?"

J.B. began to laugh.

"This isn't funny." Tears sprang to her eyes as she thought about last night's reading material. "I'm working on a case right now against a big dog track. The details of the abuse would curl your hair. These dogs need all the legal aid they can get, too. Would you consider . . . ?" She stopped at his expression. "What?"

He turned his gaze back to the road. "Nothing. It's just that you're so passionate about this."

Viv blew out a breath. "So sue me. I don't spend all my time shopping for diamonds and redecorating various houses, okay? I'm a real person who lives in the real world, not an insulated rich bitch. Did I grow up in fortunate circumstances? Yes. But I can't help who my parents are. I didn't choose them."

He was quiet for a moment. "Now *there's* a revealing statement."

"Why?"

"Do you not get along with them?"

"I get along fine with them." *I just don't speak to my father, and my mother's a little off her rocker.*

"What do they do? Where do they live? Are they still married?"

Viv got very still. "I thought you Southerners didn't pry."

"I'm a Westerner—a Texan—not a Southerner. And I figure we've exchanged far more intimate information than this."

She rolled her eyes and stayed silent.

"For example, I know just where you like my hands when you're close to—"

"My father doesn't even live in the States," she said abruptly, to head him off. "I never see him. To be frank, I don't even speak to him."

"This is the, uh, earl—that's what you called him, right? The source of your title?"

"Yes. And please forget I ever told you about that."

125

"Why don't you have a relationship with him?"

"Because he's what the English would call a 'prat.' He romanced my toothpaste heiress mother because he needed a rich American wife in order to hang on to his ancestral home. It was either that or turn it into a hotel, and he couldn't stand the shame of that."

"But haven't you had any contact with him? When you were a kid?"

*What makes you think I was ever a kid?*

She shrugged. "He knocked her up and then disappeared on vague and mysterious business. He'd pop in now and then so she couldn't divorce him for desertion. She used to get all dressed up before he arrived: do her makeup, put on her good jewelry. And then when he got 'called away' after just a few days, she'd cry and throw things. Once I went into the kitchen and our Haitian housekeeper was mixing a love spell for her."

"I guess it didn't work?"

"No. And it smelled really bad. Mummy did some other strange things . . . Finally she served him with divorce papers, I think just to scare him. But he gladly took her up on them, and got half her money, too."

"What about you?"

She sighed. "He made a half-hearted attempt to suggest that I receive a proper British education. She went *bonkers*.

"From what I understand—and this is through her attorney, who's sort of an uncle figure to me—she told him that if he wanted the money he'd better forget about me. So, to all intents and purposes, he did."

"You're kidding."

"No, I'm not. The man did have his secretary send me a card and a gift of some kind each birthday and Christmas until I was twenty-one. But to be honest, my mother poisoned any thoughts I had about him. And then I just got angry. The last communication I received from him was about four years ago. A card. I wrote 'Return to sender' on it and haven't heard anything since."

Her voice, even to her own ears, was flat and mechanical, devoid of emotion.

After a long silence, J.B. finally said, "I'm sorry."

"Why?"

"That you grew up without a father."

She waved a dismissive hand. "I never knew what I was missing, so it just seemed normal to me. Status quo. The way it was. Besides, there was an endless procession of faux uncles. Enough about me. Tell me about your little slice of all-American apple pie."

"You've met my mother, who manages my office."

*Oh, yes. The same lady who knows you curled my toes.*

"My father died when I was fifteen—heart attack. I had just left on the school bus. He hadn't felt good the day before. He was loading some Christmas packages into the trunk of our old Chevy and was going to run them to the post office on his lunch hour for my mom. He dropped with one in his arms. Our setter, Blarney, went nuts and got my mom. But by the time an ambulance got there, he was gone."

"I'm so sorry," Viv said.

J.B. stared ahead at the highway for a long time. Then he said, "The package full of presents he was holding took on a lot of symbolism for me and Mom that day. It reminded us that life and family and friends are precious gifts, and shouldn't be squandered or taken lightly. My parents—we all—were so lucky to have had the happiness we did. I see people all the time, focused on small negatives in their lives. They completely forget to be thankful for what they have. They just want more."

"Yes. And most of the time they want what isn't good for them." Viv laughed cynically. "Case in point, my mother."

"How so?"

*Phew.* This was probably getting a little too personal. But what the hell. "Mummy—"

"C'mon, you don't really call your mother that, do you?"

"Oh, yes. It's more old school and more elegant, you see." Her voice dripped with irony.

"Uh-huh."

"Mummy," she repeated, "wants a man. A gentleman with whom to share her life. The problem is, she hasn't *got* a life to share! And until she develops some interests or passions of her own, she'll keep relying on some stupid *man* to make her happy. And when he doesn't, she'll keep on with her—" Viv broke off. J.B. did not need to know about the little voodoo operations.

"Her what?"

"Her, ah, search. For The One who has multiplied until he's The One Hundredth. These pathetic faux relationships that only end up making her desperate, miserable and lost."

They got off the highway at Austin's Fifth Street, then doubled back down West Sixth, where Viv gazed around appreciatively. "This is very nice."

"Yeah. I used to own a condo on Thirteenth when I was in law school. Stupid me, I sold it. Now it's worth about four times as much."

They went another few blocks and then turned into the parking area of a two-story colonial home which housed an upscale bridal boutique: their final destination.

J.B. cut the engine and ditched his seat belt, palming the keys and staring at her speculatively.

"What?" she finally asked.

"I wish I'd known about Mummy back in New York, that's all."

"Oh, Christ. Don't psychoanalyze me." Viv slid out of the truck and slammed the door on his expression. Rude? Maybe so. Necessary to end this all-too-personal conversation? Absolutely.

"You know, some men might find you a little hard to take," J.B. murmured, out of earshot. "You like dogs better than our entire sex."

But he looked at Viv, peering dubiously through the door of the bridal salon, her arms wrapped around her body, and something inside him melted. What kind of ball-buster got teary-eyed about greyhounds and had personally placed over a hundred of them?

*Do you have acreage?* Most women would have asked him that question coveting the land or prestige for themselves. Not Viv.

She had actually begged him to take in some dogs, do legal work on their behalf. But he'd bet she wouldn't beg anyone on her *own* behalf, even if she were being boiled alive. It wasn't in her character.

Her childhood sounded extremely odd and disturbing—and he picked this up mostly from what she *didn't* say about it. He filled in the spaces between her spoken lines: a selfish bastard of a father, an emotionally unstable mother, unfulfilled in her own life, who probably hadn't been very nurturing. Love spells and histrionics . . . and yet Viv, for the most part, cultivated an icy calm.

What other contradictions were there about Vivien Shelton? He looked forward to finding out.

# Chapter Ten

Viv walked, without waiting for J.B., onto the verandah of the bridal shop. One look inside caused her to itch. White: white lace, white silk, white satin. Poofy things. Veils. Petticoats. *Yick.*

J.B. caught up with her.

"Do I really have to go in there?" she asked, aware of the plaintive note in her voice. "I'll break out in hives."

He grinned and reached for the door handle.

"Wait! I have to brace myself." Viv took a deep breath. Then another.

"You'll live. Just put one foot in front of the other and smile pretty for the saleslady."

"But . . . it's just gruesomely girly in there! I'll be attacked by a rabid ruffle!"

"Vivvie—"

"It'll sink its fangs into my ankle and I won't be able to shake it off."

J.B. laughed.

"And then the salesperson will lock me in a claustrophobic little cell upholstered in roses and unveil The Monstrosity."

"Come again?"

"The Bridesmaid Dress," Viv whispered.

J.B. took her arm. "Let me try to figure this out. You've faced entire courtrooms of people, stern judges, psychotic spouses and hostile witnesses. But you're afraid of a *dress*?"

She winced.

"This is ridiculous. Put your ego aside, Shelton, and remember that it's your best friend's wedding. If she asks you to wear a purple burlap sack and a daisy between your teeth, you will do it."

"Hmmm. I could try a little blackmail on Julia: Sign a prenup or I won't wear your icky bridesmaid dress."

J.B. opened the door and shoved her inside. "No mention of that word again."

"What word?" she asked, all innocence.

"Hello," J.B. said to a harassed-looking saleslady, with a winning smile. "We're here to be fitted for the Spinelli-Sonntag wedding. This young lady is eager to see her bridesmaid's dress. She's hoping very much that it's got lots of ruffles, and that it's pink."

Viv blanched and tried surreptitiously to kick him.

The lady clasped her hands to her bosom. "Oh, Julia's wedding! She is an absolute sweetheart. I have *so* enjoyed working with her."

"Uh, hellllllooooooooooooooo! Earth to Mrs. R! I need some help here!" an irritated, nasal voice called from the back.

Viv raised a brow and the saleslady gritted her teeth.

"You've gotta love Julia, don't you?" said J.B. "This is Vivien Shelton . . ."

"Hi, Vivien. I'm Mrs. Rundell. Excuse me for just a moment." She bustled toward the back of the shop. "Yes, Tammy dear?"

". . . and I'm J.B. Anglin," he trailed off.

"This petticoat is, like, defective or something! Could you, like, help me out here?" whined the unknown Tammy Dear.

"Oh, you've got it on wrong, sweetie. Here, let me—"

"*Owwww!* Could you watch it with your ring, please?"

"Oh, dear, sorry. Now, if you turn the underskirt like this, and—"

"I'm telling you, it's, like, defectiiiiiiive. I mean, what kind of, like, moron, designed this?"

"Well, hon, it's one of our best selling petti—"

"I don't know why," said Tammy Dear crossly. "Wait. Did you say that this is, like, a best seller? Meaning that a hundred other brides will be wearing it? Then no. I don't want it."

"Well, dear, we did, uh, special order that item for you . . ."

"So? Like, send it back."

"Let me check and see if the owner will allow me to do that. Now, just step out, one leg at a—"

"Owwwww!"

"—time, oooh, sorry, and—"

Mrs. Rundell emerged, her nerves not only frayed

but fried. She pasted another smile on her face for J.B. and Viv. "Fittings for Julia's wedding. Right." She leaped for a storage closet and yanked out a men's suit bag. "One tuxedo, for Anglin." She pointed to the other side of the shop. "Men's fittings in there. Herbert will be right with you. Excuse me." She whirled and stuck her graying head into the back. "Herrrrrr-bert! Alteration!"

Then she popped back out. "Now, I'll just fetch your dress, dear," she said to Vivien.

"Helllooooooooo! Like, Mrs. R, where are you? Can I get some service here?" yelled Bridezilla from her royal fitting room.

Mrs. Rundell hunched her shoulders. "Just one moment," she begged.

"Take your time," Viv told her.

The poor woman skittered into the back again.

Tammy Dear had a few requests. "Okay, now see where these, like, bugle beads are? I checked the lighting in the church, and they won't, like, show up at all. So my cousin thinks they should be sequins. Can you, like, pull them all off and replace them with the sequins?"

"Well, I—"

"And right here, where this, like, weird tuck thing is? We don't like that. Can you take it out so that the hem hangs evenly?"

"Tammy dear, this is a very special—as you know from the price—Vera Wang design, and if you take out the tuck and gather there, you'll ruin the lines of the gown. So I don't advise doing that."

"You know, Mrs. R, I came here because I heard

that your service was, like, implacable, but I have to say that you have been, like, *sooooo* hard to work with—"

Viv started to laugh. *Implacable? I think she means impeccable . . . Bridezilla is the implacable one.*

"I'm sorry you feel that way, Tammy. I'm doing my utmost to ensure your happiness with your gown. I really am. And I don't want to see you alter it irrevocably and then not be satisfied with the results. Please do keep in mind that we'll be happy to accommodate your wishes, but once we make changes to the gown we absolutely cannot return it. All right?"

The sound of a foot stamping reverberated throughout the boutique. "No, it's, like, *not* all right! You are here to give me good service and, like, a bridal gown of my dreams. If I want to make changes and then, like, change the changes, then it's my preposterance to do that."

*Preposterance?* Viv shook her head, and then turned at the sound of J.B. clearing his throat. "Will this do?"

Her mouth went dry at the sight of him. Anglin was one gorgeous man in boots and snug Levi's. But Anglin in a tuxedo was a whole other ball game—tall and sleek, his tousled blond hair lending the formal wear an irresistible recklessness. His wide shoulders contrasted with the narrow edge of snowy white shirt that showed underneath the jacket. His eyes held a mocking glint that utterly uncivilized the civilized attire.

She wanted to rip it off him.

Viv lowered her lids so that he couldn't read and take advantage of her desire. "Yes. I think . . . that will do just fine."

"Excuse me, Tammy. I'll be right back." Mrs. Rundell's voice preceded her and then she appeared, wild-eyed. When she caught a glimpse of J.B. she stopped in her tracks, mouth open. "Oh, my," she said. "Oh, my." Mrs. R went so far as to grab a bridal accessories flier and fan herself with it.

Anglin actually blushed, which was endearing.

"You look just like that Longview boy, Matthew McCon-whatever," Mrs. Rundell said in worshipful tones. "Only better, with those green eyes."

"Jude Law," said Vivien before she could stop herself. "With a Brad Pitt swagger."

"A cowboy 007," sighed Mrs. R.

Anglin snorted and then guffawed. "Ladies, ladies. How much were you paid to say these things?" He began to undo the studs in his cuffs, until he caught both of them staring at him like starving jungle cats, waiting for the plastic wrap to be removed from a slab of beef.

He laughed uneasily and stuck a thumb in the direction of the fitting room. "I'll, uh, be in there."

Viv and Mrs. Rundell stared at his retreating butt, Viv blatantly and Mrs. R covertly. They exchanged a long, female look of perfect understanding.

A loud, two-fingered whistle sounded from the back. "How long do I have to wait here?" Tammy Dear was back to being charming.

Mrs. Rundell assumed a hunted expression. "Just one moment, hon. I'm still trying to reach the boutique's owner about the petticoat and return policy." She scuttled in the direction of the phone, but then noticed Viv look at her watch. "Oooooh, sorry." A step-ball-change and she was scurrying toward a different back room, full of racks of plastic-shrouded dresses.

Moments later she returned with one and ushered Viv quickly to a dressing room. "I'll be with you just as soon as I can, okay?"

"I'm fine," Viv told her. "I don't do tantrums."

Mrs. R nodded gratefully and braced herself once again for Bridezilla. Viv shut the dressing room door and heard the saleslady talking with the owner shortly afterward.

Tammy Dear didn't take the news of the store policy well, and began to carry on while Viv listened in disbelief. If Mrs. R had a meltdown and assaulted the little bitch-princess, she'd defend her in court for free.

She took a deep breath and gazed in abject fear at the opaque plastic bag that held The Dress. She reached a trembling hand out for the zipper, closed her eyes and gave it a tug.

Would Julia garb them all as Little Bo Peep triplets?

Down, down, down traveled the zipper, sinking to the level of her heart. Viv braced herself and opened her eyes.

J.B. strode toward the front of the shop, the plastic-shrouded penguin suit hanging from his finger behind him. Nobody was up at the front. Viv must be meeting her fate as a bridal accessory. He ran his tongue over his teeth and smirked. He hoped the dress had lace and ruffles all over it.

His grin faded as he listened to the nasty little chick in the back fitting room, berating poor Mrs. Rundell. Violence never solved anything, but some people just needed a good slap upside the head.

"Do I have to go to, like, Dallas for my dress? Houston? Because this is ridiculous. I want to talk to the owner. Like, *now!*"

"Tammy, she can only be reached by cell phone and I'm not at liberty to give you that number."

"Then *you* call her and let me talk to her."

"I'm afraid I can't do that right now."

"Yes, you can. It's a simple little matter of, like, punching some buttons, Mrs. Rundell. You do know what a button is?"

"This is not a good time to do that. Trust me."

"Trust you? You've been giving me, like, the runaround since I came in here today. Call her and tell her to come down here immediately!"

"Tammy, calm down. I'm sorry, but the owner is in the hospital with her sister, who's undergoing minor surgery."

"You're just making that up."

Mrs. R gasped. "I most certainly am not, young lady . . ."

J.B. shook his head in disgust.

"Anglin?" Viv's voice called. "Can you give me a hand here, since the staff is on the battlefield?"

"Yeah." He walked in the direction of her voice. "Where are you?"

She waved at him from over the top of the door.

"Zip me up?" The louvered doors swung open as she pushed through them, holding the dress together, and turned. J.B. just stared.

Vivien Shelton had the sexiest back of any woman alive. Long and elegantly, sleekly muscled, it was completely bare to his gaze. Every vertebra winked at him, punctuated her sensuality. Her shoulders gleamed, smooth and soft under the boutique lighting—beckoning a caress.

Seeing her naked back brought memories of New York. How perfect her body was, except for slightly knobby knees and longer middle toes that he found endearing: the Achilles' heels of her beauty. They made her human, somehow.

She'd been voracious and almost fierce in bed, certainly not waiting for him to make the first moves. He'd finally pinned her playfully, gently, and forced her to calm down. That had surprised her: that he preferred slow and thorough to fast and furious.

"J.B.?"

He blinked. "Yeah."

She moved toward him, holding the two edges of the dress, which was a beautiful, simple, peacock blue silk with spaghetti straps and a V-neckline. Not a ruffle to be seen on it. The color set off her almost black hair and mirrored her eyes. It was a stunning dress.

He didn't want to zip it up. He wanted to push it down, puddle the bodice around her waist and palm those gorgeous breasts of hers. She had small, perfect, pale pink nipples and he still remembered what they'd felt like in his mouth, what they'd tasted like.

J.B. wanted to ruck up the skirt of this dress and slip his hands into her skimpy panties, grab two handfuls of sensual, sweet ass. He wanted to skim his hands around to the front, then, and play her cleft like a Stradivarius until she sang with pleasure.

He took hold of the two open edges, moved his hand down to take the zipper tab. And he found his fingers brushing her naked spine instead, from the base up to the nape of her neck.

Viv caught her breath and a tremor ran through her: one so deep he could feel it. She met his eyes in the mirror, her lower lip caught in her teeth, and he was gone.

He bent his head to the curve of her neck and touched his lips to her heated skin. Another deep shudder went through her, and he moved his mouth to her shoulder, the zipper forgotten. He kissed, licked, then bit.

J.B. turned her to him and saw that her blue eyes had gone smoky. He put his hands on either side of her face and held her prisoner while he took her mouth: the mouth he'd been hungry for all this time. Three long years of frustrated memories and puzzled disgust had built up a lot of passion. Viv'd be lucky to have a mouth left to argue with once he was done . . .

He wanted to love her, to punish her, to excite her all at once. It didn't make any sense, but she seemed to understand it anyway . . . because she couldn't seem to get enough of him.

He tangled his hands in her hair and shoved his knee between her thighs. *If we weren't in a blasted bridal boutique I'd take her right here on the floor, on the silly gilt stool, and standing up against the fussy, satin-upholstered wall.*

Damn it! He'd finally gotten her where he wanted her, half dressed and half crazy with desire. And they were in a semipublic place where he couldn't do a thing in hell about it.

*You're a cruel, cruel man sometimes, God. Laughing at our human antics.*

J.B. slipped his hands inside the open bodice of Viv's dress and decided he didn't give a hoot where they were. He had to feel the weight of her breasts in his palms, had to roll her nipples between his fingers.

She gasped at the contact and whispered, "Oh, yes. Please . . ."

It undid him. Manhattan's top divorce attorney, pleading with him to satisfy her, to pet her, to love her. If he got any harder—

He froze at another gasp behind them, coming to his senses. "Oh-my-God!" Tammy Dear's voice was completely unwelcome. "Would you, like, *animals* just, like, get a room?"

# Chapter Eleven

Viv yanked up her dress and clamped her arms over it. She glared daggers at the most evil bride in Texas.

J.B. raised a brow at Tammy. "I'd love to get a room," he said calmly. "That's a great idea." He turned to Vivien. "Do you want to stay somewhere on Town Lake? We'll get a nice view of the bats at sunset."

She blinked. "Bats? What are you talking about? No!"

"Austin's Town Lake bats are nationally famous."

Viv blinked, then disregarded him and turned to Tammy. "You," she said, pointing. "Bridezilla."

The girl's jaw dropped. "*What* did you call me?"

"Bridezilla. You are a piece of work! I'd advise you to pop a few Xanax and look up the word 'nice' in the dictionary, or your wedding party is going to assassinate you. With the help of a few other people."

"You can't, like, talk to me that way, you slut!"

"Yes I can, and it's about time somebody did. You

need to treat the people around you with respect and quit making their lives hell, just because you feel like it. Mrs. Rundell has been absolutely wonderful to you, and you are treating her like shit. Stop it!"

Tammy Dear dissolved into full meltdown mode, screaming unintelligible words out of a beet red slab of twisted face.

Mrs. R closed her eyes, stuck her fingers in her ears and looked as though she were praying.

Viv looked at J.B., who remained impassive. "What d'you think?" she asked. "Will her groom drown Bridezilla in the champagne fountain? Or will his mother suffocate her in her own wedding cake?"

He pursed his lips while Tammy Dear screamed some more, most of the words unprintable. "I feel certain," he said, "that it will be her maid of honor, who will brain her with an ice sculpture."

Viv brightened. "The caterer! He'll poison her cream puffs."

"No. That would kill off everybody with a sweet tooth. Only *she* should die. Everyone else should enjoy the party," J.B. joined in.

"You're right." Viv thought for a moment. "I've got it! Remember Elizabeth I, and the poisoned dress from Mary, Queen of Scots?"

"Bingo." He looked at Bridezilla, who'd stopped to gasp for breath. "Better be a lot sweeter to Mrs. R, darlin'. She'll have custody of your gown until the day you put it on." He aimed a bland smile at her while Mrs. Rundell pretended to cough in the background.

"You two are, like, *sick*." Tammy whispered the words, probably because her throat was raw from all the screaming. "Get away from me."

"Happy to oblige, ma'am." J.B. was at his most genial. He turned to Viv and grinned. "Now get dressed, you slut, so I can *un*dress you somewhere else, without an audience."

"You can't, like, talk to me that way!" Viv said to J.B., once they'd collapsed laughing in his truck.

"Did you see the look on her face?"

"Priceless. I'd probably do it again just for that, but I couldn't stand how she was treating Mrs. R."

J.B. shook his head. "I don't know why she didn't tell the little princess to shove her attitude where the sun don't shine."

Viv sobered. "Probably because she needs that job to pay her rent."

He nodded, started the truck and pulled out of the parking lot. Then he said, "That was nice work back there, Shelton. Standing up for Mrs. Rundell. Most people would have stayed out of the situation."

She shrugged uncomfortably. "It was nothing."

He glanced at her. "That's just not true. Accept the compliment."

Viv changed the subject. "I'm thinking we should write the owner a letter in case Little Miss Ugly decides to cause trouble."

"Good idea."

Viv shot him a sidelong glance. "J.B.? Something's not right, here."

"You think?"

"I think. Because we're actually agreeing. We're in harmony. We're laughing together."

"Sshhh. Don't tell anyone. You hungry? I know some great places to eat in Austin."

"It's barely eleven o'clock."

He shrugged, then shot her a look full of evil intent. "You want to go shack up somewhere in a hotel?"

*Yes. But I'm not about to admit it.* "Are you really willing to risk that with me again?" she asked. "I mean, this time I might throw you out without complimenting your performance."

He let out his breath in a hiss. "You know, you really need to be taught a lesson, Miz Shelton."

"Ooooh. By a big strong man such as yourself?" She batted her lashes at him. "Are you offering to spank me, J.B.?"

"Do not tempt me." He gritted his teeth and drove through downtown Austin, casting a longing glance in the direction of Fourth Street as they passed it. "Best Interior Mexican food to be found in the city: Manuel's. The cheese *enchiladas verdes*, the ceviche, the salsa . . ."

"Are they open at eleven?"

"Probably not." He sighed. "Best Tex-Mex: Chuy's. Best Italian: Mezzaluna. Best amazing gourmet food with a Southwest/Latin flavor: Jeffrey's. I used to walk there from my condo."

"So what you're trying to say is that you're hungry?"

"Yep. There's only one thing that could distract me from food."

"Teaching me a lesson?"

He ran his gaze over her body and nodded slowly.

"Will it be a thorough lesson, from A to Z?"

"Oh, yeah. You can bet on that."

Viv almost purred. "Really, Professor? Then let's get on with it."

He sent her a wide, slow, lazy smile. "Well, all righty then."

J.B. took Mopac to 290 and searched for the perfect location: a long stretch of country road where he could have his way with Miss Vivvie.

She gazed at him suspiciously when he slowed and began to pull over. "You're not serious," she said. "Not here."

"Good as any place, I reckon." J.B. put the gearshift in first and cut the engine. "C'mere, darlin'. Give me some sugar."

Viv reared back. "You actually think that I'm going to do this *by the side of the highway?!*"

"You got a better idea? Where else should we do it?" J.B. got out of the driver's side and walked around to her door while she gaped at him.

He swung it open and put his hand on her knee.

She jerked it away.

"What's the problem?" he grumbled. "You told me clearly that we should get on with it."

"I meant in a hotel room!"

J.B. straightened up and widened his eyes. "You New York gals sure are strange, Vivvie. How the hell you gonna learn to drive in a hotel room?"

"*Drive?*"

"Well, what other kind of lesson did you think I had to teach you?" He shook his head at her. "Ohhhhh. Why, you dirty-minded little vixen, you!" He slapped her on the ass. "Now scoot over, honey. You just grip that wheel like you were plannin' on grippin' my ears."

Viv's jaw dropped open. "You—you—you—"

"Cat got your tongue?" He slid in beside her, bumping her over with his hip.

She shot to the other side and fumbled with the door handle. "I am not staying in this car with you! You're a pig!"

He sighed and hit the LOCK button.

She shot him a Death Stare and hit UNLOCK.

He grinned and hit LOCK again. "I may be a pig, sweetheart, but you sure did wanna play with my curly little tail, didn't you?"

"Let me out of here, Anglin, or I will see your ass in court for aggravated kidnapping!"

"Naw. You came willingly and we have witnesses to that effect. All I'm doing now is taking you back safely."

"Let. Me. Out."

"You open that door and you'll get squished by oncoming traffic. Don't you want to learn to drive? How can a grown American woman not know how to drive?"

Viv clenched her jaw. She was starting to think

that her mother was onto something with the voodoo dolls. If only she had some modeling clay and a little yellow yarn in her pocketbook . . . If only!

"Tell you what," J.B. said in the most generous of tones. "If you will agree to a driving lesson, and you can get us all the way back into Fredericksburg, I'll allow you to run me over in the Marv's Motor Inn parking lot. How's that for fair?"

"*Deal.*" She said it through gritted teeth.

"Okay, then. Now: That short pedal on the left is your clutch. Put your left foot on it. You're going to push that in every time you start the ignition, and every time you shift gears. Got that?"

She nodded.

"The long pedal on the right is your gas. You will use only your right foot on that. Do not confuse it with the other long pedal in the middle, which is your brakes."

"Okay."

"Put your foot on that one now and get a feel for it. Now put it on the gas. Good. Okay, right foot on the floor. Push all the way in on the left pedal, the clutch, with your left foot."

"That's hard."

"Get used to it. Are you as far as you can go?"

She nodded.

"Then turn the key to start the ignition." J.B. popped the gearshift into neutral. "And very lightly, step on the gas."

Viv tried to follow directions, but the roar of the engine as she hit the gas distracted her, and she released the clutch. The truck choked, shuddered and went dead.

"Well, that was a good start," J.B. said after a wince.

"It was a terrible start!"

"I meant, it was a good start to a start," he amended. "Okay, let's do it again. Clutch, a little gas, and turn the key."

The truck roared, shuddered, grumbled, but stayed running this time.

"Good! Take it a little easier on the gas. Okay. Let the clutch out slowly. Now, these are your lights, your windshield wipers and your hazards. This is the steering wheel, Vivvie."

"No, really?"

"And if you turn us right into oncoming traffic, you'll kill yourself as well as me, so why not pass on that idea? You can murder me some other way."

She pursed her lips and furrowed her brow, pretending to think about it. Finally she nodded.

"Now," J.B. said. "Push in the clutch again. And fondle this joystick right here, baby." He grinned. "Now put it forward, into first gear. Good. Now step on the gas pedal, just a—"

The truck roared, lurched forward as Viv yelped, and then stalled.

"—little," J.B. finished, with a sigh. "And let out the clutch. Okay. Let's try that again, too."

"I don't think I'm very good at this," Viv told him.

"It's all practice, honey. Push in the clutch, put it in first gear, now a little gas . . ."

She finally got the truck moving in first, and then second. J.B. clapped. "There's hope for the City Girl after all! Next thing you know, I'll hook you up with a job driving a turnip truck."

Viv gunned the engine at that. "Can I try third gear?"

"Absolutely."

Unfortunately, what she thought was third turned out to be fifth, and she stalled them out again.

Finally they were bumping along the shoulder of the road at a pretty good clip. "See that double yellow line?" asked J.B.

"The one in the middle of the highway?"

"Yep. That one. Do you think you can stay on the right side of it?"

She gave him a long-suffering look. "Well, dang, how's this wheel thang work agin?" she said, in an exaggerated hick accent.

"Okay, then, smart-ass. Let's go."

"You want me to actually put your life in jeopardy on the interstate? And me without a license?"

"Do you have to phrase it quite like that?"

She shrugged.

"When you see a red light, stop. When you see a yellow light, start stopping. Poke me when we get there, because I think it's a real good idea for me to close my eyes."


"Yee haw!" Viv yelled into the wind. If only Schmidt and Belker could see her now, in command of a bona fide pickup truck! This driving thing was fun. She glanced into the rearview mirror and scanned the bed of the vehicle. *You know, there's room for a lot of dogs back there . . .*

She tried to push the thought aside. *Yeah, great idea, Vivver. You just buy a pickup to tool around Manhattan in. Throw on a gun rack and rifle, too. Wear a red bandanna around your neck.*

Maybe she should attach some spurs to her black Prada stretch boots. She got a good chuckle thinking about Belky's expression if she walked into the firm in spurs and a bandanna.

"The fiendish laughter is making me nervous," said J.B., his eyes still closed. "We *are* still on the right side of the double yellow line?"

"Yup."

"And our speed is below eighty?"

"Definitely."

"You're watching out for animals in the road, too, aren't you?"

"What do you mean?"

J.B. jolted upright and opened his eyes. "Cattle or deer sometimes venture onto the highway. Hell—I can't believe I'm sitting as a passenger in my own truck while a novice driver holds my life in her hands. You know, maybe you should pull over and let me—"

"No way," said Viv. "I'm hitting my stride. I'm just starting to have fun here!"

"Which means I should be very afraid." But J.B. smiled.

She tried not to melt at the sweetness and affection

in the curve of his mouth. *Look at the road, Viv. Not at the man.* She could get used to him looking at her that way . . .

*Stop it.* Viv did what came naturally to her: She went on the offensive as a defensive measure.

"So, Anglin. Now that I've got you held hostage in your own truck, you can tell me why you think all divorce attorneys are snakes in the grass. That was not a nice thing to say."

J.B.'s smile vanished. "I don't like divorce attorneys," he said tersely.

She raised a brow and waited for him to add to that statement. He didn't. "Why not? Why are we more evil than the rest of the population, J.B.?"

"It's what you stand for: the dissolution of unions. Marriage is meant to be sacrosanct, Shelton. And it's become a mockery. A friggin' mockery. What happened to marriage as a commitment? Huh? People these days—they go through a rough spot and call 1-800-DIVORCE." J.B. stared out the window, his mouth grim.

Vivien tried not to get angry. So her job made *her* the cause of the problem? Wasn't that a little simplistic? She asked in even tones, "And what if they're not happy?"

"You have to work at happiness sometimes! You have to fight for it. Ever hear of this phrase: 'What God has joined together, let no man put asunder?' Where the hell did that go? Huh? Marriage is a test of character and faith sometimes, and I don't see a whole lot of either these days. When I got married, I did it for *keeps*." J.B. slammed his fist down on the dashboard.

*It's what you stand for: the dissolution of unions.* Viv gripped the steering wheel hard. "Nice speech, J.B. I'd give you a round of applause but it's hard to do that and drive at the same time."

He turned and gave her a look that would have turned a lesser woman to stone.

She didn't blink. "I don't see a wedding ring on your finger, Anglin. If you got married for keeps, you must still be married. Were you somebody's husband when you slept with me in New York?"

# Chapter Twelve

J.B. froze, and white-hot anger flashed through him. "I can't believe you're asking me that."

"Well, I am," said the Ball-Busting Bitch.

"Would it bother you if I said that I *was* married that night? After all, given the wham-grrrr-thank-you-sir treatment you subjected me to, you may find it easier to screw married men. No emotional entanglement that way—hey! Slow the hell down!"

"I do not have anything to do with married men," she said through clenched teeth.

"Unless you're helping to get them divorced, and making tons of money off the whole procedure."

She cast him a look of loathing. "I happen to know that you're not a widower, J.B. So why don't you tell me all about how *you* got divorced, even though you got married for keeps. Even though you're maintaining your balance on your damned soapbox."

"I'll tell you if you slow down. *Do you hear me?* The long pedal in the middle! Hit the friggin' brakes, woman. You're going ninety miles an hour."

She finally slowed down. "So? Let's have it."

He took a deep breath. "I married my high school sweetheart, who had become my college sweetheart. I wanted to spend my life with her. I thought she felt the same way. I had an offer from the Cowboys to play wide receiver—a good offer. Two games into the season I took a direct hit to my right knee, and that, as they say, was that."

She waited.

"I went to law school. As you know, it's tough. Corinne stuck it out, even though it sure wasn't a lot of fun for her. She worked as a manager for an outlet store in San Marcos while I went to Baylor Law School. She went out clubbing with friends while I was studying all the time, and I have to admit we grew apart. We were living in different worlds; we never saw each other.

"But it wasn't until we returned here to Fredericksburg and bought a house that things really went to hell. I started a small practice and there just wasn't a lot for her to do. She'd burned out on retail and didn't want to do much else. Some friend of hers wanted to start a nightclub in Dallas, but I didn't see that as a very good use of my money, so I said no. She didn't take it well. I don't think I'd ever said no to her before, but she was talking about a lot of money.

"She left to go look into real estate anyway, thinking she could change my mind. She couldn't. She left in a huff again, and this time she talked to some fat-cat divorce lawyer there whose eyes lit up with dollar signs when he heard that I'd had a pro ball contract.

"The rest is history. I love—loved—her, but I couldn't keep her where she didn't want to be, doing what she didn't want to be doing."

"So why didn't you move to Dallas and go into law there?" Viv asked.

"I can't leave my mother alone. I won't. Corinne's always known that. I'm all my mother has. She took good care of me when I was growing up, and I intend to take good care of her while she's growing old.

"So that's my story. But you know what? If Corinne had never talked to that damned greedy attorney, we could have worked things out. Instead, she took off with my heart and half my money and started a stupid, failing business.

"And the irony of it is that she's ended up right back here now, after her second divorce. Same goddamned attorney, wouldn't you know? So now he's got more of my money than she does." He snorted.

"So it's the divorce attorney's fault that your wife left you, and moreover, he should have taken the case for free?" Vivien's voice was heavy with irony.

"You can take the sarcasm right out of your tone, darlin', because the answer to the first question is yes. Corinne is one of those people who's easily influenced."

"She knew she wasn't happy, right?"

"No. She knew no such thing. She was bored. Ever hear the saying that idleness is the devil's workshop?"

"But it doesn't sound like *you* were happy, either. Come on, admit it."

"Every marriage goes through rough spots. That's all it was."

"Hmmmm. What does Corinne like to do?"

"She's a social person. Loves people and parties and football games and action. She's got a lot of nervous energy. Adores fashion and makeup—her favorite city is LA. I don't know why she doesn't move there. I think she's scared to go alone."

"Sounds like you still keep in touch with her."

J.B. shrugged. "Only now and then." *Though it's funny how all kinds of things seem to keep breaking at her house. Things that she wants me to fix.*

"You're unusual," Viv said, her blue eyes evaluating him. "Most men don't keep in touch with their exes. Then again, most men don't take their marriage vows too seriously."

"I guess I'm not most men. What am I supposed to do, pretend Corinne doesn't exist? Pretend she was never a part of my life? I spent years dating her and then married to her. I can't erase that."

Viv shrugged.

"So what about you? Why haven't you ever been married?"

She laughed, but it was a brittle sound. "Oh, I just haven't had time."

"Had time or made time? Or do you just treat all men as sex toys, to be discarded after a couple of hours?" He knew he shouldn't have said it, but it still rankled.

"Oh, Christ." Her foot got heavy on the gas pedal again. "Haven't we had this discussion? Can't we be done with it?"

"We can be done with it once I've gotten some answers." His truck hurtled forward at an alarming speed. "Vivvie . . . the speed limit is fifty here. We're getting close to town."

She shot him an exasperated glance. "Oh, please. There's nothing out here but—"

"Oh, shit!" As they rounded a bend in the road, a trooper clocked them at roughly eighty-nine miles per hour. "Brakes, Viv, brakes!"

The roof of the squad car lit up like Christmas, and the trooper squealed off the road after them.

"Pull over," J.B. ordered. "Let me handle this."

Viv downshifted, not very smoothly, and rolled onto the shoulder. Her chin came up, and her shades came down. She lowered the window as the trooper ambled up.

"Do you know how fast you were going, ma'am?" He peered into the car. "Oh, hey, big guy. I *thought* this looked like your truck."

"Around the speed limit, I thought, Officer," said Viv brazenly.

The trooper snorted. "I clocked you at eighty-nine miles per hour, ma'am."

"Hi, Wesley," said J.B. "How's tricks?"

"And how do we know that your equipment is in proper working order?" asked Vivien, belligerently. She sounded just like a damned Yankee attorney.

"Good, good, J.B. How's your mama?" Wesley Taunton said, breaking off to frown at her. And then, "Ma'am, are you arguing with me?"

"No," said J.B., elbowing her.

"Yes," said Vivien, ignoring him.

"License and registration, ma'am."

"Well, you see, I live in Manhattan. You know, New York?" she said to the trooper's expressionless face. "And I left my license in the City."

Wesley wasn't *all* stupid. "Then how did you get on the plane, ma'am? You must have a passport at least. May I see that? I'll use it to track down your New York license. In the meantime, do you understand that driving without a license is illegal?"

J.B. interrupted. "Wesley, can I talk to you for a minute in private? Man-to-man?"

Vivien looked outraged. "Man-to-man?" she repeated. "What is this, the nineteen fifties?"

"Shut up, Vivvie," J.B. said pleasantly, "and don't be stupid."

He swung out of the truck and took Wesley by the arm while steam began to shoot from Viv's ears.

"Wes-Man. We've known each other a long time."

Wesley sighed as if he knew what was coming. "Yes, J.B., we have."

"And you do remember that my mama makes the best King Ranch Chicken in the entire Southwest region?"

"Yes, J.B., she most certainly does," Wesley said fervently. "Oh, man. I can taste it right now. I used to think it was so unfair that your mama and Alex's mama could cook, and mine burned water . . ."

"Wes, what if I was to promise you that Mama would make you two King Ranch casseroles, a meat loaf and a couple of batches of her homemade macaroni and cheese? You could freeze 'em and eat like a king for a month." J.B. prayed that his mother would take pity on him and follow through with this little piece of bribery.

The trooper began to salivate immediately. "Oh, man. Oh, man! Her mac and cheese, too?"

"You got it," J.B. said.

"That little spitfire don't have a license, does she, J.B.?"

"Mama makes those frickin' amazing *enchiladas suizas*, too, Wesley."

Taunton looked as if he might orgasm on the spot. "Tell you what. I hate to be a son of a bitch, but can she throw in an apple pie and a key lime cheesecake, too? I'm awful tired of takeout and fudge bars."

"Deal." *Oh, hell. It looks like I'll be learning how to cook this weekend.*

"Then I never saw you today, or that mouthy little Yankee that's . . . uh . . . driving away in your truck."

*"What?"* J.B. spun around as Viv gunned the engine and took off.

Wes looked sympathetic, but then crafty. "That would be grand theft auto, is what that would be. You want me to report it, or do you want to go back to the bargaining table?"

"Uh . . ."

"I always did like your mama's Hershey pie."

Viv did it just to see the looks on their man-to-man faces. How dare J.B. tell her to shut up? And call her stupid? Unbelievable. He may as well have beat on his hairy chest and thrown her barefoot into a kitchen.

She would have handled it just fine. Challenged

160

the working order of the clocking device, challenged his eyesight if necessary, and gone to court to beat the ticket. Except for that tiny problem of not having a license or insurance. She bit her lip.

So maybe J.B. had been right to call upon his friendship with the man and make some kind of closed-eyes-for-beer deal. She supposed it was only right that she supply the beer, if that's what it was.

And now that she'd made her point, she should go pick him up. Viv waited for a break in the traffic, and then performed a highly illegal U-turn in the middle of 290.

As she approached J.B. he was getting into the trooper's car. He froze and turned his normally pleasant face to her. He was almost purple with rage.

She pulled up and eyed him with a little trepidation.

J.B. slammed the passenger door of Wesley's car, gave him a brief salute and stalked to the truck. "Get out."

"No way. You might leave me stranded."

"Get. Out."

Viv unbuckled her seat belt and slid over to the passenger side. She buckled herself back in so he couldn't push her out the window.

He sent her an ominous stare and swung himself in. "Nice of you to stop back by."

"Don't ever tell me to shut up. And don't call me stupid."

"I was trying to save your ass back there!"

"I am fully capable of saving my own ass."

"Not when you pull your rude, obnoxious Yankee

161

crap on local law enforcement, you're not. You would have ended up behind bars. And now!" He was starting to turn a dark eggplant color, most interesting. "*Now* I get to spend my entire weekend swinging my dick over a hot stove."

She choked. "Excuse me?"

"Do you know what I had to promise to keep you out of trouble?"

"Beer?"

"Three King Ranch Chicken casseroles, two meat loaves, three pans of macaroni and cheese, two trays of *enchiladas suizas*, an apple pie, a key lime cheesecake and two friggin' Hershey pies!"

"No-you-did-not." She stared at him.

"I did! I pretty much had to double the original deal when you added *grand theft auto* to the list of things Wes had to ignore! You'd better be a good cook, Shelton."

She was quiet for a long moment. Not only had J.B. given her a driving lesson, but he'd bribed the trooper for her with his home-cooked food. How sweet was that? Her heart did a slow roll and collapsed into a puddle of useless sentiment. That's all it was. She was getting a little soft when it came to J.B., and it was dangerous . . . Had he just asked her if *she* could cook? *Not even.*

"I, um, am superb at cooking little plastic pouches in the microwave on HIGH." Then she started to laugh.

"I'm glad you think this is funny," he growled.

"I'm very sorry . . ." She tried to make her voice sound penitent. "So when did you learn to cook?"

"I didn't. Wes thinks Mama is making all of this! And she's going to shoot me."

Her jaw dropped. "You volunteered your *mother* for me?" *Oh, God, that's even sweeter. Except the woman's going to want my head on a pike!*

"Well . . . I figured I'd help. Or just get her recipes. How hard can it be to follow a recipe?"

"Uh-oh. From my experience, very hard." Viv chuckled. Then she put her hand on his knee. "I'm sorry that I drove off and left you. Really. Especially now that you're my knight in shining oven mitts."

He groaned.

"What can I do to make it up to you?"

"Nothing."

"Take you to lunch? A bar, so you can get staggering drunk?"

J.B. cast an irritated glance her way. "What makes you think," he asked, "that I want to spend any more time in your company?"

"Oh." She said it in a small voice. "Well, there is that. With me being a snake in the grass and a greedy corrupter of family values."

"I never said that."

"Yes, you pretty much did. You're heavy on the implications, J.B."

"Oh, hell. I didn't mean to hurt your feelings, Vivvie. That's assuming you have those, like regular people."

"Just because I'm tough and call things like I see them does not mean that I don't have feelings."

"That's good to know."

Silence reigned for the next couple of minutes.

Then Viv asked, "Is your mother going to hunt me down and set fire to me with a flare gun or something?"

His lips twitched. "Probably."

"That's very comforting, J.B. Thank you."

"Ain't nothin' but a thing."

If someone had said that to her in New York, she would have thought he was an idiot. But coming out of this big, blond Texan's mouth, it sounded just right. Even quite civilized.

They turned down Main Street and soon were at Orange, where Marv's Motor Inn was located. J.B. pulled into the parking lot and put the gear in neutral. He looked over at her.

She looked right back.

He put a finger under her chin. "See ya later, Tough Girl," he said.

"Like I told you, I can't cook. But I can buy all the ingredients, if that helps."

"Ah, the guilt is getting to you."

She nodded, with a wry twist of her lips.

Suddenly he said, "I know what you can do to make it up to me."

"What's that?"

"You can take me upstairs and let me have my revenge."

# Chapter Thirteen

Vivien gave J.B. a long, level look. "Revenge? Does that include kicking me into the hallway naked?"

"Of course not," he said. "I wouldn't do that to you."

She exhaled in relief.

"What I had in mind," he said in thoughtful tones, "was actually to fashion a harness out of the bedsheets and hang you out the *window* naked."

Viv opened her door and slid out.

"But before that, I'd make you feel real, real good." His teeth flashed white and his eyes deepened, his glance a caress.

Should she take him upstairs? Lie with him among the mustard and brown flowers? Fall with him onto the burnt orange, spongy carpet?

It was extremely tempting: to see those magnificent shoulders and biceps shirtless again; to feel him on her, under her, all over her.

A muscle twitched in his cheek and J.B. looked amused as she considered his request. She didn't like the implication that she "owed" him sex. That made it too much of a bargain, made her body a commodity. She needed to turn this situation around and get control of it.

"I should at least buy you lunch before using you for sex again," she said. "Don't you think? Is there any decent food in this walnut-sized town?"

"Walnut-sized it may be, but you'll be surprised and impressed by some of the eateries. You've already experienced Cuvée." He thought for a moment. "Hop back in . . . unless you want to walk four blocks in this heat?"

She got into the truck, since it was 101 degrees. Texas was a sauna with a sky.

"I'm going to take you to the Lincoln Street Wine Market, where we'll have a little of this and a little of that, since you've got to try everything. They've got wines from all over the world, and the food will wipe that smug look right off your face, Miz Manhattan."

They drove four blocks down Main Street and turned right on South Lincoln, pulling up to a charming, rustic little cottage with a large trellis-covered patio in back, filled with tables and chairs.

It was far too hot to sit outside this afternoon, though, so they gratefully escaped into the small but cool interior, where mingled voices and laughter greeted them immediately.

The Lincoln Street Wine Market featured a scuffed cement floor which had been given an old-world treatment in shades of beige, black and taupe. The interior walls and ceilings were plaster, hand-rubbed in warmer tones of yellow-beige, and bordered by a smoky taupe that tied in with the floor.

A long, dark wooden table, flanked by simple chairs, dominated the length of the main room and functioned as an arrow toward the bar in the back.

Every available wall hosted a black iron wine rack, stocked with every conceivable variety of wine. The curtains were a pleasing deep red velvet and the screen door stood open in welcome.

Viv noticed one private room, separated from the main area by French doors and furnished with two cozy sofas and tiny tables. J.B. glanced inside, saw that it was empty, and suggested that they take it over. She sank down on one of the sofas, which embraced her like a lover.

The air inside was seasoned with a not unpleasant aroma of good cigars, which the black ceiling fans circulated with other scents of fresh bread, unusual cheeses and general good cheer. She liked the place immediately.

Some of the wine racks were strung with amusing little bunches of artificial grapes, and the narrow hallways leading to the bathrooms and bar area had been decoupaged with newspaper and book pages. A green-and-burgundy-striped tie marked the entrance to the men's room; a little handbag marked the one to the ladies'.

The tiny marketplace seemed to have been lifted straight out of Tuscany by a benevolent tornado and spun into the Texas Hill Country.

J.B. came back with a printed list from which they

could make selections for a gourmet tray to enjoy with their wine. Since he was starving, he ordered a pastrami sandwich in addition to their complimentary fruit and fresh baked bread.

Viv chose Camembert, Gruyère and a triple cream St. Andre cheese from the list, and then in the spirit of adventure a chipotle pesto, the international olive mix, some prosciutto, and a chicken pate with black truffle mousse to be served with cornichons and mustard.

Her mouth started to water in anticipation of the feast. J.B. took her by the hand and tossed her pocketbook on the sofa. "Come on, now let's choose some wine."

She cast a glance over her shoulder at the purse.

His lips twitched. "Viv, honey, this ain't New York. Nobody will snatch it."

The owner of Lincoln Street Wine Market was friendly, knowledgeable, and possessed the most unpronounceable surname. Viv laughed as she saw that his business card proclaimed him the HEAD CORK SUCKER.

He talked with them for several minutes about what they preferred and helped them make a couple of selections from his over two hundred wines-by-the-glass. The only thing he didn't stock, curiously, was any Texas wine. He had too many friends in the local wine business and couldn't show partiality to anyone. He found it simpler to let visitors explore the local wineries on their own by taking a wine-tasting tour.

The owner gave them a brochure for the Texas

Wine Trail, and pointed out that the third weekend in August featured the Harvest Wine Trail, a tour through the newly picked vineyards to the various wineries, which were filled during that time with the smells of new wine. Viv was surprised to see seventeen wineries on the tour.

"The last one is Roman's," J.B. told her with pride. "He's really making a go of it at Sonntag Vineyards."

Viv grimaced. "Yeah, and I'm sure a capital infusion from Julia or Daddy Marv would be most welcome."

The corners of J.B.'s mouth turned down. "Let's agree to stay off that topic, Vivvie. Okay? For now, peace and wine and good eats."

She nodded.

Since it was hot outside, she chose a white to start with, the Clay Station Viognier. A California wine, it was so fragrant that it almost reminded her of a light cologne. It was also delicious.

Viv sank down into the wonderful sofa again and J.B. folded into it, too, holding a glass of the 2002 Kahn Syrah. He crossed one booted foot over another and savored the wine in his mouth. "Mmmmm. I do prefer a cold beer most days, but this hits the spot right now."

"This place is so *not* what I expected to find in Texas."

"There you go stereotyping again. I'll take you out to a place called the Salt Lick for barbecue sometime, though. It's much more Texan." He took a sip of his wine and eyed her over the rim of his glass. "Assuming you behave yourself. You should be horse-whipped for stealing my truck like that."

Viv crossed her legs and smiled. "I only borrowed it for a few minutes."

"Yeah. When you borrow something, it's customary to ask the owner. By the way, I'll be picking you up at eight o'clock sharp on Saturday to go grocery shopping. Wear gym shoes, because you're gonna be doing a lot of vegetable chopping, sweetheart.

"And keep in mind that Mama may not even let you in her kitchen—she's very territorial and it's small—so you may be chopping out on the picnic table in the backyard. Think your manicure can handle that, Vivvie?"

She blew out an unenthusiastic breath. "Yes."

"I'll hose you down with mosquito repellent, but you may get some chigger bites out there."

She squinted at him. "What exactly is a chigger?"

"Don't you have those in Manhattan?"

"No, just rats the size of city buses."

"A chigger is a little insect that gnaws on you and even burrows under your skin. They itch like a m— uh, they itch pretty bad."

"What do I have to do to be allowed to stay inside the kitchen? Sit under the table? Why is it so small?"

His eyes betrayed a flicker of irritation. "I offered to buy her a big new house, but she wanted to stay in the one she and my dad lived in. The kitchen is a closet, but she won't let me open it up and build it out for her."

"You can do stuff like that?" Then she remembered his office.

"Yeah. It's pretty easy. And no, I can bet you that you won't be allowed to stay in there with her. First of all, she won't be pleased about all the cooking, and that's *if* she agrees to help. Second, when she hears that you're the reason for it, you're pretty much toast. She wouldn't let you sit under the cabinet with the garbage."

"There's Texas hospitality for you."

"Quiet. With your cold-fish Yankee stare and your thousand-dollar suits, not to mention your little dose of prizefighter attitude, you are not qualified to make any judgments about that topic."

Viv raised a brow and thought about being insulted. Then she laughed. The wine mellowed and relaxed her, and soon she'd kicked off her sandals and tucked her feet up underneath her on the couch.

"So what do you Texans do for fun around here?"

"Any number of things. You can go kayaking or tubing nearby—New Braunfels is a good spot. You can visit the Lady Bird Johnson Wildflower Center, or Wildseed Farms and Market Center, both of which are stunning. You can hike at Enchanted Rock, or check in for a stay at the Double B Ranch and play golf at the Hidden Springs Golf Course. Book a treatment at Serenity Day Spa. Shop. Go country-western dancing in Gruene or Luckenbach. Go pick your own peaches at Hallford Orchard. Want me to go on?"

"What's tubing?"

"I'll take you over the weekend if we ever finish cooking for Wesley Taunton. You sit your hiney in the middle of a huge tractor inner tube and float it down the Pedernales River."

"Really?"

"Yeah. And generally you drink a lot of beer while doing it."

"How do you bring the beer?"

"You rent a tube just for the cooler and tie a rope between it and you."

"You've got to be joking."

"Nope. And that settles it: We're going. Just so I can send the photo to the New York papers."

"I don't think so."

Their host brought their tray in, a smorgasbord of goodies. While Viv dug into the crackers, cheese and pate, J.B. inhaled his pastrami sandwich.

"J.B., I didn't think food like this existed in Texas," she said blissfully.

He just grinned and kept munching.

She savored the taste of the rich, musky Camembert, chased it with some wine and then popped a kalamata olive into her mouth, the deep briny taste spreading over her tongue.

Sean came over to ask if everything was okay, and both of them nodded silently, mouths full, in great appreciation. They were on their second glass of wine when J.B.'s cell phone rang.

He pulled it out of his pocket, glanced at the number and frowned. Then he answered. "J.B. here. Hi, Corinne."

Viv froze at the mention of his ex-wife's name. She had absolutely no right, but a sneaky green coil of jealousy snaked through her belly, turning the appetizers sour.

"Well, call the sprinkler guy," he said. Then he

sighed. "No, we wouldn't want your roses to die. But I'm tied up in a meeting right now. Can this wait a few hours? Okay. Fine. Bye."

Viv carefully didn't meet his eyes when he hung up, concentrating on the chipotle pesto instead, and how it sank into the airy little crumb-crevices of the Italian bread. She put the piece in her mouth and found the smoky, twangy flavor delicious.

"My ex," he said.

"Mmmm," she responded in the perfect noncommittal tone.

"Wants me to fix the timer on her sprinkler system. It's not coming on."

She just looked at him.

"Yeah, I know what you're thinking, but it's not that way at all."

"I didn't say a thing."

"Don't you have any exes that you're still in touch with?"

She pursed her lips. "There's a guy from law school who'll call me every once in a while to get an opinion on a case. And one other one—he's part of a greyhound rescue I work with."

"And I'll bet that both of them are more interested in getting into your pants than they are in opinions or dogs."

She didn't deny it. "Tell me that your wife can't get someone else to fix her sprinklers."

He sighed. "Probably. But I want you to know that it's only the outdoor plumbing that I touch."

Viv tilted her head and tossed back some more wine. "And why would you want me to know that?"

"You know why." He reached out and slipped a hand into her hair, caressing her scalp and then her earlobe, stroking down to her neck. "I want my revenge, Vivvie."

She shivered under his touch, the cool air-conditioning contrasting with his warm hand.

"Cold?"

She shook her head.

"Let me warm you up. Hmmm? Finish your wine." His hair gleamed in the afternoon sun, alternate waves of bronze and pale gold. His eyes held the cool, deep color of the Pedernales River and his skin was the color of saddle leather. But it was his mouth that drew her the most, with its wicked curves and sinful cushion of a bottom lip, contrasted with the angelic golden stubble along his narrow cheeks and firm jaw.

J.B. plucked an olive from the tray and tossed it into his mouth, where he held it on his tongue, rolling it and savoring the tiny fruit. With a quirk of his lips, he watched her watch him. Finally he bit into the soft flesh of the olive and separated it from the hard pit.

She couldn't look away from his mouth, even as he covered it with a fist and discreetly disposed of the olive pit, swallowing its fruit with great enjoyment.

"You got to use me for sex in New York," he said softly. "It's only fair that I get to have you here in Texas."

It was only her second glass of wine, it wasn't even

dark outside and she couldn't say her judgment was clouded. But she felt inclined to agree with him.

She tried to wrap her mind around her feelings for him, but they weren't tidy. Since she'd arrived in Fredericksburg only a few days ago, J.B. had saved her life, publicly humiliated her, trapped her against his office door and kissed her. He'd fondled her breasts in a bridal salon dressing room, given her a driving lesson and rescued her from certain jail. He'd forgiven her for stealing his truck . . . and he made her heart sing. ·

*Whoa, what was that last part?* Viv reminded herself that her heart couldn't carry a tune. It didn't even lip-sync properly.

*He's a dog lover, too, and he's got land for greyhounds. I can soften him up, I know I can . . .*

". . . and so you should definitely take me back to your Marvelous Marv's motel room," J.B. was saying, still making his case. "It's only justice," he added. "And you and I both exist to serve Justice." He winked.

How could she not wink back at him? She felt herself melting into him on the sofa as his arm snaked around her shoulders, his fingers dipped inside her collar and he brushed his lips against her ear. She shivered with pleasure. *Serving Justice has never felt so good.*

Viv raised her glass, which held maybe two more tablespoons, in a toast. "To Justice," she said. "Let's get another bottle to go."

# Chapter Fourteen

Viv tried to ignore the ugliness of Marv's Motor Inn as she and J.B. turned in to the rear parking lot and prepared to sneak in the back entrance. She really didn't relish running into Julia.

J.B. grinned at her as he cut the engine. "We gonna count some sheep for cheap, Vivvie?"

"God, I hope not," she retorted. "Unless your technique's gotten so bad that you'll put me to sleep." She'd slid out of her seat and had rounded the front of the truck when he caught her in a firm grasp, angled his head over hers and took her mouth. He backed her up against the front of the truck with a noise akin to a growl, plucked her off the ground and sat her on the hot hood with himself between her knees.

Viv emitted a bona fide squeak, a noise very uncharacteristic of her. Warmed by both the Texas sun and the engine inside, the metal burned right through her panties, through her skirt, and practically singed her buns. She tore her mouth from his. "Hot!" she yelped.

"Feeling sleepy?" J.B. asked.

"No."

He clasped his hands around her rear end and pulled hard, so that he tugged her snug against the bulge in his jeans. Then he ground into her, watching for her response.

A flash of heat shot to her center and Viv's mouth opened slightly with pleasure. J.B. swooped down and licked between her lips, rocking his pelvis against her at the same time. He scooped her off the truck, sliding his hands under her skirt until he had two handfuls of tush. He kneaded and squeezed as if he couldn't get enough.

His razor stubble scraped her face and she gasped as he released her mouth, tipped her back, and took a large mouthful of breast right through her skimpy tank and bra.

"Room key," he said against her, his lips still nuzzling.

And he moved a hand inward, to stroke slick, forbidden parts that shouldn't be fondled in public.

A keening sound came out of her mouth but she didn't care as his thumb moved back and forth and she started to come apart.

"Oh no you don't," said J.B., and the bastard set her down on legs that now wouldn't support her. "You're not going there for a while yet." He grinned wolfishly.

She restrained herself from smacking him, exhaled in a hiss and dug into her pocketbook for the blasted key, which she slapped into his palm without a word. Her only consolation was that judging by the rocket that had launched inside his pants, he was having trouble walking, too.

They made it to her room and fell inside, J.B. kicking the door closed with his boot. He threw her onto the bed and stood, hands on his hips, looking down at her.

Her arms were spread wide, the heels of her sandals dug into the bedspread and mattress, her thighs were splayed and her skirt was rucked up. He had a great view straight up of her turquoise silk panties, and she had a serious wedgie.

A smile played over his lips. "Your panties match your eyes, Vivvie."

She had the urge to close her legs and block his gaze, but didn't. She enjoyed seeing him turned on.

"Take off everything except your panties and your sandals." It wasn't really a request—it was more a command. And nobody told Vivien Shelton what to do. But she obeyed, slipping her tank over her head and unfastening her bra.

His breathing quickened as she tossed it onto the floor, for once not thinking of the grungy, nasty orange carpet and whatever lived in it.

Her breasts were exposed to his gaze, and her nipples hardened without him even touching her. She was still so aroused that the slightest provocation would send her tumbling over the edge.

"Now take off your skirt," he said, in a curiously thick voice.

She sat up, moved to the edge of the bed and unbuttoned the waistband. She brought her knees together and slipped the skirt off, and it joined her bra on the floor.

"Open your thighs . . ."

She did.

"Touch your breasts for me."

She hesitated.

"Please."

She moved her hands awkwardly to them, lifted them and caressed them with her fingers. "But I want you to touch them," she whispered.

"You want me?"

She nodded.

"Say it."

"I want you, J.B. You can't imagine how much." She rose off the bed and walked to him, kissed him boldly and ran her hands down his own nipples, across his chest and down to his abdomen. She unbuckled his belt, undid his fly, tugged the shirt from his waistband and slipped her hands under it to feel his hot skin and all the lovely muscle underneath. He sucked in a breath at her touch and she could feel his heart beating, his pulse kicked up and his nerves on edge.

She unbuttoned his shirt and dropped her lips to a small, flat, coppery nipple, sucking at it and teasing it with her tongue. At his shaky exhale and soft groan, she switched to the other one, nipping at it with her teeth and raking her nails gently down his back.

"You're a witch," he whispered. "I haven't

stopped thinking of this for three years." He took
her by the upper arms and stared down at her. "A
witch," he repeated.

"Good witch or bad?"

He chuckled. "Some days you wear white, lacy
thigh-highs in my head. Others you've got red-
and-white-striped stockings and pointed black
shoes."

"Is that all I wear?"

"Yeah. Pretty much." He took her chin in his
hands and kissed her. "Did you think about me at
all, Vivvie? Hmmmmm?"

She closed her eyes, knowing that if she kept them
open they'd slide away from his. Her lips still under
his, she shook her head.

"I don't believe you," said J.B. when he broke the
kiss. "You at least strutted into your office and told
the girls around the watercooler about your con-
quest and how you threw him out when you
were done."

"I did not!" she said indignantly. "I never even
told Julia, until—"

"But you did think about me." He looked into
her eyes, followed them as they slid left and then
right.

"Not until I saw you again." She remained
stubborn.

J.B. ran his hands through her hair, dropped them
to her shoulders and then palmed her breasts. Instantly her body went on full alert, and when he
lifted one to his mouth and drew hard on her nipple,

she made a soft, unintelligible cry. She pressed her breast against his lips, hungry for his hunger and touched by his touch. He devoured it, loved it well and went for the other one.

When she could barely stand for wanting him, he pushed her gently down on the bed and eased her thighs apart. "So beautiful," he said, kneeling in front of her. And then he bent his head to the most intimate part of her, taking a large bite through the silk of her panties.

Viv gave a real cry this time, hoarse and helpless. "Did you think about me, honey?" he asked, and then buried his face in her again.

When he raised his head she tossed restlessly. "Tell me the truth, now." He slid the turquoise fabric to the side and entered her with his tongue.

"Yes!" She clutched at the bedspread with one hand, his shoulder with the other. "Oh, yes . . ."

"Yes, you thought about me, or yes, you like that? Remember, I can stop at any time." He bent his head to her again.

Waves of pleasure engulfed her. "Yes," she panted. "I thought about you. I almost called you . . . Oh, God! But then there was no point . . . Ohhhhhhhhh."

He stopped. "No point?"

"Please," she whispered. "Please, please don't stop. Ahhh! You—you lived in Texas, and I lived in Manhattan, and—oh, God, J.B.—"

She came apart, colors bursting behind her eyelids,

and she fell down, down and down until she opened her eyes to find him grinning in satisfaction. "Did your toes curl, honey?"

"Aaahhhh."

"I think that was an answer in the affirmative," he said. She nodded weakly.

He stood over her, between her knees, his hands on his hips again. And he frowned. "Now. You ever hear of a modern device called an airplane, Shelton?"

She blinked at the anger she saw on his face and tried to reconcile it with the generosity of the man who'd just given her ultimate pleasure.

"A large mechanical device with wings that transports people back and forth between states?"

She wet her lips as he threw off his clothes and stood in front of her magnificent and naked and not happy with her. "J.B., it's more complicated than that." She sat up and reached for him. "Come here? Please?"

He only had the willpower to hesitate so long. He stalked toward her looking as if he wielded a weapon. She kissed it, and in her hands it became even harder and angrier-looking.

Viv got up and pushed him onto the bed this time, where he sat at the corner and couldn't resist once again touching her breasts. She straddled him, rubbed them against his chest and sank down upon him. She took his anger and his sex deep inside her and let them stretch and fill her.

She rose and fell, bracing her hands on his shoulders, feeling liquid heat build within her until she thought she'd melt into a human puddle of pure bliss.

She rode his anger until it transformed into exultation and he cursed and then shouted her name, convulsing inside her and wrapping his hands around her hips as if he'd never let her go.

# Chapter Fifteen

J.B. came back to reality slowly and inhaled the sweet fragrance of Viv's dark hair, which lay in a soft curtain over his face. Her breasts pillowed her on his chest, but he could feel her heart beating triple-time against him.

He was still buried to the hilt in her, and when she tried to move off him he held her immobile. He didn't want to relinquish her soft mellowness or her muscular heat to the no-nonsense Tough Girl who ran her personality.

It was the Tough Girl who attracted him, though—drove him crazy, challenged him, made her worthwhile. To a man who'd been chased by women since he was a toddler, a guy who'd been coveted and schemed for and often embarrassed over feminine reactions to him, Viv was foreign, indomitable and supremely desirable.

Oh, he'd had women feign indifference to him as part of an act . . . but that was different. And he'd been through Corinne leaving him, which was certainly a first. But Viv was in a class by herself. In fact, she was world-class.

J.B. rolled her under him, smiled down at her, and reached a hand out for the clock radio. He clicked it on to a country-western station and moved deep inside her.

Her blue eyes widened and she caught her lip between her teeth. "Isn't he supposed to be . . . done?"

"See what you missed by kicking me out prematurely?" J.B. swelled inside her again as he traced the outer slope of a breast, careful not to touch the nipple, still probably on sensory overload from before.

Slowly, he began to make love to every part of her that was not strictly an erogenous zone, making her shiver and raising the tiny hairs on her neck, arms and thighs. Unfortunately this did require that he pull out, but he satisfied her in a thousand other ways.

He made love to her navel and massaged the muscles in her thighs. He kissed and licked behind her knees, kissing the slightly knobby caps, too. And he noticed that the entire time she should have been melting under his ministrations, she became more and more rigid. It didn't make sense.

He reached her feet and began a deep, strong massage. She sighed in bliss. Then, as if policing herself, she pulled her foot away. "The wine," she said brightly. "We should open our takeout bottle."

He analyzed her expression, which had gone from dreamy to faux cheerful—but there was something shaky and dark underneath, something he was determined to hunt down and pull from its hidey-hole, if necessary by the tail. J.B. planned to examine it gently, like a small frightened animal, soothe it and then let it go.

"All right," he said aloud. He stood, still semierect, and pulled the bottle and a corkscrew out of the bag. He felt Viv's eyes on him as he drew the cork. "Got any glasses?"

She rolled off the bed and gingerly stepped barefoot on the carpet, her expression that of a bushman about to wade through a river of water moccasins. She disappeared into the bathroom and came out eventually with two shrink-wrapped plastic cups. "Our goblets," she said, extending them.

He poured her a hefty cup, surprised to see her down half of it before he'd poured his own. It certainly wasn't like the calm and elegant Vivien to slurp her wine like Kool-Aid.

Did he make her nervous? He couldn't believe it. This woman who fought bloody courtroom battles without a blink, could rake a complete stranger over the coals without thinking about it, and brazenly steal a truck—how could he make her nervous? But there was no other explanation for her behavior. And he found her uncertainty endearing, just like her tangled cloud of normally smooth, controlled dark hair.

Then there was the fact that she'd flown down to see her friend Julia in the middle of a workweek, when he'd bet anything that she was swamped and this was inconvenient as hell. New York firms were some of the best-paying in the country, but they also sucked their employees dry.

Viv met his gaze and quickly looked away.

A slow song came on the radio and he set his own cup down and then commandeered hers, setting it down, too. He snaked an arm around her waist and drew her to him, moving to the rhythm of the music. "May I have this dance?" he murmured.

"J.B., this is a little loony, don't you think?"

"What's the matter, Vivvie? You've never danced naked before?"

"No, I can't say that I have." She was stiff and awkward in his arms.

"Dancing naked is wonderful." He dwarfed her small white hand with his. Supporting her between the shoulder blades, he dipped her backward and kissed her wine-stained lips. "Mmmmmm. Good vintage. Chateau Shelton's reserve collection, aged thirty-four years."

As he raised her again she asked, "Am I red or white?"

"Oh, definitely red. Bold, spicy and full-bodied, with unexpected hints of sweet cherry and black currant."

"Ah," she said dryly.

"You're delicious and fruity at the center."

"I've never been fruity in my life."

"Whatever you say, Tough Girl." He moved his hands over her shoulders and down her back, feeling knots of tension that hadn't been there a half hour ago. He worked them with his fingers and thumbs as he continued to sway to the music.

Vivien tensed instead of relaxing, her flesh resisting his touch, unable to accept the pleasure.

J.B. moved his hands lower, to the soft globes of her bottom, and worked his magic there for a while. She seemed to respond more to sexual touching. Viv closed her eyes, a good sign. He moved up to her hips and rib cage, then cupped her breasts and felt the nipples nestle against his palms. He moved them in circles until the peaks formed aggressive little buds that he enjoyed tormenting.

Her breath came more quickly now, and she was forgetting to tense up. J.B. turned her in his arms so that her back rested against his chest, and took both heavy breasts into his hands. He kneaded and plucked gently until she began to move her bottom restlessly against his erection. He pushed himself between her buttocks so that he just nuzzled the outside of her cleft. Her swift intake of breath told him of her pleasure, and he moved back and forth against the soft, wet flesh.

Now J.B. brought his hand down and moved tenderly into the curls below her belly. He stroked them and felt her quiver. She arched her back and let a soft moan escape while he played her with fingers, cock and simple affection.

*She can't accept the affection without sex.* The thought hit him as she begged him to enter her, fell forward onto the edge of the bed, bracing herself with her hands.

He didn't need a second invitation. He wanted to drive in hard and fast, taking savage pleasure in what a beautiful woman offered him. But instead he held back, running his hands over those gorgeous cheeks and tickling, tantalizing the delicate folds directly to the front of them. When she arched her back again, pushing against his hand, and made a sound very much like a sob, he finally rolled on a condom and slid inside her, inch by inch, while she went crazy. She tried to back onto him, but he held her forward and kept total control. Only when he was completely sheathed did he allow her to push back, joining them as completely as two people could be joined.

He began to move within her, in and out, and her entire body began to quiver. He was close to giving in to the pleasure when he grasped that something was wrong for him. He couldn't see her eyes, see her face.

This was the most impersonal position they could assume.

As close to climax as he was, and knew she was, this didn't fly with him—not right now. He pulled out, ignoring her protests. Turned her despite them. Laughed softly when she beat on his chest with her fists. Pushed her flat onto her back and mounted her again.

"I want to see you," he whispered. "I want to see those beautiful eyes at the very moment they go cloudy with pure pleasure."

Right now they sparkled with annoyance. But as he pushed her breasts together and took both nipples into his mouth, as he kissed her and drove into her again, the annoyance faded into bliss. Her hips rose to meet him and his thrusts got so powerful that he moved her across the bed.

As tension built again in him and demanded release, she let out a series of keening sounds, arched violently, and spasmed uncontrollably against him. What she did not do, he realized—even as he came himself—was open her eyes. Even in her most unguarded moments, Vivien avoided intimacy.

Viv came back to reality to find him watching her, his green eyes making a thorough emotional analysis. She tensed immediately and he noted it. J.B. reached out an index finger and gently touched her bottom lip.

She tried to squirm out from under him but she was firmly pinned. "Off," she commanded.

He frowned.

"I have to go to the bathroom," she told him. It was only half a lie. She had to go for breathing room, not for bodily need.

He rolled off her, lying lazily on his side, but continued to evaluate. It raised the little hairs on the back of her neck. The picture of calm, she rounded the corner and closed the door behind her, leaning against it. "You've got a real cute dimple right in the middle of your derriere," he called.

*No, I've got a real cute dimple right in the middle of my brain. Because I'm here with you again, naked again, and starting to panic again.*

She turned on the water and leaned her hip against the sink. She dug her knuckles into the hollows under her eyes.

*Okay. You obviously aren't going to kick him out this time. You have to be civil, even endure a little snuggling.*

*Shakiness is not an option. So what if he strokes your*

*hair, tells you you're beautiful? You will not cry. You will not even think about crying.*

*These are normal things that normal lovers do and say to each other. Now pull yourself together.*

Viv flushed the toilet, took a deep breath and straightened her shoulders. She left the bathroom. She sat on the bed, in what she thought was a passable imitation of a relaxed pose.

"Jesus," murmured J.B. "You approach afterglow as though it's boot camp."

"What? What are you talking about?" She faked a yawn and reclined among the brown flowers on the bedspread.

He reached for her and she didn't resist. He rumpled her hair and kissed her temple, drawing her close. She forced a smile. "Mmmm."

The radio was still playing, and J.B. kept time with the music by tapping on her tush. He began to hum and she discovered that he had a very nice baritone. Every muscle in her stomach had knotted, though her body adored the way he touched her.

"Why are you tense, honey?" he asked.

"I'm not tense."

"Yeah, you are. It's obviously time to dance naked again." And he tugged her, protesting, off the bed and led her into a simple, almost waltzlike movement. "What would all your New York friends think if they could see you doin' this? Hmmmm?"

"You have a serious problem with this naked dancing thing, J.B.," she said. "Have you thought about getting help?"

"Uh-huh." He spun her out on his arm and then

reeled her back in. "I've entered a twelve-step program, but I just can't get beyond the two-step. Texas Two-Step, that is."

"Very funny."

"I'm a funny guy. And charming, too." He grinned down at her. "There's a lot of women who'd *pay* to dance with me naked."

"And so modest. Should we all form a line and get some quarters ready?"

"Quarters? More like hundred-dollar bills. After all, I have it on good authority that my performance is *impressive*."

"I believe the word was *magnificent*," said Viv. "You know, we should order you a T-shirt so you can advertise."

"Word of mouth does me just fine." He kissed her, and as usual, she couldn't help but respond. The song on the radio ended and gave way to an annoying used-car advertisement.

J.B. maneuvered them over to the radio and shut it off. The silence crowded her, like the intimacy.

"What's goin' on in that brain of yours?" he asked. "You tryin' to think up a polite way to kick me out, now that you're done with me?"

She opened her mouth to deny it, but she would have been lying. She said instead, "What makes you think that I'm done with you, Anglin?" She pushed him toward the bed. "My plan is to wear you out until you collapse into a useless heap. Then I'll roll you into the hallway."

But she had a feeling that she was only postponing

the inevitable. Eventually she was going to have to face . . . the Dreaded Afterglow.

*Eventually* turned out to be a lot shorter than she thought. J.B. bounced onto the bed but caught her wrists and pulled her into his lap, hugging her against him. "No more sex for you, darlin', until we have a little chat."

He reached for her wine and put it into her hand. Then he surprised her by turning off the light. They sat in the total darkness afforded by Marv's polyester drapes, Viv frozen and wary.

"In vino veritas," J.B. said, drawling the Latin in his Texas accent. "So chugalug, baby, if that's what it takes."

"What the hell do you want from me?" Her voice sounded metallic and hostile even to her own ears. "My life story? My medical records?"

"I want you to relax," he said.

"I'm sitting in the dark with a crazy man," she retorted. "Would *you* relax? And why *are* we in the dark, anyway? We had sex with the lights on."

"I want you to trust me. I want you to talk to me. And the lights are off because I thought it might help. You're different from any other woman I've known, Vivvie. You'll show every inch of skin in broad daylight, but you won't show your heart. You'll have sex, but you won't make love. Why is that?"

"Oh, hell." She tossed back the wine out of sheer frustration. "Are we getting into the semantics of romantics again?"

"What do you mean by semantics? I don't know all your Park Avenue terminology."

"Meanings of words. Hairsplitting. Sex versus making love. Same thing, J.B.! Insert the male into the female. Animals do it all the time. Inseminate and run."

"That's not what just happened here and you know it. Why can't you look at this as a thing of beauty and not science? Why are you reducing making love to crude mechanics?"

"Love," she snorted. "The many-splendored thing. The great eternal . . ."

"Yeah, *love*." His voice was hard and uncompromising. "Tenderness. Et cetera. Ever hear of it? Or are divorce attorneys immune?"

"Nice crack about my job again. Of course divorce attorneys aren't immune. I see divorce attorneys get divorced all the time! I've even done a couple of the divorces myself, out of professional courtesy."

"Don't any of them stay together? Come on, they must."

She sighed. "Yeah, but are they happy? J.B., romance may lead to marriage, but marriage kills romance, okay? Romance does not equal love. You're talking about illusion. Temporary blindness."

"You are such a cynic."

"And you are a poor, misguided idealist."

Viv reached for the wine bottle and splashed some more into her cup. She took another mouthful and let it slide down before gesturing with the cup.

"Come on, J.B. *Making love*? Are you honestly

going to tell me that we're here in this room because you *love* me? Because I *love* you?" She laughed.

"I don't know." His tone was quiet but angry. "What do *you* call it when you can't stop thinking about someone for three years after just one encounter?"

"Obsession. Unhealthy." She got off the bed and paced around it.

"No. I didn't obsess about you. I didn't think about you every day, or spin endless fantasies about you in my head. I went on with my life. But your image, your voice, your smile—they'd drop into my consciousness every once in a while.

"I wondered about you, and what made you tick, and why you'd done what you'd done. Then I wondered if your actions had hurt you, too. Whether you thought about me. Obsession? No. I'm not a nut. I'm not a stalker or a psycho. But I'm not a liar, either. I'm telling you, I feel something here and I think you do, too. But you're treating it lightly and cynically. That pisses me off."

She said nothing—just put the cup to her lips and tipped it back yet again.

"That 'something'," he insisted, "can be fostered. The 'something' is a seed. It can become love. A precious gift. One that you don't look in the mouth."

"J.B., you don't even know me."

"Because you won't share anything."

"What do you want to know? You can't force sharing. That's . . . it's practically oxymoronic."

He was still and quiet in the darkness.

She drained her cup and set it down with a little hollow *plonk*. She hesitated and then spoke. "My mother once urged me to write a letter to my father. I think she thought it might remind him of domestic bliss or some such crap, and bring him back. I told her that I had no idea what to write." She wet her lips.

"Mummy said, 'Just *share* your life with him. Go on. Do it.' And so I chewed on a pencil for a while and wrote about the funny smell of the silver polish, and how I was allowed to taste the party hors d'oeuvres, but only the broken or cracked ones. And how I loved it when Mummy gave holiday parties, because she looked so pretty and wasn't crabby like usual."

J.B. was quiet and didn't interrupt her.

"Well, my mother didn't like what I *shared*. So she ripped up the letter and told me to write another one, all about ice-skating and pretty holiday lights and hot chocolate. I did. She sent it to him. He never responded."

"I guess you didn't think too highly of *sharing* after that?"

She shrugged. "I suppose that's a little simplistic, but yes. After that I shared my grades. I shared my school photos. I shared my awards and achievements. But not too many private thoughts. I found that Mummy either edited or invalidated them."

"Who else was around?"

Viv shrugged again. "Gerta, the housekeeper. Various 'uncles' and friends of my mother's."

"What was Gerta like?"

"She was wonderful and warm, used to kiss and hug me all the time. But I think Mummy got jealous of my feelings for her, because she sat me down one day and told me about how 'one' didn't kiss and hug 'the help.' She must have said something to Gerta, too, because after that day the physical affection stopped and Gerta seemed quiet and moody. I think she was petrified that my mother would make a voodoo doll of her and—"

"*What?*"

Viv realized she'd slipped. "Ah, yes. Didn't I tell you that the ex–Lady Shelton, wearing her cashmere pajamas, practices a little black magic? You don't want to make her angry. Ooops. Shouldn't have shared, I see."

"I'm speechless. You're not saying it works, are you?"

"Well, that's the creepy part. It does."

"God Almighty." He didn't seem to want to know any more.

She supposed that was understandable. Viv thought about J.B.'s mom, who seemed sweet and normal and actually cooked. Mrs. Anglin looked like she gave good hugs. She wasn't rail thin, with bones that clacked together when she moved, like Anna Shelton. J.B.'s mom had probably been the nurturing type, praising his every action.

And he seemed to be a lot like her. Her heart melted again as she reflected that it wasn't every guy who'd wheel and deal a woman out of jail with pies and casseroles. *And* plan on seeing the bargain through even after she'd stolen his truck . . .

"Viv," he said, "come 'ere. Your parents may have put the 'fun' in 'dysfunction' but not all marriages are like that. I wish you could have seen my parents. And you should see my friend Alex's parents. His mom's lost half her mind to Alzheimer's, but she and his father are still in love."

She didn't respond.

"Look. I don't know what I feel for you. And you don't have to be in love with me. The bottom line is that I actually did come up here partly to get my revenge. But that urge is gone now.

"The urge that *isn't* gone is this: I want to show you that you've been missing out on the best part of sex, Vivvie. And it's not the lust or the climax. It's the unspoken connection between two people. It's the harmony of skin on skin and the pleasure of giving someone else pleasure; it's the sharing. Maybe you hate that word, but it fits."

J.B. had walked to her in the darkness, and now he actually picked her up and carried her back to the bed, while her heart moved into her throat and she almost gagged on it. She was paralyzed by his sweetness, not knowing how to accept it.

He settled them onto the bed, his arms around her, and tucked her head under his chin. She tried not to hyperventilate.

He stroked her hair and kissed it and murmured nonsense to her: sweet, comforting nonsense. The words ran together in her mind, but the sentiment got through. Still . . .

"What if I don't know how to share, J.B.?"

"Ssshhhh. Sure you do."

"No . . . I snatch before anything can be shared, because I'm afraid it'll be taken away."

"We're sharing right now, baby. We're sharing right now: space, and breath and comfort."

*Is this man even real? Or have I gone mad and conjured him?* Emotion drowned her, but she didn't dare reveal it. She ate her sobs whole without a single spasm, but the section of pillow under her eyes got soaked. She fell asleep in his arms.

# Chapter Sixteen

Vivien awoke to a tinny little refrain from a rock song, repeated over and over. It took her a moment to realize that it was J.B.'s cell phone, and that they'd been asleep for . . .

She squinted at the clock radio. One a.m.? Not possible. They'd slept for hours. She'd . . . she'd actually *snuggled* with the man. It had been . . . nice. Better than nice. So why was the panic rising in her again at the sight of him, relaxed and rumpled on her bed?

*You've been missing out on the best part of sex, Vivvie. And it's not the lust or the climax. It's the unspoken connection between two people.*

His words echoed in her mind. *Yeah, but the problem is that the connection doesn't last, or it gets old and moldy and you end up breaking it anyway. I don't want to get used to this. I'll only miss it so much it might kill me.*

The tenderness and affection was all great and wonderful, except that it snuck up on you, caught you unawares and made you vulnerable as hell. That vulnerability equaled messy emotions and then eventual victimization.

*I refuse to be a victim. It is just not my style.*

So she yawned and stretched and said, "Good thing we woke up. I'm a thrasher and a blanket thief, and I'm sure you'd be more comfortable at home." She got up and threw a long T-shirt over her nakedness while J.B. eyed her with an inscrutable expression.

Had the man really talked to her about love? When she lived in Manhattan and he lived in the Texas Hill Country? He was such a sweet, old-fashioned idealist—nothing like the New York men who, as she did, gave ninety-seven percent to their careers and just got in a quick encounter when they could.

J.B. was hot. He was truly gifted in bed. But he was an alien. He may as well have been green with little antennae.

*Uh-oh.* And right now it looked as if he was one pissed-off alien. His face darkened, his brows drawing together and his mouth thinning. "You're kicking me out."

"I'm not kicking you out. I just—"

"You used me all over again."

"—sleep better alone, that's all. And you will, too."

"Unbelievable! I'm *so* done trying—" J.B.'s cell phone rang again. Without another word, he picked it up and answered it. "Yeah." His face remained impassive as he listened.

It took Viv about three seconds to figure out who

would be calling him at one a.m. J.B. wasn't the type to have a girlfriend on the side. It had to be his ex-wife.

"Get a broom," he said.

*A broom?*

"You can use a broom just as well as I can, Corinne. And that creature is a lot more scared of you than you are of it." He ran an impatient hand through his hair.

"I'm out," he said. And then, "Does that really concern you?" He sighed. "Well, how about you? I'm sure there are other people you can call."

The completely unjustified green coil of jealousy came back and took root in Viv's stomach as he spoke to the unknown Corinne. Suddenly she hated the woman with a violence that shocked her.

"Yeah. I'm such a goddamned nice guy. That's why I get *used*." He shot a glare in Vivien's direction. Then his face softened and his tone gentled. "Okay, okay. I'm sorry. Just close the kitchen door. I'll be right there." He hung up.

"What was that all about?" Viv asked, as he tugged on his boxers and jeans.

"There's a rat in my ex's kitchen."

"She calls you at one a.m. and you come running?"

"What do you care?" He pulled on his shirt and rounded up his socks.

Whether justified or not, her anger grew. "You've just spent the entire evening with me, and now you're going to her? I don't believe this!"

He shoved his foot into one sock and shot her a

scathing glance. "Oh, no, darlin'. You are not allowed to get territorial *now*. You had your chance. And you made it crystal clear that you weren't taking it. May I remind you that you were in the process of kicking me out when my damn cell phone rang? You've got a nerve, woman." He got his foot into the other sock and jammed on his boots.

She just stood there with her mouth open. What could she say? How had she gotten herself into this, anyway?

J.B. stalked to the door and opened it, his expression bitter. "What the hell better do I have to do?"

J.B. drove away from Marv's Motor Inn too fast, trying to leave Viv, his conflicting emotions about her, and the tasteless neon COUNT SHEEP FOR CHEAP sign behind. From Main, he took South Adams toward Kerrville and turned off at the winding entrance to what had once been his home. Two minutes later he sat in the driveway, looking forward more to seeing the rat than Corinne.

He sighed and got out of the truck, remembering how they'd looked at endless plans and blueprints, chosen a special oversized lot and paid a hefty sum for the house to be built out of Texas white limestone. He'd been so sure he would have children in this house, grow old in it, perhaps even die in it if he was lucky and went in his sleep.

He looked at the place now with regret tinged by growing indifference. As he climbed the steps to the front walkway, he bent to pull a few weeds from between the concrete slabs, but then straightened without doing so. It was her problem to deal with the weeds. It was her house.

His boots scuffed a couple of times on his route to the door, he guessed because he was dragging his feet. Impatient with himself, he jammed his index finger onto the bell.

She opened the door wearing very short satin tap pants and a very skimpy matching camisole, her hair tumbled ingenuously around her bare shoulders.

She hugged him as he stood impassive.

"Where is it?"

"Behind the stove."

He disentangled himself and made the familiar trek over the polished marble in the foyer, the parquet living room floor and the ceramic tile of the kitchen. Though she'd deliberately dressed for the occasion, Corinne wasn't lying, or she'd have followed him into the room.

Instead she hung back, letting him deal with the rodent. J.B. opened the back door and found a broom. Then he pulled the stove away from the wall and banged at it with his boot so the creature wouldn't run back under it.

After a bit of back and forth, scurrying and sweeping, the small rat made for the open door. J.B. gave it a little help on the way outside. Then he shut it out.

Corinne's voice traveled into the room as he looked around at the same red stand mixer, the same flowered tea cozy and the same bulletin board that had been there when he was. "Did you kill it?" she asked.

"He's gone."

"But is it dead?"

"No." He hunted occasionally, but he didn't like killing for the sake of killing. He ate what he shot.

"Don't tell me you just shooed it out the door? Won't it come back?"

He shrugged. "Not if you get a pest control place out here to make it uncomfortable for him."

"What's the matter, J.B.?"

"I'm just tired."

"You want a beer? A bourbon?" She was already moving toward the refrigerator.

"No thanks."

"You came all the way out here—you should at least have a drink."

He sighed. "Corinne, what do you want?"

"Nothing." She stood too close to him, though, and her makeup was perfect. Corinne was a beautiful woman, with all that sun-streaked blond hair of hers, and her wide hazel eyes. But she'd lost her charm for him. He just didn't feel anything.

"Are you seein' Mindy Baker?"

"What?"

"You heard me."

"No! You know me better than that. She's a married woman. Besides, what's it to you?"

"Are you seeing that Yankee chick, the attorney?"

Despite his anger at her, his mouth twitched at what Vivien would say if she heard herself referred to as a "chick."

"Why the questions, Corinne? Why the sudden interest?"

She looked at him for a moment in silence. Then she blurted, "I still love you, J.B."

"Corinne—"

"Don't say anything. I just—I know I was wrong, running off to Dallas like that. I just expected that . . . well, when we got married everything was so exciting. We traveled and we partied and we had fun. And then the whole knee thing happened and it was so tough for both of us. Your law school—it was so hard on me. I never saw you. Then you opened the practice and I just sat around. I was so bored, and I felt ignored and unimportant to you."

"You were never unimportant to me, Corinne."

"I know that now. I know now that it wasn't you that was boring. It's just life. Life is boring, you know? And we all just have to make the best of it."

"Well. I'm so glad you've decided that I'm not boring." He brushed past her on the way to the door.

"Wait. J.B., that came out wrong. What I meant was—"

"Life is what you make of it, Corinne. If you choose to sit around and be bored and not do any-thing with your time, then you're not going to be happy. There are thousands of ways you can help people or be creative or productive."

"You said once that you'd always love me."

He looked at her for a long time: her lovely face, her earnest expression, those killer legs she'd always had. "I didn't lie."

"Then can we . . . ?"

"Can we what?"

"You said I gave up too easily. What if I said I wanted to try again?"

He'd desperately wanted to hear those words come out of her mouth four years ago. Now they just made him angry. He wanted to hammer and split and twist every letter of every word in that sentence and make her take them back.

*God damn it. I must have a sign on my back that says* PUPPET. FEMALE'S PLAYTHING. He looked at her levelly. "What if I said it's a little too late?"

He had Mindy chasing him for recreation, Viv there just for sex and now Corinne wanted him to banish her boredom. They could all three just go to hell.

An hour after he'd left, Viv could still smell J.B. in the room. He was on the sheets, on the bedspread and in the bathroom on a towel. Worse, she couldn't even decide if his scent was disturbing or comforting.

If she knew she hated it, she could throw open a window and let the hot Texas air blow every remnant of him out of there.

If she knew she loved it, she could rub her face against the pillow he'd used.

But she did neither, just stared into space and reflected on the irony of the situation. She'd tried to protect herself from getting hurt, only to enrage him into hurting her.

Finally she decided that she didn't want to analyze things any further. She was only making herself crazy.

She went into the bathroom, splashed water on her face, and dried off with a clean towel that was so rough it left red marks on her face. As usual, the thing was like sandpaper. She hoped Julia would replace all of the Motor Inn's linens, and fast.

She picked her way over the icky carpet and as usual turned to work, since she wasn't able to sleep. Viv opened her laptop and checked e-mail.

She quickly answered about ten messages from clients, two from Andie that were also work-related, and stalled over one from Belky that made her see red.

It was a quick reminder that all employees of Klein, Schmidt and Belker were to go through Human Resources before using any personal days, and take into consideration the needs of the firm when they did so.

Gosh, how sweet. Belky missed her! The poisonous little prick. She almost hit REPLY to inform him that a fictitious uncle hadn't had time to notify HR before dropping dead of an aneurysm, so sorry. But next time she'd be sure to discuss keeping her dead rela-

tives on ice until such time as the firm could spare
her for a funeral.

Viv decided that it was best to ignore the e-mail,
but she spent a pleasant few minutes thinking about
quitting, particularly in the middle of an important,
publicity-drenched trial, and leaving The Belk high
and dry.

She'd leave the hassle of New York behind, buy a
ranch out in the middle of nowhere and start her
own greyhound rescue. She wouldn't have to see another human being all day long, if she chose not to.
No tearful, drunk or psychotic clients, no miserable
children caught in the middle of divorce, no negative
energy at all whatsoever.

She could grow bluebonnets, work with her dogs
and hang dozens of wind chimes on a back porch
with a rocker. She could wear cowboy boots and
drive a truck! One with an automatic transmission,
though.

Viv sighed and scanned her e-mail in-box again.
Tabitha wrote that the vet had put Mannie on antibi-
otics for an ear infection, poor little guy. And there
was a note from Mummy.

Subject:   Noblesse Oblige

To:        vshelton@kleinschmidtbelker

From:      AShelton

Darling Viv-Ant,

  Regarding the day care for these Displaced
Homemaker females: it does seem to be a good tax

shelter. But I must tell you, love, that I'm afraid you're carrying the concept of noblesse oblige a bit too far.

It's all very well to be compassionate and to volunteer oneself for a couple of hours per week, but frankly you're a bit obsessed.

Do keep in mind that obsession causes unsightly wrinkles and all sorts of tension headaches. Truly, it can make one's life a misery, so do avoid it.

On other topics, my gentleman friend is too charming! However, on his last visit Paolo positively glared at him from the solarium and insisted on working shirtless out there. You know how he is: "Eet eez too hot, Meesus Anna!" (I do love that accent of his, don't you?)

Pow thought he'd hidden himself behind the orchids, but he was quite impossible to miss. Dear me, he did look a bit murderous with that trowel . . .

Don't you dare tell a soul, Viv-Ant, but his behavior gave me the tiniest thrill! Even if he is only the gardener.

Well, darling, must motor. Having lunch with Gisela and Lou . . . I must say that I enjoy this computer contraption, especially when I can dictate to Dolly from the bathtub and don't have to hunt and peck.

Toodles, darling! See Gerald for the day-care funds. He'll work out the details. Xoxoxo, Mummy

Speechless, Viv typed back a quick reply. She told herself to be thankful that her mother was at least human enough to find her gardener attractive.

Subject:  Re: Noblesse Oblige

To:       AShelton

From:     vshelton@kleinschmidtbelker

Dear Mummy,

Thank you so very much for your generous contribution to the Displaced Homemakers' Day Care project. You will have the eternal gratitude of these deserving women. I'll get in touch with Gerald as per your instructions.

As for your gentleman caller, I'm glad that he is amusing you . . .

Paolo is very fond of you and only wishes to protect you. Yes, I like his accent, too.

If you and the G.C. run out of things to talk about, you could always dress Paolo in an animal skin and release a live leopard into the solarium with him. They could go mano à clawo for your entertainment one rainy afternoon while you shriek with laughter . . .

Viv forced herself to erase this last paragraph, though she dearly wanted to leave it in. She wrote instead,

Hope your lunch with Gisela and Lou went well. Please send them my regards and same to Dolly.

Julia asked after you and I told her how fabulous you're looking these days. She's sticking by her "cowpoke," but thanks for offering to introduce her to the B-list boys.

xoxoxo, Viv

She hit the SEND button and closed her laptop. Her thoughts returned unbidden to J.B., his ex-wife and the supposed rodent in her kitchen. What kind of guy still slew minidragons for his ex? And how could Viv persuade him that she hadn't been kicking him out?

# Chapter Seventeen

The morning brought no change in J.B.'s rotten mood. He went out to the woodshop at five a.m. and finished sanding the pieces of the console table, getting himself good and gritty with sawdust.

Harley tried to join him once he turned off the sander, but ran off again to chase chipmunks as soon as J.B. pulled out the Shop-Vac for cleanup.

The dull roars of the sander and vacuum soothed him— they were the sounds he felt like making himself: angry, mechanical, drowning out the world around him. Women!

*Dogs make a whole lot more sense. You always know how a dog feels about you. They're loyal and obedient.*

He finished sucking up all the sawdust, wiped off the pieces of the console table, and decided to wait on staining them until the next day. He hung his safety goggles back on their peg, threw away the paper mask he wore to protect his lungs and wiped his face on his sleeve. Then he slid the door of the shop closed and went outside, into the gorgeous, blue and gold Texas morning.

Harley ran to him and wagged his tail, lolling his pink Lab tongue out of his mouth.

"You lonely, boy?" J.B. found himself thinking about greyhounds, in spite of his anger with Vivien. They were sweet dogs, they really were. And he did have several fenced acres. They liked to run.

He eyed an old shed a couple of hundred yards away, shoved his hands into his pockets and walked toward it. He'd been meaning to rebuild it for storage, but he didn't really have all that much to store. Could it serve as a shelter for greyhounds? How many?

He circled it, evaluating the corrugated metal roof, the weathered boards, the lack of insulation and the dirt floor. Pull off the existing roof . . . redo it, lay plywood. Tar paper on top of that, and shingles.

Most of the two-by-four framing was still sound, but the walls had to be rebuilt, an elevated floor put in, decent bedding added.

Ventilation, too; that was important. He'd have to think about that.

*Are you nuts, J.B.? Are you really getting yourself into this? Why? To impress some squirrelly New Yorker who don't give a damn about you?*

He kicked at a decrepit board on the ground and pulled a disintegrating bag of charcoal out of the shed. Harley danced around, seeming to egg him on. "You'd still be king, buddy," J.B. reassured him.

The Lab sat down and scratched at his ear with a back paw. *Of course*, he seemed to say. *But we have to do our part for the canine race. No excuses. You've got the land, you've got the means. So have at it.*

J.B. drank the rest of his now-cold coffee by the lake on his property and tried to de-grouch a little, but it wasn't working. Where exactly had he gone wrong with his life? Why was it that Roman, and now Alex, by the sound of things, were happily coupled, when they'd been roving tomcats for years? And he, J.B., the stable, family-oriented guy, was divorced and single, living the bachelor life with his dog?

Life just didn't make any sense sometimes. J.B. threw a last stick into the lake for Harley and retreated inside to shower.

The hot, steamy water ran down his body like Viv's hands, the soap felt like her skin and his towel hugged him afterward like he wanted her to do. Hell.

The woman was a witch. A gorgeous, cold, blue-eyed witch who valued dogs over men. While he was beginning to understand what made her the way she was, he didn't have to like it. She aroused his protective instincts as well as his body, which was ironic, since she'd die before accepting a man's protection. This was part of her mystique, part of what drew him to her.

He threw on an overstarched white shirt from the dry cleaners that crackled when he moved. How many times had he asked for light starch? *Grrr.*

He got dressed in a pair of jeans that Mama had suggested were no longer appropriate for anything but mowing. Who cared? He jammed his feet into his boots so hard that he put his big toe through the seam of his sock, and decided he didn't care about that, either. And of course, his belt was nowhere to be found, so he left without one.

J.B. went to work and squatted over his papers and files like a big, bad-tempered crow.

When his mother buzzed through and told him that Corinne had been trying to get hold of him yesterday, he barked, "She found me."

His mother didn't tolerate that tone from him, not even at age thirty-six. "Well, John Bryan, if you expect me to spend my weekend in the kitchen cooking for Wesley Taunton so he won't arrest your Yankee gal, then you'd best say 'please' and 'thank you.'"

"I'm sorry." He ran a hand through his hair. "I'll buy the groceries and I'll make her help." Not that he wanted to see Viv.

"You don't know the brands of the things I'll need. And she can write me a check for the groceries, but neither one of you is stepping foot in my kitchen. You'll drive me crazy, and she doesn't look like she knows her elbow from a potato peeler. You can just paint the garage for me when it cools off."

He was getting off easy and he knew it.

He also knew it was a bad sign when she buzzed through with Julia Spinelli on the line. Another woman wanting something from him. This time it was errands.

"So," she said in her sunny voice, "since Syd and Alex are out tasting cakes and Roman's not available, I thought I'd ask you again. You don't mind, do you?"

She wanted him to drive Viv to meet with the band for the wedding. She wanted them both to look over the contract. "Because I've heard horror stories about people making deposits with musicians, and then them not showing up. I need you two to make sure they get thrown in jail or something if they do that!"

"Thrown in jail?" J.B. snorted.

"Oh, you know what I mean. Just that there are consequences due to violation of contract, et cetera, et cetera. You're the attorney. And Viv. I just need you guys to lock it up tight and sort of . . . intimidate them. You know, with a little legal muscle."

"Uh-huh." This was a load of—

"Roman said you'd be more than happy to do it for us, not only because you're his attorney but because you're our friend."

He was being hornswoggled and he knew it. "Are you sure that Vivien is even available? She might be bus—"

"She is. Can you pick her up at ten? Oh, and I told her that you'd probably show her the Riverwalk and all, en route."

*Oh, you did, did you?* "Julia, I can't afford to take another day—"

"Gotta fly!" she said. "The other line! A customer! Bye!"

J.B. hung up the phone and stared at it. *I wonder if Roman understands just how Machiavellian his bride really is. Maybe I should advise him to sign a damn prenup . . .*

\* \* \*

Viv watched J.B.'s blue pickup turn in to the parking lot with mixed emotions. She felt a quickening of her pulse and then a rush of panic, followed by unjustified suspicion. Had he slept with Corinne last night?

It really wasn't her business, and yet it was. She had no claim on J.B., but she *hadn't* taken him up to her room to use him again, as he seemed to think. Somehow she had to get that through his head.

She left the Inn and walked toward the truck. J.B. emerged, looking unfairly handsome with his blond hair blowing in the breeze. He nodded curtly at her and opened her door. She swallowed. Even when the man was barely speaking to her, he was a gentleman. She got in and said one word. "Julia."

He met her eyes in agreement. "Julia."

"You'd think she'd be busy enough planning her wedding and have no time to interfere in the lives of her friends."

"Why don't you just tell her she's painfully obvious and that it's not going to work?" J.B. eased them out of the parking lot. "By the way, you can write my mother a check for around three hundred dollars," he said. "But she won't let us in her kitchen."

"Is that enough for all of the ingredients?"

"I doubt it, but it's a start. I think she's secretly pleased that her food is in demand."

They drove in silence for a few minutes and Viv tried to figure out a way to tell J.B. that she hadn't used him. Unable to think of a decent segue into that particular topic, she asked, "So did the big, stwong man take care of the nasty, evil wat?"

J.B. snorted. "Yes, he did."

"And was he thanked properly?" She knew she was skating close to the edge, but she couldn't help it.

He shot her a look. "Like I said, that's none of your biz."

*Ugh. True.* But she said, "Corinne wants you back."

He shrugged. "Next topic."

Viv sighed. "Okay. After we meet with the band, we have to pick up some crystal swans."

He looked revolted.

"It's a Julia thing. She loves swans. The long, graceful necks."

"We've got plenty of long-necked birds right here n Fredericksburg. She can have live emu at the wedding, for an added touch of elegance."

"I don't think it's quite the same thing."

"By the way, I hear that Uncle Ted's Shrub is quite aken with you." For the first time that morning, J.B. aughed. "I hear that he wants you to lay his eggs."

"Not funny," Viv said.

"Very funny."

She glared at him before finally cracking a smile herself. "His wasn't the usual come-on."

"Oh?"

"Yeah. He was smoother than most."

J.B. grinned. "Hey, well, what can ya do?"

"Sleep alone," she retorted. *Ooops. Well, there's a egue of sorts . . .*

The grin vanished from his face.

"I want you to know that I didn't take you back to my room to use you for sex." She threw it out there baldly and waited to see what he'd do with it.

"Oh? Why, then?"

"I . . . like you. When you're not being righteous and annoying."

"*Righteous*? About what?"

"Your whole marriage-is-a-commitment-blessed-by-God shtick."

"It's not a shtick," he said in a tight voice.

"Philosophy. Whatever."

"No, not whatever. That's how I feel and it's very important to me, Shelton. Your problem is that you hold nothing sacred. Your religion is cynicism. Don't tell me I'm 'righteous' in that worldly, amused tone of voice . . . that tone that says *You poor unenlightened provincial*."

She started to speak but he wasn't done.

"If more people worked on their marriages instead of running to the nearest divorce attorney and treating them as disposable, then more kids would have stable homes and society wouldn't be so screwed up."

"You can stop right there, Anglin. Divorce attorneys are not the cause of marriages dissolving! That's just BS. It's the people involved who are the cause. All we do is help clean up the legal and financial and emotional messes involved in the split."

"And you profit from that!" he shot back. "The

more divorces, the more cash for you. You profit from the breakdown of the family."

She actually punched him in the shoulder. "I am not the root of all evil! Do you have any idea how many women I've helped to get out of psychologically painful—and even physically painful—situations? Do you know that I spend a lot of my free time donating legal aid to a chapter of Displaced Homemakers? I'm in the process right now of establishing a day-care system for my local chapter!"

"Look, I'm not advocating that women stay in abusive marriages. But every marriage goes through rocky times. And I repeat: People should not give up so easily! Marriage involves a commitment, a bond, loyalty. And the loyalty isn't just from man to woman and vice versa. The loyalty I'm talking about is loyalty to *we* over *me*. It's called not always being selfish and looking out for Number One."

"Sorry, but that's just counter to human nature," Viv said, barely restraining a snort.

"Yes, it is." J.B. surprised her by agreeing. "That commitment to *we* requires us to evolve. To rise above self-interest. To love, honor, cherish, and *mean* it."

"So do you still love, honor and cherish Corinne?"

He took a deep breath. "Yes."

The simple three-letter word had her reeling. She felt sick to her stomach. "*Yes?* Then what were you doing with *me?*" Her voice rose, in spite of her efforts to keep it calm and measured.

"All I'm saying," J.B. told her, "is that in spite of

everything Corinne did to destroy our marriage, she's a human being and not a four-letter word. I won't turn my back on her. Partly because I want her to understand what she threw away."

Viv stared at him, feeling her pulse pound in her ears. The man was still serious about his wedding vows even after a divorce? After his ex had left him flat, taken half his money and had been married to two other men?

When Viv got control of her nausea and it turned to a dull, vague pain, she said quietly, "You're still in love with her."

# Chapter Eighteen

"No." J.B. refuted Viv's statement. "I'm not in love with Corinne."

"But you'll go chase a rat out of her kitchen at one in the morning."

"Yes."

"That just doesn't add up."

"I made a promise once, in a church, in front of God, to take care of her. If she needs help I'm not going to deny her."

Viv just stared at him, uncomprehending. "That promise is *over*. You're not married to her anymore."

"I keep my promises. It's important to me. Your honor is all you've got in this world."

*Christ. He sounds like a knight of the Round Table. He's a walking anachronism.*

*In fact, he's more loyal than a dog. I've discovered the one man on the planet that even I could marry without a prenup.*

The thought flashed into her mind without warning.

But typical of life's irony, his doglike loyalty belonged to another woman, not her.

Aloud she said, "You haven't kept your promise to forsake all others. You were just with me. So I guess you're selective about which promises you keep?"

He turned an angry gaze on her. His green eyes had darkened to a more forbidding gray. "Just lay off for a while, okay? Just leave it."

She stared out the window. They were approaching the San Antonio city limits now. It looked like any other city until J.B. drove them into the historic downtown area, where they parked near the historic Menger Hotel.

They had about forty-five minutes to kill before meeting the band, so J.B. fell into tour guide mode and hauled her first to the Alamo, and then to a little shop of horrors called the Buckhorn Saloon and Museum.

Viv found the Alamo small, pokey and unimpressive, but J.B. shushed her when she said so aloud. "They'll take you out back and hang your Yankee ass from a live oak tree!" he told her. "It's sacrilegious to insult the Alamo in Texas. Ozzy Osbourne once peed on the wall and he's never been allowed back into the city again."

Viv laughed.

"Hey, disrespect for the Alamo is no laughing matter. Every schoolkid in Texas is taught the legend of the Alamo over and over again. I remember even having to reenact the damn battle in fourth grade . . ."

Next he hustled her off to the Buckhorn Saloon on East Houston Street.

As they approached, she looked up to find a long

horn head staring down at her. "Ugh." In fact, there was a longhorn head between every window of the place. To Viv, an animal lover, it might as well have been the Tower of London, with human heads on pikes.

J.B. held the door open for her and Viv walked inside only to come to a standstill. There were dead animals everywhere. Animals with fangs, fur, claws, horns and fins. Animals of every size and species. A huge potbellied bear menaced her from his platform, while a wolf prepared to attack her from another. Countless deer had been beheaded and watched visitors with lifelike eyes.

It was probably a cowboy's or hunter's paradise. As someone who didn't even like zoos because the captivity of the animals depressed her, Vivien felt sick.

"There are over four thousand horns here," said J.B. "Frontiersmen used to come in and barter antlers for drinks. Those were the days before credit cards." He pointed. "See the bar back there?"

She nodded, feeling bile rise in her throat.

"Teddy Roosevelt actually sat there to recruit Rough Riders. Pancho Villa may have planned the Mexican Revolution over liquor at this very bar. A lot of the other furnishings are original, too."

Viv "met" a wolverine, a coyote, a nasty-looking boar (J.B. called it a javelina), a giraffe, and numerous other wild animals that she'd seen only on nature programs.

"Wanna beer?" J.B. asked. "You gotta like Texas. Can you get a beer in a museum in any other state?"

"No. I don't really want to stay here."

"But this place is chock-full of Texas history."

"I'll buy a book. To me, it's 'chock-full' of horrible death. I'm not kidding, I have to get out of here before I throw up on the floor."

It reminded her of unspeakable pictures she'd seen of greyhounds in Spain, put to death by their owners when they didn't hunt well. Viv turned and booked for the door.

J.B. followed. "Tough Girl, you're not looking so tough right now . . ."

She ignored him and ran to a nearby trash can, retching over it. Thank God nothing came up. She got control of herself.

"Oh, hell, I'm sorry, Vivvie. I thought maybe you'd get a kick out of the place. It's a famous San Antonio landmark."

She looked at him without speaking.

"Kids love it . . . so do most tourists . . ." He rubbed her back. "I'll take you over to the Riverwalk for a bit. I know you'll like that. Everything's alive and well and cheerful."

"You promise?"

"Yeah."

"J.B., I often work with the Animal Legal Defense Fund. I'm not a radical—I don't run around throwing blood or red paint on women's furs—but I do what I can to stop cruelty to animals. Greyhounds may be my personal crusade, but I hate to see any animal mistreated or killed for its skin."

"If it's any consolation, most of those animals in

the Buckhorn were probably eaten . . ." His voice trailed off as he saw her face.

"Why don't we change the subject?" she suggested.

"Okay."

They walked the few blocks to San Antonio's most popular area: the Paseo del Rio, or Riverwalk. Two and a half miles long, it consisted of stone pathways that followed the river under the bridges and streets of downtown. On either side were umbrella-shaded cafés and shops, bars and historic hotels—even an entire mall area. The water was the deep, mossy green of J.B.'s eyes.

"We'll meet with the band, pick up those stupid crystal swans and then come back over here for lunch, okay? We'll have a margarita and I'll take you over to La Villita, the arts district where the original 'little village' of San Antonio sat. It was built by the Spanish in the 1700s."

She nodded.

"Then we'll make a run over to El Mercado, the outdoor Mexican market."

"Okay. That sounds fun." She looked up at him. "Can you afford to take all this time off work?"

He shrugged. "Work will always be there." His unspoken comment was that she wouldn't be, which touched her.

"If we had more time I'd take you to the old Lone Star Brewery, which now houses the San Antonio Museum of Modern Art." He stopped and caught her chin in his hand, examining her face.

"You feeling better now?"

"Yes." She took a deep breath of fresh air, savoring it—so different from the air in Manhattan. She even liked the fetid, musky smell of the river. "Thank you."

He chuckled. "So now I know the two things feared most by the Ball-Busting Bitch. Bridesmaids' dresses and taxidermy."

She grimaced at him.

"Nope," he added. "I forgot one."

Viv looked a question at him.

"Intimacy. I think you'd rather put on a pink, frilly bridesmaid dress and dance with that stuffed bear in the Buckhorn than share your deepest thoughts with any man."

"That is so untrue," she retorted, knowing that it wasn't. "Oh, look at the time—we've got to meet the band."

"Yeah, look at the time," J.B. repeated sardonically. But he let it slide.

The band Julia had chosen had the dubious moniker of Ten Gallons o' Luv. Viv exchanged a meaningful glance with J.B. as they walked into the agreed-upon bar and were met by a man in painted-on black jeans and an acid green cowboy hat.

"Miz Shelton? Mr. Anglin?" Acid Green asked.

"Yes." Viv looked at his hat with undisguised horror.

"Hidey," he said, looking her up and down with blatant appreciation. The man almost smacked his lips. J.B.'s face darkened.

228

"Excuse me?" Vivien said.

"I'm Boogey, manager of Ten Gallons o' Luv."

"Er, charmed to meet you, Boogey."

J.B. just nodded curtly at him.

"So whut kin I do you for?"

"I am Vivien Shelton and this is J.B. Anglin. We are the attorneys for Julia Spinelli and Roman Sonntag, respectively. We're here to look over the contract for your gig on their wedding day."

"Jayzus." Boogey looked taken aback. "That cute li'l blonde sent her *lawyers*?"

"Yes," Vivien said evenly. "That cute li'l blonde sure did." He'd known their names but not their professions?

"Well." Boogey scratched at his scraggle-haired chin. "We don't rightly have a *contract*, you know." He then reached down and adjusted himself with great elegance. He shifted from one boot to the other. "We just have a verbal agreement and she writes a check."

"I'm sorry, but Ms. Spinelli doesn't do business that way." Vivien opened the flap of her leather satchel while J.B. looked on in amusement and said not a word. She removed a sheaf of papers about a quarter-inch thick.

"Now. Boogey. Er, do you possess a surname, Boogey?"

"A what?"

*Unbelievable.* "A last name."

"Jones."

"Thank you. Mr. Jones, if you'll read this document through completely and initial each page, indicating your comprehension of and agreement with the terms, we'd appreciate it."

He stared at the papers as if they were covered in anthrax, and adjusted himself once again. Viv thought about suggesting that he might be more comfortable in pants that were three sizes larger, but decided it wasn't her problem.

"Miz Shelton, I really ain't the person to sign those papers. I just met you to pick up a check from Julie."

"Julia."

"Right. Her. If you're talkin' legal papers, you need the lead vocalist."

*Such* a good sign that the band's manager refused to vouch by his signature that they'd show up. Viv didn't like this at all. "And the lead vocalist's name is . . . ?"

"Dizzy."

"Dizzy," she repeated. *Who named these guys?* "Oh-kaaaay. Where might we find this . . . Dizzy?"

"He don't get up until after two."

Viv sighed. "Mr. Jones, I thought we had an appointment to get this done today."

"All I knows, I came here to get a check because Miz Spinelli said she'd be down here anyway, and she wanted to meet—" He broke off, realizing that he was about to screw up.

"She wanted to meet the band in person. Yes. That would indicate that someone told her the band would be here today, would it not?"

Boogey looked at her with an "Oh, shit" expression.

"We've driven here from forty minutes away. So

would you consider waking up Dizzy? So he can come over here and sign this?"

He pursed his lips. "Not a real good idea."

Viv stared at him with growing wrath.

"He can be violent when woken." Boogie eased off his acid green hat and ran his fingers through hair that was not well-acquainted with shampoo.

She took in the ridiculous ridge left around his head from the band of the hat, the visible red capillaries in his eyes and the black under his fingernails. Also a nice touch was the black T-shirt he wore with the ripped-off sleeves. His tattoos didn't bother her, but the image of a bound, grossly endowed, nude woman on the T-shirt did.

Viv exchanged another glance with J.B., who shook his head. "Mr. Jones, we don't have a lot of time to waste. This wedding is in less than two weeks. Now, either you call this Dizzy person right away or the deal is off."

"I'm tellin' you, this is not a good idea." But at her steely glare, he walked as best he could in the ridiculously tight jeans to the phone, set it on speaker, and dialed a number. It rang and rang and rang.

Jones hung up and repeated the process twice.

Finally a voice snarled a string of words having to do with violators of mothers, crude body parts and impossible physical acts.

Viv's brows rose.

"Hold up a minute, Diz! I got two fancy lawyers here about the Spinelli-Sonntag gig. Wantin' you to sign some contract."

The voice told him exactly what to do with the Spinelli-Sonntag wedding, the lawyers and the contract. It added that Jones was, himself, a stupid violator of mothers and had a voracious taste for male sexual organs.

"Diz, I kind of forgot to mention that you're on speakerphone."

A resounding silence followed—then a single, breathless stream of obscenities followed by a dial tone.

J.B. began to laugh heartily while Viv packed her document back into her satchel.

"I think we've reached a perfect understanding," she said crisply to Boogie, who wore a sickly grin. "Ten Gallons o' Luv will *not* be playing the Spinelli-Sonntag wedding."

"Julia's going to kill us," Viv said to J.B. over margaritas at Casa Rio. It was the oldest, and arguably the best, restaurant on the Riverwalk, and they sat outside under an umbrella. "But what other choice did we really have?"

"None. She doesn't want those guys, no matter how much she liked their tape. She never saw them live, did she?"

Viv shook her head. "I don't think so. When would she have had the time?" She took a large, soothing mouthful of potent 'rita and let it slide deliciously down her throat. As usual, the heat had wilted her, flattened her hair and sucked most of her energy dry. The drink was refreshing, and she wanted about a gallon more.

"How did she choose these jackasses, anyway?"

"A cousin of one of them did her eyebrows."

"Huh?" J.B. looked at her over the rim of his 'rita glass. "What exactly do you women *do* to an eyebrow?"

"Lots of things. Shape it, arch it, tint it . . ." His puzzled expression made her laugh. "Never mind."

J.B. ordered something called *flautas* and a chile relleno to follow their ceviche. Viv dug into the fresh, spicy salsa with an oversized tortilla chip and relaxed against the cushion of her chair. Below them, a barge packed full of tourists went by, while a guide on a microphone narrated colorful details of San Antonio history.

J.B.'s boot knocked against the cardboard box full of little crystal swans they'd picked up nearby.

"Be careful," Viv told him.

He cast the box a dismissive glance. "Never seen anything so useless in my entire life."

"They'll look beautiful on the tables at the reception," she said, though privately she agreed with him. Still, they'd be a pretty and very Julia-like touch.

He rolled his eyes heavenward. "You know what people will be focusing on at the reception? Julia and liquor, in that order. And then within an hour, the focus will all be on the liquor. Things may start out elegant, but the party will degenerate into a hoedown."

Viv found herself wondering what J.B.'s own wedding had been like, but didn't dare ask him. "If the wedding is at the vineyard, won't the focus be more on wine than liquor?"

"Yeah, I suppose." He flashed her a grin. "Depends on how many pocket flasks make an appearance. Not everybody around here is a wino like Roman. We tease him and call him the Grape Ape."

Speaking of Roman, Viv had still not found a way to get Julia to sign a prenup. As she sipped her margarita, she reflected that she'd have to go for the "protect your children's inheritance" angle—if Julia didn't kill her for bringing up the topic again.

Their food came, and it was a little spicier than she'd bargained for. Viv broke out into a sweat at the first couple of bites, while J.B. laughed at her, his even white teeth flashing in the sunlight.

She dove for more margarita, fanning herself with a napkin, and this became a trend for the rest of the meal. The Riverwalk started to achieve a pleasant blurriness which only added to its charm.

Feeling fat, relaxed and happy, she allowed him to take her hand and walk her along the banks of the river until they got to La Villita, an absolutely charming area full of tiny shops, galleries and restaurants. J.B. smiled at her delighted expression as they walked along Villita Street and King Phillip V Street, poking their heads in here and there on a whim.

Viv loved the colorful rugs at Village Weavers and admired paintings at the River Art Group and Little Studio Gallery. She looked at silver concho belts and a bracelet of running greyhounds at another shop. And J.B. talked her into trying on a beautiful, hand-embroidered turquoise Mexican dress at a little boutique.

She came out of the dressing room barefoot to model it for him, laughing self-consciously.

J.B. looked at her for a long time without saying a word.

Disappointed, she said, "Well, it does look a little like a big blue sack on me."

"No." He shook his head. "It doesn't. You look gorgeous. It matches the color of your eyes. And you should never wear shoes . . ."

He turned to the saleslady. "We'll take it. She'll wear it out."

"J.B., you can't just buy this for—"

He took out his wallet.

"J.B., I'm not going barefoot along the Riverwalk! And I can't wear these shoes—"

The saleslady held up a pair of natural leather thong sandals. "These are perfect."

"Yes," he agreed. "They are. We'll take a pair of those, too."

"No—"

"Don't listen to her," he told the saleslady, who beamed and was only too happy to obey. "What size, Vivvie?"

"No."

"Okay, she's not being cooperative. I'd say she's about a seven? Let's take a seven."

"Eight," called Viv, deciding it was hopeless. She came out of the dressing room with her clothes and pocketbook to find him signing the credit card slip. The lady handed over her new shoes and packed her belongings in the store's shopping bag.

"Thank you," she said to them. "Y'all come back, now. You are such a cute couple. Enjoy your time in La Villita."

"Did you hear that, Viv?" J.B. took her by the hand again and steered her back outside. "We make a cute couple."

"You can't just be buying me things," she said, ignoring that statement.

"What you mean is, *Thank you, J.B., you sex god and all-around great guy. I'd like to kiss you all over now.*"

She eyed him, with her hands on her hips. "Thank you, J.B. That was very . . . sweet."

"And?" he asked hopefully.

"And you get *one* kiss."

"Stingy," he sighed. "But I'll just have to make the best of it." And so saying, he backed her right up against the wall of Villita Stained Glass and swooped down on her.

His mouth was hot on hers and he still tasted of margarita, his lips tinged with lime and salt. Though her impulse was to push him away, she couldn't find the willpower, and she melted into him.

A throng of middle-aged women clucked and giggled as they exited the shop and came down the three little steps. "Makes you remember when, doesn't it?" said one. "How romantic," said another.

"I'd like to hike this dress up around your hips and take you right here," said J.B., tearing his mouth from hers. "But it would be a tad exhibitionist."

"Just a tad."

"I'll have to wait till later." His tone was regretful. They went on to El Mercado, the marketplace at

Commerce and Santa Rosa, where he bought her some *dulce de leche*, or Mexican candy. It reminded her a little of butterscotch.

She had a ball wandering through the stalls with him and looking at the huge variety of goods: pottery, ceramics, turquoise jewelry and blankets. Here, among the hustle and bustle of people, jokes and laughter, they saw more embroidered dresses and peasant blouses, colorful striped blankets, rugs and leather goods. Viv also saw shellacked frogs drinking beer or playing musical instruments. They reminded her of Belker, the little toad.

She averted her eyes. She didn't want to think about work. She just wanted to enjoy herself and the limited time she had left with J.B. When would she return to Manhattan?

She was surprised at the level of resistance she felt toward going back. Not only was she adapting to the heat and the casual, friendly people in Texas, but she loved the open space, the vast blue sky and the sense of possibility here.

New York was electric, alive and exciting . . . but New York was also demanding, exhausting and unforgiving, at least in her circle.

She didn't know when she'd return to the City. And if she got too used to J.B. and that killer smile of his, she might not return at all.

# Chapter Nineteen

J.B. couldn't keep his eyes off Vivien in her embroidered Mexican dress. She looked like an entirely different being than the one who terrorized Manhattan courtrooms. She'd tucked her dark hair behind her ears, and it hung loosely down her back. Her eyes held the warmth of the sun and top-shelf tequila, not coolness and wariness.

He was seeing a glimpse of the real woman inside her professional shell. The question was when she'd snap the shell closed again, don the suit and the eyeglasses with the heavy, rectangular black frames. They sat on her delicate nose like a big bird of prey, a symbol of her readiness to hone in and snatch whatever advantage she could from an opponent. And as far as he could tell, with the exception of Julia, pretty much everyone was an opponent to Vivien Shelton, even her own mother and father.

But now, as they left El Mercado and headed back toward the truck for the ride home, she appeared lighthearted and sexy. The leather sandals and loose, pretty dress lent her a festive, carefree attitude that suited her. He could actually see some skin: pale and curiously vulnerable, unused to the Texas sun. He noticed the tiny blue veins along the tops of her feet and the delicacy of her exposed elbows. Her ears were just a little too large for her face, something he'd never noticed before. This gave her a sweetly goofy appearance that held enormous appeal.

He'd picked up another gift for her while she waited in line for a cappuccino, and he was tempted to give it to her but decided to wait.

They drove back to Fredericksburg in companionable silence, the little crystal swans nestled at Viv's feet. As they approached the town's outer limits, J.B. turned to her. "Do you want to come back to my place for a drink?"

Her lips twitched. "Does that mean you're going to show me your etchings?"

"Nope. I don't etch. But I do make furniture. I could show you that." He smiled.

"You make furniture? What kind?"

"My kind. You'll just have to see it."

"Okay. We do have to tell Julia she's lost her band, but I guess it can wait until later."

J.B. turned onto the road that led to his little country estate, as his mother called it. When he'd bought it only a simple three-room cabin stood on the property. This he'd expanded, and then he'd added a large separate studio for his woodworking, a three-car detached garage and finally a little guest cottage. To him it was paradise. An old stock pond now functioned as a tiny lake with a rock-waterfall, the sound of which he loved. He'd fashioned some unusual benches and a stone-topped table nearby where he often drank his coffee and read the paper in the mornings. He'd also rigged a hammock for truly lazy days.

Viv exclaimed as they turned down the gravel drive. "You have your own little compound here. And it's beautiful!"

J.B. had to agree. He'd had a professional landscaper come in to help him xeriscape and set the atmosphere. The result was total charm. The one thing that he and the landscaper had disagreed on was the ivy that climbed up the trellis on the main house and was working its way around the back wall, too.

J.B. loved the ivy in spite of the man calling it an awful weed. He loved it even though ants and other pests used it to crawl up onto his roof.

"It's all so picturesque," Viv said.

"It should be. There wasn't much out here when I bought the place. This is the result of four years of weekends and not much social life."

"You did all of this yourself?" She gaped at him.

"I had some structural help pouring foundations and putting up walls. But the rest I did, yes."

She pointed to the little benches and table by the water. "Those?"

"Yes, I built those."

She got out of the truck and wandered over to them, running her hands over the stone surface of the table, then the bentwood legs that supported the slab. "J.B., this is wonderful! I knew from what you'd said that you built out the shelves in your office, but this . . . you're an artist!"

He laughed. "No, I'm just a craftsman."

She shook her head. "A craftsman builds other people's projects. You conceived of this, too. And it's gorgeous. Can I see the rest?"

He nodded. "Yeah. But first . . ." He bent his head and kissed her, kissed all that was good and light and appreciative in her. This was the Viv he'd somehow seen, even through the suits and the heavy glasses and the mocking sarcasm. She was the woman he'd made love to there in New York, until she'd done the about-face and kicked him out.

Viv's lips were soft and yielding under his and she responded wholeheartedly. Her arms came around him, hands kneading his back. God, he wanted to pull up her dress and have her right there on his outdoor table . . . There was something about her that was addictive and touched a part of him nobody had ever touched. This woman, who'd essentially been betrayed at an early age by the man who should have loved and protected her—she needed him. He broke the kiss and gazed at her beautiful, flushed face, finally understanding that.

It undid him and he fell the last 20 percent of the way in love with her. He'd already been 80 percent gone, stupid or not.

She needed him in a way that cosseted and adored

Corinne never had. Viv might challenge him, verbally toy with him and never admit her vulnerability . . . but it existed.

Something inside him needed to nurture—it was just who he was. And something inside her needed to *be* nurtured.

Viv needed, on some very basic level, to be adored and cherished and comforted as she never had been. The question was, did she realize this? It saddened him. Because he wasn't at all sure she'd ever let anybody close enough to do that.

"Show me your house," Viv said, before she lost her mind, whipped off her simple cotton dress and dragged him down into the grass. J.B. once again had turned her personal switch to ON. How did he do that with a single kiss, a simple gesture?

He took her hand and walked with her to the door of the main living space, which was unlocked.

"You leave your door unlocked?" She tried and failed to imagine anyone doing that in Manhattan. It would be criminally stupid.

"Yeah. Everybody around here knows everybody else. Nobody's going to come in and take anything."

A series of cheerful barks sounded from the back of the house, followed by scrabbling claws on the wood floors. A large black Lab came bounding to the door and leaped on J.B., who patted him and ordered him down. He then leaped on Viv instead. He was all happiness and slobber and big paws.

"Hi, there!" she said, hugging him. "What's your name?"

J.B. laughed as the dog wagged his tail so hard that his back legs almost fell from under him. "This is Harley. He doesn't understand that his name calls for him to be more badass. He's irrepressible."

Harley slurped her face, almost knocking her nose off with his enormous pink tongue.

"Get down, critter. You trying to kill her?" J.B. physically hauled the dog off her.

"He's fine. My dogs are the same way—they just have less hair." She grinned and brushed at the mass of black fur on the new dress. Harley kept all four feet on the floor but continued to wag his entire body and tried to shove his nose into her crotch.

"No!" J.B. told him. "Sit, varmint." Harley obeyed reluctantly, and Viv finally had a chance to look around.

The interior of J.B.'s home took her breath away. It was utterly simple, with the emphasis on the richness of the natural wood everywhere. There were very few sharp angles, which pleased her; even the built-in shelves weren't the normal rectangular sort. They were natural, undulating shapes, no one shelf the same as another.

The space inside was full of light and air, thanks to the placement of skylights everywhere and few solid walls. It was very masculine, yet very warm. Books and turned-wood bowls populated the shelves, and vibrant rag rugs punctuated the rooms with color, as did the light apple green walls.

But it was J.B.'s rough-hewn furniture that stole the spotlight. A sofa, love seat and chair gathered around a low coffee table had all been fashioned out of . . . trees. Literally. Not wood that had been cured and smoothed and turned, but heavy, raw branches that he'd notched and placed carefully—almost sculpted together. Then he'd stained and shellacked the wood, sealing its natural beauty. He'd had overstuffed, shaped cushions upholstered in a textured beige fabric and placed them onto the seating areas.

Viv fell in love with it immediately. She ran her hands over the wood, loving the feel of it and the duality of rough and smooth. She sank into the cushions, which had to be some combination of down over foam because they were like heaven. Harley eyed her, obviously wanting to join her.

"Don't even think about it," J.B. said to the dog.

"I'm speechless," she told him. "This is stunning. How do you do it?"

He shrugged. "Some simple power tools and a whole lot of messing around."

"But who taught you?"

"Nobody really taught me. I learned how to use the tools from my dad when I was a kid. Took shop in high school, and learned some more. After that it was just talking to some local furniture makers and looking at books. A lot of trial and error." He was modest about it, but she could see the pride in his eyes. J.B. might be a lawyer by profession, but this was his true love.

"These pieces could go into galleries, J.B."

He stuck his hands in his pockets. "I don't want them to be in galleries. I want them right here."

"You've never made pieces to sell?"

He shook his head. "No. I've made things for friends. For my mother. That's it." He started toward the back of the house. "Come on. I want to show you my bedroom."

She chuckled. "Oh, that's subtle."

"No, really. I want you to see it."

His bed was massive and spectacular. Again, rough-hewn branches made up the frame, headboard and footboard. The walls were midnight blue and the spread was a handmade quilt large enough to cover a village.

"No, I don't belong to a sewing circle," J.B. said in answer to her unspoken question. "I commissioned that from a local artist."

But he had made the large armoire that stood against one wall, as well as the dresser. She tried to imagine the hours these pieces must have taken him.

Instead of curtains he had fashioned shutters out of wood from an old barn. He'd stained everything the same rich honey color of the furniture in the living room.

"You'd better get away from my bed before I throw you into it and have my wicked way with you, darlin'," he told her. "Do you want to see the studio?"

She nodded, although J.B. having his wicked way with her sounded tempting. She followed him through the kitchen, which was another work of art in itself: granite countertops, modern appliances and glass-fronted cabinets.

"Did you make those, too?" she asked.

"No. I don't have the patience for doing that kind of work—they're factory made."

"I think you have more patience than anyone I've ever met." He had it with her, with furniture and . . . ugh. With his ex. Now there was a path she didn't want to go down.

"It's not really patience," J.B. told her. "I'm just really damn stubborn. I refuse to give up."

His studio was scrupulously clean, even the bare concrete floor. Two walls were lined with waist-high cabinetry with big tools bolted to it, and one full wall was floor-to-ceiling cabinetry. A huge dust collector dominated one corner. J.B. explained to her how dangerous it was to breathe sawdust, and that it was also combustible. One spark from a big power tool and you could have an instant fire on the premises if you didn't clean up.

She loved the smell of the place, the essence of raw wood and machinery. It was the scent of nature and creativity, the odor of a man and his urge to produce things of beauty from simple materials.

In contrast, the smell of her law firm was all about money, leather and strong disinfectant. The place gleamed oppressively, Belker's dour minor-master paintings surrounded by six-inch gilded frames that took away the focus from the art and put it on the price tags.

She'd been proud to get their offer, proud of the

names on their letterhead. They hired only the best, like her. Now she wondered what her pride had been all about.

As J.B. showed her his drill press, his band saw, his table saw, his sanders, she looked at his big hands and how honest and capable they were. They were hands that gave back to the world, hands that made love, hands that she wanted to hold when she walked somewhere.

And they were so different from her citified, manicured ones. She truly lived on a different planet— one faster paced and with alternate priorities.

He touched her back and she felt his heat through the thin cotton of the dress. "Do you want a drink?"

"Sure." She should be drinking water in this heat, but the light was growing a little softer and he had some excellent bourbon.

He bribed Harley into good behavior with a rawhide chew, and they took their drinks out to the little lake with its waterfall. They sat at his table.

"My dogs would love this," she said wistfully. "So much room to run."

Harley grinned a toothy doggie grin at her and slobbered over his chew. J.B. prodded him in the backside with the tip of his boot and was rewarded with a look of adoration.

"You watch. He'll be done with that in about a half hour and go right into the water. He's a mess."

She laughed and sipped at her bourbon. "He's a dog. That's what they do best."

He eyed her lazily. "If you hadn't told me about your greyhounds, I'd *so* have pegged you for a cat person."

"I like cats, too. But people don't raise them in horrific conditions, feed them raw meat and then discard or destroy them when they're not fast enough." She set her glass down with a snap and was then afraid she'd cracked it. "Sorry."

She sighed. "I'm currently involved in a big suit against some people who hired the equivalent of a hit man to kill off a bunch of their racing dogs. They got too old, or had injuries, or just weren't fast enough. So this guy would take them out to his farm, shoot them and throw them into a mass grave full of thousands of other dog carcasses."

She stopped, picked up her drink and tossed some of the bourbon back. "But being a budget-conscious guy, he only allotted one bullet per dog. So if he missed, he'd just toss the poor thing into the grave and *bury the dog alive*."

She slammed her glass back down and said through clenched teeth, "It's somebody else's job to make sure these bastards rot in hell, but it's *my* job to try to get them punished while they're still on earth."

J.B. shook his head in disgust.

Her mouth quivered. "I'd have twenty greyhounds if I could."

"What's stopping you?"

"The size of my apartment. But as I told you, I've sponsored a lot of other dogs, found them homes. By the way, have you given any thought to—"

"Yes," J.B. said, his mouth quirking. "I'm going to

work on modifying that shed out there, and I also have a spare bedroom in the house. I can take a few. And I'll even work on Roman and Alex for you."

She jumped up and threw her arms around him. "You are not only a knight in shining· oven mitts, you're a knight with a shining leash!"

"Boy, do I have you snowed." J.B. reddened slightly. He kissed her, then stood up and dug into his left pocket. "I was going to wait and give you this before you left, but what the hell." He took her hand, dropped something heavy into it, and closed her fingers.

She opened them to find the gorgeous silver bracelet of linked greyhounds she'd admired in La Villita. "J.B.," she whispered. It was warm from his body heat, since it had sat snug in his pocket for most of the day.

He fastened it around her wrist.

"Thank you." She would have gone on, but he put a finger to his lips and pointed as a deer poked its head around the edge of the small waterfall. Cautiously, it took a few steps forward.

"Harley, stay," J.B. said in warning tones.

The dog's nose came up and he saw the deer immediately. Though Viv sensed that he wanted with every fiber of his canine being to charge the other animal, he obeyed his owner.

The deer had a fawn with it, and Viv felt warmed by the simple pleasure of watching the animals. They munched here and there while Harley vibrated like an egg sizzling in a pan. "*No*," J.B. said to him again.

Viv was amazed that he listened. She watched the

deer and tried to imagine one in Manhattan . . . It would immediately become venison, courtesy of a taxi.

"What are you thinking?" J.B. asked her. She told him and he chuckled.

"I love the city and I hate the city," Viv said. "On the one hand, it's exciting and vibrant and alive. On the other hand, it's a hassle. The best of the best live there, and yet sometimes they're the worst of the worst."

"Meaning?"

"Take my firm, for example. More Ivy League, law review overachievers than you can squeeze onto one floor. The combined brilliance of these people would probably run a whole power grid. And yet most of them are such . . . assholes."

"Those exist everywhere, Vivvie. You can trust me on that."

"Not of this caliber. These people are the crème de la crème of assholes."

He laughed.

"It's really not funny. And I fit in there perfectly: two Ivy League degrees, law review, top of my class. What does that make me?"

J.B. let out a breath. "You make you who you are. Only you decide that. But I can tell you what I see: a Tough Girl who's got a good heart. Cares about the underdogs, quite literally. Even if you treat those dogs better than you treat your men . . ." He shot her a provocative look.

She'd had too much relaxation and fun and bourbon to get mad. She winked at him. "Watch your mouth, J.B., or you might not get your Scooby Snack."

There was nobody around at all besides him and the animals. Viv stood, pulled her dress over her head and tossed it at him. She unhooked her bra and threw that, too. Then she headed for his bedroom wearing nothing but his bracelet, a thong and a smile.

# Chapter Twenty

Viv's thong did not stay on long. J.B. had her on his big bed in seconds flat and kissed her everywhere a woman could be kissed, while Harley roamed free outside.

"Counselor," he said, from between her breasts, "I'd like to make a motion for permanent nudity on your part."

She wasn't in the mood to deny him anything. Especially not when his mouth encircled her nipple and he tugged gently on it with his teeth before moving into pleasure, full throttle.

"I can't seem to get enough of you," he whispered. She knew the feeling. As she opened her mouth to his, and opened her legs to him, she was awfully afraid that she was opening her heart, too. But sensuality shoved panic out of the way for now, and she spun away from all logical thought.

She guessed it had something to do with having a large, handsome, naked man looming over her and moving deliciously inside her, wanting her with a fierceness and a possessiveness to which she was unaccustomed.

"Look at me, Vivvie," he said.

She opened her eyes. His own were heavy lidded, and he'd caught his lip between his teeth as he drove into her and pulled out, the rhythm building more and more tension. Sweat beaded on his forehead and under his jaw as he stroked in and out between her thighs.

She took his face in her hands and kissed him while her body met his in every possible way. She ran her hands along his jaw, to his neck and up to his ears, where she felt again those soft, velvety lobes.

He took her nerve endings and tied them into little knots of fabulous sensation all over. And when she climaxed, eyes open and looking deep into his, she was possessed by a single thought: *I love you*.

She loved the way he kissed her, the little bump on his nose where it had been broken in a college football game, and the feel of his warm breath on her cheek. She loved his stubbornness, his amazing loyalty, and the fact that he made beautiful furniture with his own hands. She loved that he'd taught her to drive, was converting his shed for needy greyhounds, and saw through all her defenses and postures to the person she really was inside.

This simple country boy had stolen her big-city heart.

She lay in the big bed with him spoon style, turning his bracelet on her wrist and feeling her body begin the inevitable stiffening process. Was she crazy? She couldn't love this man. They lived over a thousand miles away from each other. He was an idealist and she a cynic. She didn't believe in happy endings.

But for the first time, she wanted to stay overnight with a man. She wanted to fall asleep, and stay asleep in his arms. Not be so alone . . .

"You're doing it again," J.B. said into her ear.

"Doing what?"

"Going into postcoital rigor mortis."

"I am not." She sat up and shoved the hair out of her face. *"Rigor mortis?"*

"Yes. What is up with that?"

She stared at him. "I . . . don't know," she admitted. "I guess I just come back to the real world."

"You get defensive." He propped his chin on his hand and looked up at her. "What are you defending yourself from?"

*You. Me. My feelings. The idea of an actual relationship, because it won't work. We are just too different.* But she didn't say any of this aloud. She just shrugged.

J.B.'s face shuttered. "Still won't talk to me, huh."

"It's not that. I just—" She threw up her hands. "I just don't know what to say!" She could have been five years old again, being told to "share herself" in a letter to a man who could care less.

He shook his head. "Nobody hands you a script, Vivvie." He looked sad. "You've got to develop your own character."

"What the hell is that supposed to mean?"

"Whatever you want it to." He rolled out of bed and headed for the bathroom, looking curiously vulnerable for such a big man.

When he returned she'd huddled under the quilt, missing his warmth and still shell-shocked at what she'd admitted to herself. She was in love with the big, naked Texan frowning down at her. How had she let this happen? How had she left a chink in her armor big enough for him to get through?

Of all the stupid, moronic, idiotic things she could do, falling for a guy like J.B. was the crowning glory. Because, all other issues aside, no matter how much he denied it, or how sexually attracted to Viv he might be, he was still hung up on his ex-wife.

The idea of it burned like acid inside her.

He sat down on the bed and touched her hair. "When are you going back, Viv?"

"I don't know. Soon," she said bitterly. "As soon as I can get Julia to wake up and sign a damned prenup."

His hand froze on her head. Then he removed it. He got up and pulled on his jeans in frozen silence.

Finally he said, "I'll take you back to the Motor Inn now."

She sat up and stared at him. "I—but—I thought I'd stay . . . I wanted to wake up next to you in the morning at least once before we said goodbye."

J.B. fished his shirt off the floor, his actions weary. "Don't strain yourself, Vivvie. It would take more out of you than you're willing to give."

Her mouth dropped open.

"But as usual, the sex was great, your performance magnificent."

His words knocked the breath out of her and she couldn't say a word.

"I was guilty, I guess, of forgetting that we were just using each other for sex—indulging in a purely animal act. But when all is said and done, we each have opposite values. We should cut this off right now, shouldn't we? You were right all along. We can't let feelings get in the way.

"You go get Julia to sign that prenup, Viv. But I can tell you that Roman will sign it over my dead body. You go on back to Manhattan and bust balls. Dissolve more couples. Perfect your ironclad pre-nups."

His voice dripped with as much contempt as it had that night in Cuvée, and she found herself shaking.

"Was this all an act of revenge, J.B.? Get me back in bed and soften me up so that you could do the kicking out this time? Teach me a lesson?" She tried to keep her voice calm but to her humiliation it broke.

He just narrowed his eyes at her. He seemed about to deny it. Then he exhaled and nodded.

"Good job, then. Congrats. I hope you're happy. But you know what? All this anger and contempt you've got inside you has come out in a very twisted way. Because it's not me you're mad at. No, J.B., you've taken your revenge on the *wrong woman*!"

She gave up on keeping calm and screamed it at him. "It's your damned ex-wife who deserves your revenge, not me! But instead, I get it. Because I'm the evil bitch who damaged your ego three years ago.

"I didn't damage your heart the way she did. But you're obviously still in love with the woman, and it makes me sick because she doesn't deserve you!"

Viv took a ragged breath and kept yelling at him. "You want to know why I kicked you out, you stupid son of a bitch? I may as well finally tell you . . . I mean, why not mortify myself even more?

"I kicked you out because I was afraid of falling for you. But it was too late. Two hours, you bastard, and you stole my heart!" She was automatically hunting for her clothes now, and tears blinded her.

Then she remembered that her dress was outside. "Give me a robe!"

He stood there like a statue.

"I kicked you out because I didn't want to miss you. I didn't want to get attached to you. It was going to end anyway, and I didn't want it to end like *this*." She dashed a hand over her eyes. "Give me a robe! I don't want to be naked in front of you. Not ever again."

When he still didn't move she grabbed the quilt off his bed, wrapped it around her body and stormed out of his house. Harley ran over to greet her, his tail wagging uncertainly, and this made her cry even more. She wrenched open the passenger side of his truck and pulled out the bag of clothes she'd worn to San Antonio that day.

God only knew where her underwear was, and her bra was still by the lake, but she pulled her shirt over her head and was in the process of unfolding her pants when a BMW 700 Series, driven by the gorgeous blonde she'd seen once in his office, pulled down the driveway. The woman stared at her. Viv stared right back, holding her pants in front of her. It was not her proudest moment.

"You can have him!" she yelled. "I hate the bastard."

Corinne's eyes widened and her mouth formed an "O." The BMW went into reverse and began to back away, down the driveway.

"I said *you can have him!*" Viv screamed. She ran after the car while the blonde took one look at her, the bottomless lunatic, and sped backward, squealing out onto the macadam. Harley, who had followed right along with her, barked madly. Then he stuck his cold nose up her butt.


Of all the screwups in all the screwed-up situations in the entire screwed-up nation, J.B. reflected that this one had to rank in the top ten.

He stood at the screen door watching as half-naked Viv chased his ex-wife down his driveway *trying to give him back to her*. Like he was a freezer-burned piece of meat.

"That's just priceless," he muttered out loud. "Priceless." She deserved more than Harley's nose in her rear. She deserved to be kicked there by a steel-toed boot. He had one of those real handy.

Viv unconsciously mooned him as she put on her pants. He supposed he deserved it. Or did he?

J.B. wasn't sure who deserved what at this point. If, as she claimed, she'd fallen for him in New York, she'd had a damn funny way of showing it.

But he'd paid her back in spades at Cuvée.

Since then it had pretty much been tit for tat, no pun intended. And his tat had been very happy about it.

Until she'd brought up the prenup again and he'd lied about a revenge strategy. Or had he?

He wasn't too sure about that anymore, either. Because originally he *had* set out to teach the high and mighty Miz Shelton a lesson. But that goal had faded away as he'd fallen for her all over again—at least that part of her that was fun and human and not a divorce attorney android.

He sighed. Viv had her shoes on by now and he half expected her to go ahead and steal his truck for the second time, since the keys were still in the ignition. But instead she dug into her purse for her cell phone and started walking down his driveway. She'd tossed his quilt on the hood.

He might not know exactly what to say to the woman, but he would not allow her to walk the two miles back to the Inn. Dusk was fading into darkness and he had some standards of behavior, which included making sure females got home safely after they were out with him. Or in with him. Or—oh, hell and damnation.

He pondered her accusation that he'd taken his

259

revenge on the wrong woman. He rejected the idea, but then turned it over and over in his mind.

Had he, in his efforts to be the good guy, the guy who would prove marriage could succeed, just gone passive-aggressive and then released his rage for Corinne at someone else? The problem was, he no longer felt any rage for her. He felt pretty much nothing. Maybe a little curiosity about why she'd been coming to visit him.

He did feel rage about something, though. Maybe . . . maybe his own failure at not being able to hold together the life he'd constructed.

J.B. was just tired right now. Not to mention confused. He jammed his feet into some shoes and banged out of the screen door, making his way to the truck. He got in and told Harley to stay put. He started the ignition and eased down the driveway, only to find Viv sitting on the ground by the entrance.

He lowered his window. "Viv?"

She extended her middle finger in reply.

He sighed. "That is an eloquent argument, Counselor, but I'm more likely to take it as a come-on than an insult."

She stared straight ahead and didn't reply.

"Look, would you get into the truck so I can take you back to the Inn?"

No answer.

"Viv, I can sit here until you get into the truck, or I can physically throw you into it."

She turned her head and shot him a Death Stare. "I don't advise that you lay a finger on me."

*Fine.* And so they sat, not speaking, until Julia

pulled over in her rented Mercury and looked, bewildered, from one to the other. Viv got up, brushed the dirt off her rear, and got into Julia's passenger seat. She again refused to look at J.B., and the two women drove away.

He turned around and went back to his house, his dog and his thoughts.

Julia turned off the radio and Viv waited for her inevitable questions.

"Sooooooo?"

"So we picked up your crystal swans," Viv said.

"Right now, I am not interested in my crystal swans, but thank you very much. Now spill!"

"And I should tell you that we fired your band, for very good cause."

"You *what*?" Julia put a hand to her forehead. "Never mind. I'll kill you after I get this out of you. Now tell Mama Julia what's wrong with you kids."

"Nothing's wrong. I just hate him, that's all."

Julia audibly counted to three. "Vivver, if you hate him, then what exactly has happened to your bra, honey?"

*Crap.* She'd forgotten that small detail. "It broke."

"Uh-huh. It just popped off in public, and fell to your feet. Viv, quit avoiding the subject and just tell me what's going on. Please."

"Well, let's see. J.B. and I had a wonderful time in San Antonio and then we went back to his place for a drink and et cetera. The et cetera was fabulous until he asked me how long I was staying and I laughed and said until I got you to sign a prenup."

Julia's mouth tightened. "Which I will not do, so you might as well buy a house here."

*I'd have loved to. Maybe even a ranch. But not now.* "That was when he got pissed off and then got even and kicked me out. He slept with me for revenge." Viv's voice started to shake. "Which I suppose I deserved, but I told him the person he was really mad at was his ex-wife and he'd taken revenge on the wrong woman because he still loves her." To her horror, she started to cry again.

"Which is so utterly, cosmically unfair, because she doesn't deserve him. And I told him that, too," she sobbed.

"Oh, honey . . ." Julia touched her shoulder with the hand that wasn't steering.

"And guess who should come gliding down the drive when I had no pants on?" Viv's voice rose and she started to laugh at the same time she cried. "Corinne herself, in all her blond Texas glory. So I screamed at her that she could have him . . ."

Julia pulled over to the side of the road and stared at her. "Oh. My. God. You didn't!"

"Yes, and then"—Viv hiccupped—"I chased her down the driveway like a dog, half-naked."

Julia put her head down on the steering wheel. "Oh, honey. Mummy would be so proud . . ."

"Wouldn't she?" Viv's laughter escalated into full-blown hysterics.

Julia gathered her into her arms. "You know, for a logical, practical, Ivy League lawyer, you sure are nuts. What am I going to do with you?"

"I don't know," Viv sobbed.

"What are *you* going to do with you?"

"I don't know that, either . . ."

"What *do* you know?" Julia's tone was softer than the words themselves.

Viv raised her tear-streaked face. "That I've met the one man in the entire world that *I* would marry without a prenup. But he despises me, he's still in love with his ex, and we live hundreds of miles away from each other. Oh, and I hate my miserable life. But other than that, everything's p-p-perfect."

# Chapter Twenty-one

J.B.'s cell phone rang insistently. He glared at it, wanting to lob it into the waterfall. But instead he answered it to find Corinne on the other end of the line.

"John Bryan, can I ask what that half-naked psycho was doing in your driveway?"

"Sure. If I can ask what *you* were doing in my driveway."

"Well, I . . . I was coming to bring you a casserole."

Along with a professional-grade seduction, no doubt. "How nice of you," he said dryly. "And here I was just craving Tuna Surprise."

A telling silence greeted him, and he almost laughed out loud. She really did have a Tuna Surprise in her car. Good guess.

"J.B., if you're going to be a jerk about it, then—"

"Pardon me?" He held the phone away from his ear and stared at it.

"I said, if you're—"

"I heard what you said. I'm just having a hard time believing that came out of your mouth. You don't even know the meaning of the word 'jerk,' Corinne.''

Vivien's words came back to him. *You've taken your revenge on the wrong woman!*

It floored him. But she'd hit the nail right on the head. He had.

And his ex thought she could crook her little finger and he'd come running back. Rage ignited in him and he was glad not to be face-to-face with her, because she'd be wearing her damned tuna and noodles.

He said evenly into the phone, ''Listen to me, Corinne. I haven't been nearly as much of a jerk as I should have been. I gave you my heart and my ring and everything else, but you got bored with them. *Bored!* It wasn't enough for you. I guess your daddy's given you everything all your life, and so you just take it for granted.

''You also took for granted that I'd always treat you right, because my dad taught me to cherish a woman, and I do my utmost to follow his example. But you did not deserve it. Still, I didn't give up.''

J.B. took a deep, angry breath and continued throwing his words into the void of her silence.

''So then you took half my money, and chump that I was, I continued to keep trying to prove to you that things could have worked between us. I didn't care about the money that much. I did think I cared about you.''

''Huh,'' she said. ''You slept with that psycho in New York!''

''Don't call her that. Don't call her anything at all.

I'm not perfect, Corey, and we were divorced! You dare to say that to me? I've slept with one woman in four years, and you've *married* two other guys?"

"What*ever*."

"No, not whatever. I thought maybe I did still love you for a while, but now I realize that I was just being stubborn—trying to show you that I was a better person than you. I took the high road, I was superior, I wasn't as shallow as you." He laughed bitterly.

"But what the hell is the point? Corinne, the high road has just come to a dead end! *I want nothing further to do with you.* I don't want to be friends, I certainly don't want to be your lover again, and I sure as shit don't want to be chasing rats out of your kitchen at two a.m.! Understand?"

She blew out an audible breath. "Yes. But J.B.—"

He cut her off. "So call some other chump. Dress up in your lingerie for him. Get *him* to fix your sprinklers. I'm done. By the way, do you not understand how frigging *insulting* it is that you think a Tuna Surprise makes up for everything?"

"Stop yelling at me! You've made your point. I—I guess I won't bother you anymore." Then she added in a small voice, "I know that I was wrong, okay? I messed up real bad the day I left you, J.B. I'm sorry."

For the second time during the conversation, he held the phone away from his ear and stared at it. Had she really just said that?

Viv made Julia stop at Judy's Liquor on Washington, where she purchased a large bottle of Scotch. Not bourbon, Scotch. If she drank most of the bottle, she could banish J.B. from her mind and grow hair on her chest by morning. Then she'd sleep on the plane all the way back to JFK.

"Schtupid, wife-loving bastard," she said to Julia an hour later. "What kind of scum-sucking pig still loves his wife after she leaves him and they're divorced?"

Julia looked up from filing her nails. "The kind of scum-sucking pig that you should marry, because he's loyal and sweet."

Viv felt her face crumple again. "You're supposed to be on my side, here. Agree with me that he's evil. That he's the worst man in the entire world." She put the plastic cup full of Scotch to her lips again.

Julia sighed. "Would you set that down and quit poisoning yourself? I personally don't think J.B. is still hung up on Corinne. I think he's got a thing for you. Or he did until he saw your naked butt running down his driveway, and heard you trying to give him back to her."

"I've been told that my naked butt is ver' niccce," Viv said with great dignity.

Julia just raised a brow.

Viv looked into her Scotch and frowned. "Though I've notished way too much cellulite lately. Think he saw that?"

"Every woman has cellulite. And I'm sure if you were halfway down the driveway, and your buns were bouncing as you ran, he did not notice any orange-peel effect." She lost it and cracked up. "The only thing he'd have noticed was your mental instability . . ."

"Did you know," said Viv conversationally, "that Mummy doesn't want you to marry the cowpoke? And that she thinks you should snare a better guy while *you* don't have any cellulite?"

"Give me that," Julia said, and snatched the cup of liquor off the nightstand.

"Hey!"

"Your mother is very disturbed, Vivver. And frankly, it's a wonder that you have turned out somewhat normal. I use the term 'somewhat' loosely." And Julia marched into the bathroom and dumped the contents of the cup down the sink.

"I take ex—ex—exception to that," said Viv, following her.

"Roman is not a cowpoke. There *is* no one better. I already have cellulite. And any guy who marries a woman for her airbrushed derriere is not a guy I want in my life. Now, let's talk about you."

"Me?"

"Yes. Why would J.B. have slept with you three years ago if he was still carrying a torch for Corinne?"

"Distraction," Viv said promptly.

"Unlikely, but I'll let you have it as a possibility. Then why would he have slept with you here in Fredericksburg if he was still hung up on her?"

"I told you, revenge."

"Nope. I don't buy it. He got his revenge in Cuvée. And he's not a guy who holds a grudge. Look how Corinne has treated him. So why did he sleep with you?"

"To use me for sex. We talked about it."

"That is warped. And again, I don't buy it. Why would he give you a driving lesson? Why would he save you from being arrested by putting his poor mother in the kitchen for an entire weekend? By the way, you need to send her some flowers."

"Already done."

"Answer the question, Viv."

"Jeez, I'm not on the stand here! I don't know."

"He did all this because he has a thing for you. And you have a thing for him. Now how about you guys talk this out? Put Thing One together with Thing Two and make a couple?"

"You're such a mash-maker." Viv wandered back out of the bathroom, plopped down on the brown-and-mustard comforter and curled up.

"Oh, I think it's you who's made the mash."

"Hmmmmm," said Viv, closing her eyes. She never had been able to drink much. "Will you make me a reservation for tomorrow?" She waved at the corner of the room. "Don't think I can focus. Laptop. Airline flequent frier number stored . . ."

She felt Julia pull the corner of the bedspread up and over her, and was vaguely aware of her saying something more. Then she drifted off to sleep.

The next day, on the other side of town, Wes Taunton had been awaiting the call from heaven, aka J.B. Anglin's mom.

When it came, he began to salivate immediately. Would he taste the key lime pie first? Or her King Ranch Chicken? A cheesecake, or the *enchiladas suizas*? Wes wondered if, at age thirty-five, it was too late to ask her to adopt him. He could move right into her back guest room. He could help her out by chopping wood, maybe even rub her feet after a long day.

If that didn't work out, he could always take to arresting J.B.'s little Yankee gal a lot—maybe once a week if she stuck around—although he'd heard that they'd had some kind of big fight. Something about her chasing Corinne down his driveway with no pants on.

Wes brightened. Bingo! Having no pants on in public was a misdemeanor. He could probably get him a Mississippi Mud Pie just for that one. He'd delay it for a couple of weeks, though, since he was going to go pick up an entire trunkful of food right now.

He hummed as he drove, idly listening to the chatter on the radio. Suddenly something flaming orange caught his eye in the distance. It disappeared quickly, but he'd only seen that shade of orange on one person in town.

Wes squinted, and then saw a flash of steel. What on God's green earth? As he got closer, he pulled over to the side of the road and got out of his car.

Yep. His eyes hadn't deceived him. There was the blob of orange, accompanied by a swatch of floral material, a pudgy, suntan-colored, hosiery-encased leg, and a mustard yellow orthopedic shoe—all poorly concealed behind a clump of cedar.

"Come on outta there, Miz Grafton. And bring the wire cutters with you. I saw 'em."

"Oh, Wesley. You always were a nice boy. Give an old woman a break."

"Thelma Lynn, you know I can't do that. Not now that I've caught you, red-handed, cutting Ted Kimball's fences. Those loose-runnin' emu have caused a lot of accidents! You should be ashamed of yourself."

"They've only caused two," she argued, emerging from behind the cedar. "One was an out-of-town woman, and one was that trashy little tramp Mindy Baker. She was speeding like the dickens, too. Who cares?"

Wes put one hand on his hip and the other on his holster. "You are showin' a grave disregard for the lives of other human beings, Thelma Lynn! Not to mention those poor defenseless birds, and Ted Kimball's livelihood. Now would you like to explain to me why you've been doin' this?"

"Ted Kimball's livelihood! That man's got piles of money. How would he like to live on a widow's social security like me? No, he's got to start messing around with face creams. I've been selling Avon for years around here, but now nobody will order moisturizer from me because of some emu-oil crap that the Kimballs and that redheaded Jersey gal are marketing in baby-food jars!"

Wes stared at her and shook his head. "That's why you've been cutting his fences?"

She stuck out her chin. "Yes! My moisturizer sales numbers are down in the dumps! I wish I could flatten *all* of those smelly birds into roadkill . . ."

Wes took her by the arm and led her to his squad

car. "Thelma Lynn, I'm sorry, but I've got to take you in. This is serious mischief you've been up to."

Her eyes narrowed and flashed under the orange hair. "You make one move to arrest me, son, and I'll tell everyone in town how you're accepting bribes for looking the other way. Oh, yes, I know about you and that Yankee attorney gal and the deal with J.B.'s mother . . ."

Wes felt the blood draining out of his face and pooling down at his hot, swollen feet in the black, police-issue shoes. How did the woman, town gossip that she was, find out everything in Fredericksburg? Had she bugged his car? "Now, Thelma Lynn! There is no need to be stirring up trouble."

"Oh, no need at all, Wesley." She batted her green mascara-encrusted eyelashes at him. "How about I make you some nice ambrosia and a box of Turkish delight?"

He swallowed and tried not to blanch. If possible, Thelma Lynn was a worse cook than his own mother. Her ambrosia, a puke green Cool Whip and Jello-O mixture with stale walnuts on top, had been known to condemn a man to the bathroom for days. Nobody knew what she put in it, but it wasn't safe.

On the other hand, it would be all too dangerous for his career to offend her. And if he was going to have Internal Affairs suspend him and investigate him, shouldn't it be for something more badass than casseroles?

Irritation dawned over her powdery cheeks, and Wes realized he'd hesitated too long.

"That'd really be something, Thelma Lynn. I'd love

some ambrosia, and I never turn down delight, no matter what nationality it is. Thank you."

He escorted her to her old Bonneville, parked behind some mesquite trees, and shook a warning finger at her. "But you stop cutting Ted's fences, you hear? Or I will turn you in, even if I have to eat frozen dinners for the rest of my days." He tapped on the roof of her car as she drove off, and looked at his watch. He was now late for his pickup at Mrs. Anglin's.

He had just strapped himself back into the squad car when Corinne's BMW pulled over beside him. He rolled down his window and drank in her blond beauty.

"Wesley!" she exclaimed. "I am so glad to see you here. I was just thinking about you this morning, and how you must get tired of bachelor food. So I made you a Tuna Surprise! I have it right here."

He blinked. Besides Thelma Lynn's ambrosia, there was nothing he avoided more than a canned tuna casserole. It sure was his lucky day. He was going to have to get a dog.

# Chapter Twenty-two

J.B. holed up in his office and found himself absolutely fascinated with a dirty blue rubber band instead of the piles of work on his desk. He laced his index fingers through it, then his pinkies, and pulled in opposite directions, stretching it out.

He let it retract again and put his thumbs inside it this time. Stretch. Retract. Stretch. Retract. It occurred to him that the blue rubber band was a lot like his relationship, if you could call it that, with Vivien Shelton. Every time they seemed to stretch and come to an understanding, something got screwed up and they retracted again.

J.B. made a gun out of the rubber band, lacing it around the tip of his index finger and pulling back with his thumb. It shot across the room and almost hit his mother when she knocked briefly and opened the door.

She looked at him much as she had when he was ten and threw a football inside the house.

He shot her a sheepish glance. "Sorry."

"Here's the Zigler file and the Chapman release, which is signed, dated and notarized."

"Thank you."

She nodded and turned to leave. "I have mixer's elbow because of Wesley Taunton. He picked up all of his food. Hope your little Yankee lawyer is worth it."

He got up and went to give her a hug. "Thank you, Mama. You're an absolute gem."

"She did send me the prettiest flowers."

"Good."

"Are you okay, son?"

"I'm fine. Couldn't be better," he lied.

When she retreated and shut the door again, he stared into space. Was Vivien Shelton worth it?

Yes.

He could still see her eyes, looking into his the last time they'd made love. It had taken him a long time to get past her defenses, but he'd done it. They had connected. She'd wanted to stay the night.

And how had he reacted? He'd lost his temper over the prenup issue and betrayed her growing trust—the worst thing he could have done, considering her background. He'd kicked her out, and lied to her about why. No wonder she'd run down the driveway and told Corinne she could have him back.

He still saw her face as she'd told him why she'd turfed him out in New York.

*Why not mortify myself even more? . . . I was afraid of falling for you. But it was too late. Two hours, you bastard, and you stole my heart!*

J.B. walked to the door of his office and picked up the blue rubber band again. He stretched it between his fingers. Viv's words had been her Tough Girl equivalent of saying that she was in love with him.

The rubber band snapped back to its original shape and J.B. realized that he'd been very, very stupid yesterday. She had come as close as she humanly could to reaching out to him, to sharing with him.

And he'd stood stock-still, unable to process it, only aware of her anger, her accusation that he'd taken revenge on the wrong woman.

J.B. stretched out the rubber band one more time. Then he slipped it onto his wrist and walked out the door.

"She's worth it," he said to his mother.

She took off her glasses and rubbed her nose. "Well, it's about time you found one who is."

He drove the few blocks to Marv's Motor Inn, unsurprised when he found Julia at the front desk. "Hi," he said quietly.

She looked up and smiled her angelic smile. "Hi."

"Can you call Viv's room for me?"

Her face fell. "J.B., she's already left. I just got back from taking her to the airport."

"I see." He hadn't considered this possibility.

Julia hesitated. Then she said, "Oh, well. I did learn meddling from the Blue Ribbon Interference Queen herself: my sister Sydney."

"Excuse me?"

"So I'll just rip out a page from her book. Listen to me, J.B., Viv is special . . ."

"I know that."

"She's got issues. Family and trust issues. But she is so incredible underneath that cool, tough, lacquered shell. And here's the thing. She came flying down here to protect me and get me to sign a prenup, for God's sake, but the person who really needs protecting is Viv herself. She needs protection from the hardening process that's going on in her. I hate what that job is doing to her, and I think she hates it, too. But she doesn't see any other way to live."

She looked him square in the eyes. "I'm going to tell you something that she would actively kill me for revealing."

"Shoot."

Julia expelled a breath. "Yeah, that's what she'll want to do to me if she ever finds out. No, that wouldn't be personal enough. I'm pretty sure she'd want to throttle me and drown me in a toilet bowl."

"I get the idea," J.B. said. "I won't betray you."

"Okay. She told me that you are the one man in the entire world that *she* would marry without a prenup."

"She did not," he said, grinning hugely.

"Yes, she did," Julia insisted. "But she thinks you're still—"

"I am not in love with my ex-wife. Not even a little."

"That's what I thought. So then would you do us all a favor and go get Viv? Shake some sense into her and tell her what you just told me? Before it's too late and she petrifies into stone or something?"

"Yeah."

"She needs warmth and love and a normal mom who'll stuff her with food, not that whacked-out countess who plays voodoo. I'm hoping she can borrow your mother."

He nodded.

"Well, what are you waiting for?" Julia asked.

"Her address and phone number. That would help me out a lot."

Viv stared at the ceiling of her Manhattan apartment and ignored the irritating buzz of the alarm clock, her mind far away. Finally Brooklyn's nose appeared from under the covers, where he always slept. Another push and wriggle and his entire head emerged. He blinked at her, pinned his ears back, and gave a sharp, staccato bark.

"You're right. I need to get up and turn it off." She raised her head enough to kiss him on the nose but then flopped down onto the pillow again.

Mannie, Ellis, Queenie and Longo joined in the barking and jumped all over her, licking and prodding her with their noses.

"Okay, okay." She fumbled up onto her elbows, stuck a depressed toe out from under the blankets and found the floor. She staggered over to the clock and turned off the noise. How had it gotten to be 7:14 already?

The dogs sat outside the door while she went to the bathroom and followed her into the kitchen while she started the coffee. They had obviously missed her while she'd been in Texas and now didn't trust her not to leave again.

She opened the cabinet where she kept dog food and treats, sleepily amused when Mannie and Ellis stood on their hind feet like elongated, big-eared prairie dogs. She passed out five gourmet dog "bagels" and was rewarded with canine ecstasy.

At 7:23 she poured her first cup of coffee, reflecting that in exactly two minutes she would receive a cranky call from Maurice, wondering why she wasn't downstairs and getting into the Lincoln for work. She'd given Tabitha the day off and sent an e-mail to Belker and Schmidt at midnight that she'd be in late but had an issue to address with them. She intended to quit.

Right on schedule at 7:25, as she took her third sip of coffee, the phone rang. She picked it up, pressed the ON button and said, "Vivien Shelton."

"Miss Shelton, it's Maurice."

"What a nice surprise, Maurice. How are you this morning?"

"Late to pick up Mr. Fontaine, is how I am, if you're not down here within ninety seconds."

"I'm so sorry, Maurice—I didn't want to bother you after eleven last night when I got in, but I'll be going to the office late today." She could almost hear his scowl through the telephone.

"Very good, Miss Shelton."

*Yes, it is, isn't it? It's about damn time I stopped having to look at Belker and his peeling, reptilian skin.* She would now do all the pro bono work she wanted to do, spearhead the day-care project at the Displaced Homemakers' Association, and maybe start her own rescue shelter for greyhounds. She'd devote her life to good causes and animals, since she definitely hated all men.

Viv took her coffee back to bed, a luxury to which she was not accustomed. She fell back asleep after a quarter of the cup, burrowing under the covers and surrounded by her dogs. An hour later she became vaguely aware of the phone ringing, but ignored it just like she had the alarm.

It was almost certainly the office, and she had no desire to speak to anyone there. She just wanted to hole up and lick her wounds.

Something had changed for her in Texas. She'd returned a different woman, tired and sad and no longer sure of her place in the world. Everything had tilted slightly—not upside down but enough to shift her center of gravity.

The new tilt had to do with J.B. Anglin.

Her phone rang again, insistently, but she just turned off the ringer.

As she drifted into a sleepy haze again, it occurred to her that she didn't want to live in New York anymore. She loved the City and always would, but she'd been here too long. Maybe she'd rent out the apartment and go off to Taos or Santa Fe with the dogs . . .

Viv awoke an hour later and took a luxuriously long shower. She pulled on a simple skirt, tank and thong sandals, took the dogs out a couple at a time, and then headed to the office with a Diet Coke in one hand and her letter of resignation tucked into a beach bag she'd slung over her shoulder.

She took a cab to midtown, relishing the smell of

falafels and too much Stetson cologne on the driver instead of Maurice's wintergreen gum and putrid, tropical fruit carpet freshener.

She smiled at Cleo, grimaced at Belky's gilt-strangled, framed sourpusses and cruised into his office without knocking. The door was open, but he was on the phone, barking at someone while pieces of his skin flaked onto his leather blotter.

*Ooooh, I am so not going to miss that.*

She sank down into his leather visitor's chair while he frowned at her and continued his conversation with the poor unfortunate on the other end of the line. He made no move to end the call.

Viv took a sip of her Diet Coke and waited. And waited some more. She stared at a photograph of The Belk with his arm around a past governor of the state, and another photograph of him with a well-known socialite at a charity fund-raiser. Finally there was one of him grinning like a jack-o'-lantern at the attorney general.

At last, thinking of all the times he'd done the same to her, she just started talking to him, utterly disregarding manners and protocol. "Belker, I'm sure you'll feel that I should have run this by Human Resources first and checked to see if it's convenient with your schedule, but I'm leaving the firm." She slid her letter of resignation onto his desk.

"What?" She finally had his attention.

"I. Am. Leaving."

"Harris, I'll call you back." And Belky hung up the phone. He steepled his fingers and leaned back in his chair. "This is a sudden decision."

"Yes." She didn't give him any reason; she'd make him ask.

"You're going to be letting down a lot of people here. This firm has made an investment in you."

*Oh, you're going to try to guilt me into staying? You don't even like me, Belker.* "And I've made an investment in the firm. I've sacrificed vacations, sleep and social life to billable hours, and I've brought Klein, Schmidt numerous clients. I would think that makes us even."

"What firm are you going to? What have they offered you? We can match it."

"I'm not going to any firm. I'm going to be doing pro bono work on my own."

"Come on, Vivien. Don't BS me."

"I'm being straight with you."

"You expect me to believe that you're leaving a solid six-figure income to go play around with dogs and housewives for free?"

"That's right."

"Are you feverish, Shelton, or just stupid?"

She stood up. "Neither. I'm just not happy practicing law here. And I don't care about the money."

"Ah, yes, I'd forgotten: the heiress factor. I do hope that your people are selling a lot of toothpaste these days to support your little hobbies." He gave her a nasty smile.

"That was completely uncalled for," said Viv, pouring her now-warm Diet Coke into the potted plant by his desk.

His mouth opened in outrage and she derived great satisfaction from it.

"You know damned well that you and the firm benefited from my family connections. So I'm not taking that kind of crap off of you, got it?"

The little weasel had no response to that.

"I'm taking the next couple of days off. Then I'll be back for two weeks so that we can assign my cases to other attorneys and smooth the transition."

"I do hope you won't expect a reference from me."

"Belker, I don't expect a thing from you besides the headaches you've always instigated. Now, goodbye."

"Goodbye, Vivien. Don't let the door hit you in the butt on the way out."

She was free! Free! Someone else would have to deal with drunken Klempt and crazy Mrs. Bonana. She'd no longer be taking the Maurice-mobile. And she could give all of her attention to causes that were dear to her heart. Viv hunted down Andie, told her the news, and gave her a hug, promising to see if she could place her somewhere else.

She grabbed another cab to the Displaced Home-makers' Association on Lex and went in to talk with the director about the day-care program, funding and liability insurance. They sat down and began to draft a plan of action, Viv working feverishly so as to keep her mind off J.B.

It was late afternoon when she finally headed back to her apartment to take the dogs for a walk in the park. Unable to handle all five at once like Tabitha somehow did, she took Brooklyn, Mannie and Longo on one run and then returned for another with Quee-nie and Ellis, who didn't take kindly to going second.

She was so tired after the second run that she put on her jammies, collapsed on the sofa and fell asleep. Sleep would block out the stress of the day, the uncertainty of the future and her unwelcome thoughts about J.B.

But Murphy's Law worked against her. Half an hour later, the doorman leaned on the buzzer and her dogs went nuts, barking.

"Oh, for pity's sake," Viv said. "What?" Her tone was anything but warm and fuzzy.

"Miss Shelton?" Timmy the doorman said. "There's a gentleman here to see you. Name of Anglin?"

"No-he-is-not."

"Yes, he is." J.B.'s voice came clearly through the intercom.

*He flew all the way from Texas to see me?* Viv tried to absorb this, blanched and cast a look of horror at her faded, crummy pajamas. Wait a minute. Who cared? She hated J.B. "Tell him to go away."

A coughing, retching noise came through the intercom, and then Anglin's voice crackled through again. "He would go away, but he's choking on an apology. It's, uh, stuck in his throat. He needs you to come down and perform the Heimlich on him."

*Oh, ha ha. Very funny.* Viv hung on to her sense of outrage that he'd used her for revenge. She hung on to her embarrassment that he'd seen her running down the driveway bare-bunned after his ex. J.B. was persona non grata.

"As far as I'm concerned," she said, "he can go ahead and choke to death."

"Damn, that is cold." Timmy's voice this time.

She had to agree with him. Viv slumped over the buzzer. *Yup. That's me, cold ball-buster.* But the alternative was hurt. She'd told him she wanted to stay the night with him, and he'd kicked her out anyway. She'd made love to him, and given her heart to him, and he was hung up on another woman.

"Vivien." It was J.B. again. "I am *not* in love with my ex-wife!"

"I think you are," she said.

"I'm not," he insisted. "I doubt I ever was in love with Corinne. I married her as the logical conclusion to years of dating. It was a rubber stamp."

"But you wanted to *stay* married to her."

"Yeah, because I am one stubborn son of a bitch."

"You chase rats for her, J.B.," said Viv sadly. "At two a.m."

"Would you let go of the rats already? Rats are not dragons, and I am no white knight. I have been a chump. I have acted out of habit. When Corinne wanted something, I used to give it to her. She was the girl, I was the guy. I provided. Do you understand?"

Viv was silent.

"I have been a martyr for her. But worse, I've been self-righteous. I've been busy proving to the world and her that I'm a better person than she is—that I wouldn't turn my back on her when she needed something. Worst of all, I've just been stupid. Because I don't need to prove anything to her. I don't love her. I love *you.*"

The breath caught in Viv's throat. "What?" she finally said, but her voice was gone and it came out as a whisper.

"Hello? Did you get that? I. Love. You."

She stood there stupidly trying to absorb the concept, and finally burst into tears.

J.B.'s voice said to Timmy, "What the hell? You bare your soul, you tell 'em something that should make 'em happy, and they cry! I give up . . ."

"Don't give up," she said unsteadily. "Please don't give up."

"You gotta meet me halfway, Viv. How about letting me past the door? That would be a good start."

"He can come up, Timmy."

"Hallelujah!"

Moments later, she opened her apartment door to J.B. Anglin, who stood there in his Western boots, rumpled and unshaven. Viv's heart did a slow roll. Then it sat up and begged.

She wiped at her eyes and held out her arms, but her dogs got to him before she did. They'd followed on her heels and immediately rushed him. Tails wagging, noses seeking, tongues slurping, they had their canine way with J.B. while he gazed ruefully at her, scratched their heads and patted them. "You gonna introduce me?"

"Mannie, Brooklyn, Ellis, Longo and Queenie. Not necessarily in that order, since they won't stay still . . . okay, guys, enough!" She pulled two of them back by the collars.

Then she lunged at him and wagged her tail, too. He smelled like clean Texas air and mesquite, like heaven.

"I'm so sorry, Viv," he said, and then he kissed her. All she cared about was the feeling of his lips on hers, the fit of his arms around her, the mysterious human chemistry that just spelled r-i-g-h-t. She didn't give a flip about his apology, only the fact that he'd jumped on a red-eye flight and come to find her.

He raised his head and stroked her hair back from her forehead, then kissed her brow.

She tried to swallow the emotional tidal wave that his simple affection brought, but she couldn't. She sobbed into the crook of his neck, feeling like an unattractive wet dishrag, but unable to control it.

"Viv," J.B. said, "I didn't use you for revenge. I swear I didn't. I set out to, it's true. But somewhere along the way, I lost my heart to you."

When she could take a breath, she asked, "Why did you kick me out, then?"

He sighed. "You mentioned the prenup issue again, and it triggered years of pent-up frustration in me. All of a sudden it hit me: Here I was trying to change yet another woman, force her to fit into my life, when we had such different values. I thought I could change you from a cynic into an idealist like me. And there you were, being as cynical as they come. I just thought, screw it! What am I doing?"

She wiped her face with her pajama sleeve. "So . . . what *are* you doing here? I can't help but love you. You say you love me. But I am who I am. You are who you are. I live in Manhattan. You live in Texas."

"Vivvie," he said slowly. "What is a cynic, really, but a disappointed idealist?"

She stared at him. "Come sit down," she said.

They walked into her living room, with its comfortable sectionals and purple cushions. They sank down into the upholstery and he took her hands in his.

"I can't change you, honey," J.B. told her. "But I can watch as you transform yourself. I can be amazed and honored at the trust you put in me, and I can promise to never let down that trust.

"When we had sex the first couple of times, you came alone with your eyes closed. The last time, you came for me and with me, looking right into my eyes. I'm still floored by that, by how beautiful that moment was."

His hands tightened on hers. "That was making love. And what did I do? After my big song and dance about you missing out on the best part of sex . . . I was a total bastard and lost my temper, kicked you out. That was some afterglow, wasn't it?"

She looked away.

"I'm sorry," he said again. "And you wanted to stay. I couldn't have hurt you worse if I'd tried."

Viv leaned forward and kissed him. "So when you say that a cynic is a disappointed idealist, you mean . . . ?"

"I mean that I'm going to take the disappointment out of your life, Vivvie—at least regarding men. If you'll let me. I'll bet you'd look real cute in a pair of rose-colored glasses."

"You think?"

"Yeah."

"How about rose-colored glasses and a cowboy hat? Maybe even some boots?" Viv grinned at him.

"I think you're gonna get some *real* funny looks here in the City in a getup like that, but I don't care if you don't."

She cozied up to him. "Well, here's the deal, Tex: I just quit my job and I'm thinking of buying a ranch."

"You what?" He stared at her and then grinned so wide that his ears almost disappeared behind his teeth.

"But instead of filling it up with cattle, I want to fill it up with greyhounds."

He laughed out loud. "Why am I not surprised?"

She twisted his bracelet on her arm. "Up until about fifteen minutes ago, I was going to find this ranch in New Mexico or maybe Colorado . . ."

"What's wrong with the Texas Hill Country?"

"Nothing at all. Not now. And it has the added benefit of fields of bluebonnets." She kissed him again. "So it wouldn't scare you, huh? If I followed you down there."

"Do I look scared?" He looked elated, as a matter of fact.

"Well, I do have a reputation as a Ball-Busting Bitch. And we've only really known each other for a week, and it's not like we're engaged or anything . . ."

"You've never scared me, we've been acquainted for three years, and you know damn well that we'll be engaged before a fourth year has gone by."

"I do? Aren't you presuming a lot?"

"Yup." He began to unbutton her pajama top.

"What are you doing?"

J.B. let out a long-suffering sigh. "Preparing to have my way with you before you whip out a prenup and piss me off. You can keep your damned toothpaste." So saying, he took her left breast into his mouth.

Viv gasped as electricity shot through her, igniting her inner Mata Hari in spite of her scruffy pajamas.

Mannie and Brooklyn barked.

"Mine," J.B. growled at them. "Get your own Scooby Snack."

They barked again, and Queenie jumped up between them.

"Down!" said Viv.

"Jeez," J.B. complained. "You're already treating me like a dog."

"I didn't mean you."

"That's good, since I'm not the obedient type."

"Loyal, though. And I love you for it." She stroked the rough stubble on his cheeks and fell into those moss green eyes. She bent and kissed the bridge of his broken nose, and then the corners of his lips.

"I love you, too, Vivvie," he said seriously. "Always and forever . . . no matter how many hundreds of greyhounds you make me adopt."

# Chapter Twenty-three

"Vivien Anthea!" Mummy said, when Viv reluctantly answered her phone.

"Hi, Mum."

"I just got off the telephone with Mrs. Blount, who is across the street and one floor up from you."

*Uh-oh.*

"She wanted me to tell you that you and That Man are clearly visible to God and everyone in her building! She says you are naked as plucked game and dancing some sort of waltz in your living room!"

"The two-step," corrected Viv.

"I beg your pardon?"

"We're dancing the Texas Two-Step."

"Well, for heaven's sake, can you do it with some clothes on?!"

"Doing it with clothes on is no fun."

"I have to live in this town. Would you have some regard for my feelings and reputation?"

"Let 'em look," said J.B., striding to the window and waving.

"Mummy," said Viv. "You know this is all your

fault. I found the two little naked, embracing dolls on the heart-shaped doily. How long have those been under my bed? And while I appreciate your interest in my love life, I was a little creeped out after I stopped laughing. I think you should stick to your own love life."

"Mine's been going swimmingly, thank you." Mummy's tones were stiff with disapproval. Children, in her book, never offered unsolicited advice to their parents.

"Swimmingly? Have you been in the hot tub with Paolo again?" .

"Just a turn of phrase, I assure you." Mummy was admitting nothing, especially not that she was boinking such a social inferior as the gardener.

"You should be very careful what you teach your children by example, Mum."

"Vivien Anthea! What have you done?"

"Oh, nothing . . ." Viv fingered the little dolls on a bookshelf. One had dark hair and no shirt. The other wore a dress made out of an excruciatingly expensive embroidered hankie with the initials AS on it. They were tied together with a lacy blue garter and a bit of tulle.

"Listen, Mum. J.B. and I have half a CD to go. No clothes until the last notes of the last song. Mrs. Blount will just have to take some Xanax and enjoy the show."

"Vivien Anthee-ah! I demand to know—"

Viv clicked the OFF button on her phone and set it back in the cradle. She smiled at J.B., who had now added cowboy boots to his birthday suit.

He took her by the hand and led her to the window. "May I have this dance?"

"Absolutely," she said, kissing him. "And many others. I'm sure we'll dance 'til dawn at Julia and Roman's wedding."

Since you've just finished watching Vivien Shelton's *First Dance* with her true love, you're ready for the bride's story . . . unless you haven't met the other bridesmaids in Julia Spinelli's wedding party. If you haven't, you'll definitely want to read the first two books in The Bridesmaid Chronicles: sister of the bride, Sydney Spinelli's *First Date* and Kiki Sonntag's *First Kiss*.

If you've been part of this series from the beginning, you're now ready for . . .

## *First Love*

### BOOK FOUR IN

## THE BRIDESMAID CHRONICLES

Available from Signet in September 2005

Here comes the bride, or so the saying goes, but is Julia Spinelli truly ready for her big wedding day? Turn the page for a quick sneak peek as Julia takes on the biggest challenge of her life. . . .

*"Don't rush your wedding . . . savor it. Overcome the cliché of the stressed-out bride by focusing on your secret weapons—time and planning. Pick a date that will allow you to blossom along with your plans, each step in the planning process bringing you one calm, smooth, and organized step closer to that final, wonderful day."*

—From *The Guide to the Perfect Texas Hill Country Wedding,* Summer 2005 edition

"I'm screwed," Julia Spinelli said miserably. "Absolutely, totally, and completely screwed."

Across the table, Sydney stabbed some sauerkraut onto the end of her fork, then looked at it dubiously. "Maybe it would have been smart not to fire your wedding planner."

Julia shot her sister a scathing glare, then rocked forward, banging her head rhythmically on the picnic table and the bridal magazine she had open in front of her.

Maybe if she banged hard enough, she'd wake up and realize this was all a dream. It wasn't really five days to the wedding, it was five months. And instead of a laundry list of details left to attend to, she'd awake to discover that everything was ready and in place, and all she had to do was have a facial, shave her legs, buy something sexy for the wedding night, and then go marry the man she loved.

She opened her eyes, clinging to the hope that this

was a bad dream and she had more than five days, five hours, and thirty-two minutes to pull together the ultimate wedding. But instead of a reprieve, all she saw across the table was an amused pair of brown eyes. The sauerkraut, she noted, was back in the dish, having never made it past her sister's lips.

"Dammit, Syd," she said. "This isn't funny."

Syd's mouth curved up into a smile, but she was smart enough not to laugh. As Julia's big sister, she knew well enough that any misplaced chortle could easily earn her a kick in the shin. "You're right," she said. "Not funny at all."

Behind them, children frolicked on the playscape that dominated this corner of Market Square, a lovely little park with a small museum, a charming garden with an arbor, and lots of covered picnic tables. After a morning of prowling through the Main Street shops for welcome basket goodies, Julia and Syd had grabbed take-out bratwurst from Auslander Biergarten and walked the short distance to the park. She didn't really have time for a break, but Julia knew that if she didn't eat, she'd probably pass out. Of course, if she continued to eat bratwurst—a wonderful sausage that had never crossed her lips back home—she'd have to add finding a new wedding dress to her list, because the one currently scheduled for delivery tomorrow would rip to shreds the second she tugged it over her ever-widening hips.

Since the dress was the one part of her wedding plans that had yet to dissolve into disaster, Julia didn't intend to tempt fate. She'd eaten just two bites,

then pushed it away to pick at the garden salad—
without dressing—that she'd bought as an after-
thought.

Syd, Julia noticed, didn't try to talk her little sister
into consuming anything more nourishing than
wilted leaves of iceberg lettuce. In fact, once it was
clear that Julia was done with the salad, Syd had
reached across the table, nailed the sausage with her
fork, and started to chow down.

Julia scowled, ignoring the blatant food theft. She
pushed the magazine across the table, her manicured
nail tapping on the article that had plunged her into
this bout of misery. "Right there," she read. "See?
I'm supposed to be savoring." She repeated the word
for emphasis: "*Sa-vor-ing.* Instead, I'm suffering."

Syd took another bite, then closed her eyes, doing
a good impression of someone entering nirvana. "I'm
savoring," she said.

Julia rolled up the magazine and smacked her
sister.

"Hey! Don't take it out on me! I'm not the one
who got engaged and set the wedding date for just
barely a month later. And I'm not the one who set
you up with a wedding planner with an agenda."

"It wasn't his agenda, it was Kiki's."

"Exactly. Too bad your future sister-in-law is a little over-exuberant."

Julia raised an eyebrow. "Over-exuberant? She had
Breckin wasting hours researching destination wed-
dings instead of following up on *my* list. It took him
ages just to rent the tables and chairs, and he was

absolutely no help at all with the photographer or with finding me a morning-of makeup artist and hair designer."

"You're going to design your hair?" Syd looked completely baffled by the concept. "You've spent the last twenty-some-odd years putting your hair into every possible style. What could anyone possibly do better than you can manage yourself?"

"Syd . . ."

Her sister held up her hands in surrender. "Whatever."

"My point is that Breckin was spending so much time doing Kiki's bidding he wasn't focusing on me." At first, Julia had been patient because she did need the help. Putting together a wedding with over three hundred guests required a ton of planning, especially a whirlwind wedding. But she'd reached the end of her rope when Breckin admitted that he hadn't confirmed the photographer because Kiki'd had him running interference for *her* wedding. If Kiki hadn't already stepped up to the plate and arranged for Vera Wang gowns for her bridesmaids, Julia might have had to throttle Roman's little sister.

"Despite all her trouble, though," Julia had to admit, "Kiki did come through in the end." In fact, at the moment, Julia considered Keeks a goddess, since she hadn't been blowing smoke about the Vera Wang thing. The dresses had already arrived at the same shop in Austin that Julia was using for the groomsmen's tuxes, and Syd and Viv had already been fitted, and Kiki was bringing her dress with her. Fabulous, sleek gowns in peacock blue silk with spaghetti straps and a plunging neckline. If Julia hadn't already fallen madly in love with another dress in a San Antonio shop, she would have snagged a Vera Wang gown, too.

"She did good by the gowns," Syd agreed. "But overall, you have to admit that by comparison, I've been the voice of reason from the beginning."

"Voice of reason? Have you gone mental? You wanted me to call off the wedding!"

Syd looked only slightly abashed. "Well, yeah, but I thought that was reasonable at the time."

"You thought Roman was some sort of con artist! You thought I was being flighty and naïve." She tried for a light tone, really she did, but her voice held more accusation than good humor. She'd forgiven her sister for trying to sabotage her engagement, but the incident still stung.

"I had justification," Syd said, getting her back up and slipping into her know-it-all persona. "You hadn't even known the guy a month, and suddenly you were making wedding plans? Of course I was concerned. How could you fall in love so fast? Be so sure that he was the one?"

"You did," Julia pointed out, thinking of her sister's recent tumble into l'amore. And her sister's fall had given Julia such pleasure. Not only was it poetic justice after the way Syd had doubted the strength of Julia's feelings for Roman, but Julia was genuinely happy for her big sister. Syd might be a real pain at times, but Julia loved her anyway.

She flashed a grin. "Yes, indeed. I'd have to say that the ever-stalwart and reasonable Sydney Spinelli fell hard and fast."

It was Syd's turn to scowl, but the sour expression was marred by the light shining in her eyes. "Yeah, I did. But," she added, sitting up straighter and sliding easily into big-sister mode, "*I* don't have a history of collecting men."

"*Collecting men?*" Julia repeated. "God, Syd, you make me sound like Hannibal Lector. And for the record, I never collected. I dated. And also for the record, Roman's the first man I've been in love with. If you'd put any thought into it before you rushed from Jersey to Texas to save your poor helpless little sister, you would have realized that I'd never been engaged before. Roman's the first and the only and we're getting married with or without your approval or Daddy's approval or anyone else's for that matter."

"Touchy much?" Syd countered, without a hint of remorse.

Julia huffed, feeling a little martyred, but, dammit, ever since she'd told her bridesmaids about the wedding, everyone seemed to be planning sabotage. First Syd, then Kiki, then most recently Julia's best friend Vivian. It was enough to give a girl a complex.

"At least tell me you understand," she finally said. "And that you approve."

"I do, and I do," Syd said, and despite her lousy temper, Julia smiled.

"Practicing?" she asked.

"I take the Fifth," Syd answered, but her eyes told

another story, and Julia wondered if Alex had popped the question yet.

Across the table, Syd leaned forward and took Julia's hands. "Seriously, Jules, I do understand how you fell so hard so fast. I didn't when I came, but I do now. You know that, right? That I only wish you the best?"

"I know." It had been a little rocky when Syd had first barreled into town. But after a few missteps, they'd finally come to terms, and now Julia was genuinely grateful her sister was in town to help with the wedding details and, well, to just be a big sister.

"Then don't take this the wrong way." Syd took a deep breath. "But maybe you should postpone the wedding. Get married at Christmas instead of next Saturday."

"Are you insane? Kiki already tried to manhandle us into a winter wedding, and we are *so* not doing that." A fresh jolt of anger cut through her. "Dammit, Syd, every time I think you're on my side—"

"I *am* on your side, sweetie. You're the one who said you're stressing out. You're the one who said there's no way you can get everything done in a week—"

"Less than a week," Julia cut in morosely.

"And you're the one who's going to have to deal with Marv when he gets here."

Julia sighed heavily. She loved her father, really she did, but Marv Spinelli was Jersey born-and-bred, living proof that all clichés and stereotypes had some basis in fact. If Julia didn't know better, she would have easily believed that Joe Pesci had used her father as a case study when he'd boned up on his character for *My Cousin Vinny*. And Julia knew with absolute certainty that Marv's brash, bull-in-a-china-closet manners weren't going to blend seamlessly with the Southern charm of the small Texas town. Left unattended, Marv would clear a path through Fredericksburg as wide as Sherman had cleared through Atlanta.

"If you think you're going to be able to focus on wedding details with our father stomping around town, then the Texas sun has seriously fried your brain."

Obviously, Julia didn't intend to leave her father to his own devices. Which meant she had to add "Babysit Daddy" to the top of her list of last minute wedding tasks.

"I almost wish I hadn't told him. Or that his memory wasn't so long." Marv hadn't been thrilled when she'd called yesterday to finally tell him about the whirlwind wedding. But what had really smoked his goose wasn't the short engagement, but the identity of the groom.

Marv hadn't ever met Roman, but he'd butted heads with Robert Sonntag, Roman's father, over a real estate deal some fifteen-odd years ago. That wouldn't have been a problem if Marv had won the battle, but he hadn't. Not only had Sonntag managed to hold onto his property, but he'd also won in court. Always a sore loser, Marv had bought a neighboring parcel of land and plunked a Marv's Motor Inn at the corner of Main and Orange, a reminder to everyone in the town that what Marv Spinelli wanted, he got.

The irony, of course, was that if he hadn't later shipped his youngest daughter off to manage that very motel, Julia would never have met and fallen in love with the enemy. Fate's twist amused Julia, but her father hadn't seen the humor. As soon as he'd heard the Sonntag name, he'd barked into the phone that he'd be out there soon to "smash some sense into that dreamy-eyed blond brain of yours." Nice, Pop.

His plane was scheduled to land in Austin the next morning, which meant that Hurricane Marv would be arriving before lunch. One more day of sanity, and Julia intended to savor it. Of course, she'd considered expanding that to two days by spending tomorrow at River Center Mall in San Antonio for a little credit card therapy, but she'd talked herself out of it. She was a grown-up, now. And grown-ups stayed for the fight.

"You *had* to tell him," Syd pointed out reasonably. "You want the big wedding, right? That means that the father gives away the bride."

"The Elvis chapel in Vegas is looking better and better," Julia muttered.

"Would to me, too," Syd said. Then added, "Seriously, why *don't* you just postpone? Roman's the one, right? It's not like you have to get married before the love wears off."

"No, it's not like that," Julia admitted. "But I'm not going to France as Roman's girlfriend." Roman's business was wine, and he'd recently scheduled a trip to the south of France to meet with a group of vintners. The trip was important to Roman, and that made it important to Julia. "I'm going on the trip, and I'm going as his wife. And that's all there is to it."

As Julia lifted her chin defiantly, Syd nodded, resigned. The one truth throughout their childhood had been that what Julia wanted, Julia got. This wedding wouldn't be any different. She might suffer a few bumps and bruises along the way, but in the end, Julia would be exactly where she wanted to be: smack dab in the middle of a fairy tale wedding with several hundred guests admiring the efficiency, grace, and classy elegance of what would surely be the most fabulous social event in the history of Fredericksburg, Texas. Or South River, New Jersey, for that matter.

"So you'll help me?" Julia asked.

"You know I will," Syd said. "But maybe you would have been smart not to fire Breckin."

Julia grimaced. "He tried to move the wedding to Disney World! And he *insisted* on Snapdragons, when I made it perfectly clear that I wanted Birds of Paradise and South African Orchids."

"Yes, but now that A Floral Affair's gone out of business, you don't have snapdragons or orchids *or* Birds of Paradise or even daisies. You've got—as they so charmingly say down here in the South— bupkiss."

"The florist didn't close its doors because I fired my wedding planner," Julia said.

"No," Syd agreed. "But Breckin might know another florist that can pull together exotics in less than a week. As it is now, you're stuck. Unless you want to just forget about flowers altogether."

"You're kidding, right? Without flowers, the ceremony, the reception, *everything* will look totally naked."

"Or natural. You know, back to nature. Ra-ra the environment?"

"Are you insane? What would I carry down the aisle? Grass clippings? And if I wanted *au naturel*, I'd get married in the buff. This is an *event*. And flowers symbolize everything I want in a marriage. A thing of beauty and endurance. Something with inherent beauty that blossoms over time."

Syd blinked. "You say the weirdest shit."

"Dammit, Syd. This is my wedding. I've been fantasizing about this day since I was nine years old. I think I know what I want. And since I'm the bride, what I want is what matters."

"Julia, honey, you've never been a bride before, but you've *always* gotten what you want."

Julia frowned a little at that, but she had to concede the point. Of course, she hadn't wanted her father to ship her off to Texas, but at least the end result had turned out to be fabulous.

"At any rate," she continued, "what I want now are flowers. I'm not worried about the Birds of Paradise; those are easy. But they were only for accents, anyway. The orchids are the real focal flower." She started to tick items off on her fingers. "I need bouquets for me and the bridesmaids. Some sort of spray for my hair. Roman's boutonniere and the same for all the groomsmen. Mom and Sarah's corsages. We don't need anything for the arbor since it's already so lovely, but I need floral centerpieces for the tables at the reception and something with flowers and ribbons decorating the chairs that line the aisle." She pressed a finger to her lips as she closed her eyes, picturing the ceremony and the reception. "Yeah. I think that about does it."

"And you're telling me this why?"

Julia didn't answer. Instead, she just rested her chin on her hand and smiled, waiting for the light of realization to shine in her sister's eyes.

"What?" Syd said. Then her eyes narrowed. "Oh, no . . ."

"Oh, yes," Julia said. "You just promised to help me. First thing you can do is call every florist in Austin and San Antonio until you find one that can step up to the plate."

"Julia . . ."

But Julia just shook her head, ignoring all protests. "Don't even try, Syd. I'm not listening."

"But—"

"*No.*" She held out her hand, and Syd closed her mouth. "The one thing I did right was get my invitations out first thing. Now I have a box full of over two hundred rsvp cards confirming over three-hundred and fifty guests. If you think I'm going to walk down the aisle holding a spray of carnations and babies' breath, you are sorely mistaken."

"Sweetie," Syd said, taking Julia's hand between her own, "the flowers really aren't your major problem here. Marv is coming. *Tomorrow*. If you want to focus on a crisis, focus on that."

"I'd rather not," Julia mumbled, then shut her eyes as if that could block out the knowledge that her tacky—and tactless— parents were about to descend on and tarnish her shiny new life.

That her parents would show up for her wedding had, of course, been inevitable. In fact, knowing that Marv and Myrna would fly to Texas for the nuptials had been the only reason that Julia had truly considered—however briefly—eloping to Mexico or Monte Carlo or anyplace else exotic and far away.

But, no. Julia wanted the fairy tale wedding too badly to make that kind of sacrifice. Had wanted it all her life, in fact. And she had to acknowledge that her father had been the one who'd firmly planted that dream in her head.

At the same time, she deeply resented that Marv had always seen—and treated—her as "the pretty one" while Syd had been "the smart one." He'd never failed to tell her how pretty she was or how dear or how easily she'd snag a rich and worthy husband. Depending on her mood, she'd been alternately flattered and irritated. Over time, irritation had settled in as the primary emotion, coupled with a desperate need to prove to her myopic father that she had more than a model's face and debutante's knowledge of all things fashion.

That frustration with her father, however, had never edged out Julia's gut-deep desire for the pageantry of matrimony. She wanted it, needed it. She wanted to be a bride and walk down the aisle. She'd been treated like a princess for much of her life, and she wasn't about to turn her back on what she considered the ultimate royal treatment simply because her father exasperated her.

She and Roman had made the decision to have a big, Texas-sized wedding the weekend after he'd proposed to her. She'd seen in his eyes that he would have been just as satisfied with a quick visit to the Justice of the Peace, but in the generous way she'd come so quickly to love, Roman had insisted that she plan the wedding of her dreams. And—bless the man—he hadn't even flinched when she'd laid out for him the vast expanse of those dreams.

From the beginning, Roman believed Julia could pull off anything she set her mind to, whether it was making a success of the tacky Marv's Motor Inn her father had banished her to or pulling off a dream wedding.

Roman supported and helped her. More important, he had faith in her even while her own father had never once believed that Julia could do anything more than be a pretty bauble. Well, this time, Julia intended to show her father what she was made of. She'd not only convince Marv that Roman wasn't the spawn of Satan, but she'd throw the wedding of the century. Seamless, perfect, and dripping with class. No tacky blue tuxedo for her father; she'd clothe him in Armani even if she had to fly the designer here herself.

And in the end, she'd prove to her father that she was capable, confident and worthy.

She only hoped that she could prove it before he drove her absolutely and completely crazy.

One wedding.
Three bridesmaids.
Four sexy tales of modern-day romance.

# The Bridesmaids Chronicles

Now available
### First Date
by Karen Kendall
0-451-2155-9

### First Kiss
by Kylie Adams
0-451-21581-8

Coming September 2005
### First Love
by Julie Kenner

Available wherever books are sold or at
penguin.com